THE ORPHANS
OF DOUGERES

BY

EDAN JAMES

For Mum.

For her interest and support.

CONTENTS

I would like to acknowledge my family and friends for their interest in *Orphans of Dougeres* and for their encouragement. In particular, Damian and Bernadette Rameaux who have made France my second home.

Also Jean-Luc Morrison, my protagonist, who embodies the best in all of them.

Chapter 1

Dougeres, Pays Basque, France, 2014.

As if by magic, the front doors to the three adjoining cottages opened at exactly the same time. The three elderly ladies smiled and kissed each other as they slowly made their way towards the well opposite their dwellings. They each took out needles and wool from their bags and settled down to continue knitting the garments for the baby that was expected soon to the granddaughter of one of the trio.

They smiled as they grumbled about the arthritis that afflicted them. The three ladies had been great friends for many years. Not one of them minded that they had heard each other's stories many times. They had never moved from the village for many years nor had they wanted to. They made disparaging comments about the weekly market that would arrive the following day, and yearned for the days when the produce sold was so much better than now. They had raised their families together, helping each other out in times of hardship, and cried for one another through the inevitable widowhood as it touched each one of them. They tended the graves of the men who had shared so much with them and spoke fondly of their children and grandchildren. And now another generation was about to be born, bringing joy to the tiny hamlets that surrounded Dougeres. The trio looked back into their memories; each of them knew that they had many years behind them and that in their long journey, time was slowly but inexorably catching them up.

Caeserea, 44 BC.

As the hour of their execution approached, the two very different men tried to come to terms with their impending doom.

Over the last few hours, one of the men had gone from an air of disbelief at his capture and the subsequent verdict of death by beheading. He had protested his innocence to the walls of his cell and to the unmoving companion who would shortly share his fate.

Yacov had tried to shut out his fellow prisoner's moans. Sometimes the man's complaining had verged on hysteria. The fisherman had tried to reason with his companion, but to no avail. Dismissing the other man's whining voice, Yacov closed his eyes and allowed his mind to wander back to happier times.

He smiled sadly as he remembered the time that his boat had been blown off course as he and his companions set out to carry their teacher's message overseas. Instead of making safe harbour on the Galician coast, they had finally beached their damaged boat many miles down the coast. They were warmly welcomed by a small friendly community that upon seeing the tools of Yacov's trade, set about repairing the craft and thus endearing themselves to the strangers in the process.

The Galileans had rested there over the winter, making friends, and with much laughter on both sides they had managed to communicate with their hosts.

An elder of the village had offered Yacov a bed in his tiny cottage. A rapport had grown between the two men, many years apart in age, but with a similar outlook as they explained to each other, their hopes for the future. The older man's granddaughter had been captivated by this quiet, dignified stranger, and the two of them spent many hours together.

Finally, with their boat once again seaworthy, the Galileans made their reluctant farewells. Yacov embraced the young woman that he had come to care about so deeply, and explained to her that he had to fulfil the promise that he had made. He assured the tearful woman that he would come back to her as soon as he was able.

Strands of pale light filtered through the tiny window of their cell and the two men realised that death was imminent. The sound of a key turning in the door proved too much for Yacov's cellmate. The man prostrated himself on the floor, begging for mercy. A look of distaste flickered across the face of the Roman soldier, followed by a wrinkling of his nose as he realised that the pathetic wretch had soiled himself. He looked at the silent Yacov with admiration and thought that this was indeed a man. The prisoners left their cell, one walking with his head held high, and the other was dragged, crying hysterically.

A crowd had gathered; anxious to see the executions, they clamoured to be let in. The commander of the invading forces knew that as long as they had no personal involvement with the prisoners, the spectators would enjoy the executions. At a nod of his head, the gates were opened and a large group of people rushed in, jostling for the best position.

Outside the gates of the compound, the uncle of Yacov waited. His hearing had started to fail, but he felt the buzz of the crowd as the executions were carried out. A tear ran down his cheek as he realised that his dear nephew had lost his life. Rumours coursed through the crowd that although one of the prisoners was a habitual criminal, the only wrongdoing of Yacov was that his quick temper had got him into trouble with the authorities on more than one occasion. His uncle smiled sadly as he remembered telling the boy that his red hair and the temperament that went with it would prove to be his undoing.

Shortly the huge gates to the compound were opened and a soldier appeared, asking for the relatives of the dead men to step forward. The old man quickly made his way to the soldier and thought how sad it was that no-one came forward to claim the body of the other victim.

Recognising Yacov's corpse from the scars on both his arms that were testament to the hard life of a fisherman, the old man asked for permission to take his nephew's body for burial. A look of compassion appeared on the soldier's face as he saw that the frail old man could not possibly move the corpse. Bending down, he whispered into the older man's ear. Nodding his head in gratitude, Yacov's uncle watched as the two bodies were loaded onto his cart. Taking up the reins of the horse, he quickly drove the cart through the gates and made for the harbour.

The boat had been made ready to sail. The two bodies were loaded quickly onto the deck and the boat pulled away from the harbour.

As he looked at his homeland for the last time, Yacov's uncle thought how the friends of his nephew had spread far and wide at the insistence of the young man who had become their teacher. He remembered a humble man, just a few years older than his students, but he had inspired such loyalty among Yacov and his friends.

For the first, but not the last time on that voyage, the old man looked at the object in the sack that Yacov had insisted that he take to a place of safekeeping. He wondered why his nephew had attached so much importance to the gift from his teacher.

During the long voyage, as he cleaned and dressed the two bodies an idea came to fruition in the elderly man's mind. He remembered his nephew telling him many times of the idyllic few months that he had spent in the tiny community across the sea. As the Galilean fishing boat neared Galicia, the elderly uncle of Yacov asked three members of the crew to put the body of his nephew's cellmate onto the prepared board and lower it overboard. He smiled as he thought that wherever the body ended up it would give people something to talk about for years to come.

Seventy years later.

He was close to death. He had no fear of dying; indeed he had lived far longer than a man had a right to expect. Sadness crept over him as he remembered his three wives and his five children. All of them had passed over before him and he thought that no man should outlive his own children. Now there was just him and his two grandsons.

He marvelled that he could remember quite clearly events from many years ago, when he couldn't recall what he had eaten for breakfast, or even if he had eaten anything. He smiled toothlessly as he recalled waiting wide-eyed with his tearful mother as his father's body was carried gently from the boat. In the tiny cottage that he shared with just his mother, he had watched as she washed and anointed the headless corpse and readied it for burial.

Just after the quiet, dignified funeral attended by the small community, a merchant had appeared. The man was a busybody who wanted to know everybody's business. This wasn't surprising as he spent many hours alone on the roads with only his donkey for company. The merchant wondered why the entire village looked so glum. In a tale that was repeated many times over the years, the elder of the village quickly replied that the people were not sad, they were shocked by what the young men of the village had witnessed that very morning. The merchant's jaw dropped as he was told in hushed tones of the crew of fishermen seeing a boat being steered by a headless corpse, sailing towards the Galician coast.

In his haste to spread this juicy piece of news to anyone that would listen, the merchant left his sack of wares behind as he bullied and cajoled his donkey to carry him with all speed along the coast road.

The old man cackled as he remembered his mother telling him the tale many times over the passing years. She had laughed as she explained how that story would become very different with each telling.

His mind came back to the present as he heard the soft footfall on the staircase. His sightless eyes turned towards the door. He knew that his unwanted visitor was his eldest grandson. The elderly man was relieved that he had made his younger grandson leave the day before. He knew that the young man had been trying to find a safe place to keep the object that his own mother had insisted that his family were the guardians of. Many times he had told the boy not to tell a soul, not even his grandfather, for fear that the eldest boy would beat it out of him.

He had listened patiently as his youngest grandson had told him of the place a full day's walk from here at the foothills of the great mountains, where he was sure that the tiny community would find shelter from the cruel sea that regularly battered their homes and had claimed many lives from the small group of people. The old man had laughed aloud when his grandson had exaggerated how the fish would happily jump from the river into his hands.

He cried out in fear as he was lifted bodily from the bed. His frail bones shattered as he was slammed against the door. 'Where is my snivelling brother, old man?' his grandson shouted. He had often wondered how two boys so alike in looks could be so different in their natures. He shuddered as he remembered how before he had lost his sight, he had looked fearfully into his eldest grandson's eyes and seen nothing. The small boy had looked back at him with an almost reptilian gaze. A freakish accident of nature had ensured that the boy had been born with completely black eyes. Throughout his childhood, the boy had shown that his heart was just as black.

The younger man raged against his grandfather as he demanded to know where his brother had gone, and why he had been given the family heirloom that belonged to him by birth right.

The elderly man was relieved that he had insisted that the gentle, caring youth should leave. The younger man had cried as he left, stating that one day he or his descendants would return to the tiny community of people that he loved so much. His parting words to his grandfather had intrigued the old man, the boy had simply stated that he would look ever homewards.

He lay on the floor and tried to curl himself into a ball in anticipation of the kick that he knew was coming. Mercifully he never felt it as the shock of the rough treatment at the hands of his eldest grandson proved too much for his frail old bones and the life passed from his body.

Chapter 2

Avignon, France, 1348.

He cursed as he realised that he had seen the same two men for perhaps the fourth time that day. He knew that they had been following him. Usually so alert, he had allowed his sadness to become his principal agenda.

Grief threatened to engulf him as he felt his armpit for perhaps the fifteenth time that day. From the moment that he had felt the lump in his body, the man had known that his life would soon be over.

Mathieu Charpentier gazed to the heavens as if to ask God why he should be struck down with this terrible sickness that was to cut a huge swath across the whole of Europe. Common sense prevailed and Mathieu reasoned that he had no right to expect to live when hundreds were dying each day. Indeed it had been a miracle that his wife had survived the pestilence. Nobody could understand why some people should recover from the dreadful sickness, while all around them, friends and family members succumbed.

The master carpenter had nursed his wife back to

health, grateful that a neighbour had offered to look after the young couple's small son.

He knew that before he died, he must make arrangements to get his family to safety. Mathieu was grateful that outwardly he looked well, but he also knew that would change very quickly as the sickness spread through his body.

Taking a circuitous route through the city, his pace quickened each time he turned a corner. He doubled back on himself several times as he sought to lose his pursuers. Smiling grimly, Mathieu realised that the two men were not very fit as he heard their laboured breathing as they ran to keep him in sight.

Dusk was beginning to fall before he was satisfied that he had managed to shake off his enemies, as he was convinced that they meant him harm.

Slowly, he made his way to the small forest just outside the city where he had lived with his family for two years. These last two years had been good ones. His skill as a master craftsman, honed in some of the great cathedrals in the south of France, had quickly been realised and he had found well-paid work in the Palais des Papes. The immense gothic building had inspired Mathieu to produce some of his finest work. A man not given to idle boasts or posturing to be noticed, the quiet man was soon put to work producing carvings and making fine furniture along with the elite craftsmen of the age. Money had never been an issue for the present Pope, Clement VI, who had provided Avignon with the best that money could buy in his desire to make the Palais des Papes envied throughout Europe.

Tears filled Mathieu's eyes as he stood in the small clearing in the forest. There was a scattering of huts occupied by craftsmen, such as himself, and their families. This small community had come to rely on each other and had become great friends. As he looked around the little clearing, he was gratified that the group of inhabitants were for the most part, self-sufficient. Practically the whole of France was struggling to grow enough wheat to feed the population, but here with good husbandry and a thriftiness that came from years of going hungry, the small group had managed to produce enough vegetables, that along with a steady supply of meat and fish from the forests and rivers, ensured that none of the small group starved.

As dappled light began to filter through the trees, Mathieu busied himself by scratching a line in the soil along the length of the clearing that formed the entrance to the collection of huts. Taking a small spade from his tool bag he dug a shallow trench, which he then filled with dry kindling that was in plentiful supply in the vicinity.

The young man picked up a collection of small stones that he proceeded to throw onto the roof of his hut, hoping to attract his wife's attention. Presently, Eleanor came to the door, alarm etched on her face. A small boy tried to squeeze past his mother; he was not scared, just ready for a great adventure. His eyes lit up as he saw his father and he doubled his efforts to escape his mother's grip. The young woman who was still quite weak from the terrible sickness looked enquiringly at Mathieu. Her shoulders slumped in dejection as she realised why he hadn't simply walked into their hut.

'Eleanor, I have the sickness.' His resolve wavered as his wife began to cry. 'We spoke about the chances of this happening. With God's mercy, I may survive and we will be together again. My love, there is a small amount of money beneath the bed. If I do not return in one week, then I will have perished. Take the boy and leave this place. You must stay away from big cities as I feel that the filth and squalor that people live in must surely contribute to the spread of this terrible disease. I have told you about my ancestor's beginnings far to the west, I would hope that you can manage to reach his birthplace and that you and the boy can make a new life for yourselves.'

Mathieu knew that his wife had a strong character and he felt that she would eventually reach the small fishing community that his ancestor had left hundreds of years before.

Despite the early hour, people had begun to stir. Alarm, mingled with sadness filled their faces as they saw their good friend Mathieu talking to his wife from a distance. As they listened curiously to the young couple, a few of them decided that they would try to help.

Eleanor smiled her gratitude as her husband's best friend came to the door of his hut and promised that he and his family would accompany the woman and her son wherever they chose to go.

Mathieu's heart lifted as he saw some hope for the future of his small family and their good friends. Quickly, he told his wife that when their son was old enough to understand, she must never let him forget the origins of his family.

He looked at each of his friends in turn, nodding his head to some and waving to others. He told them that as they prepared to leave none of them should approach the trench that he had recently dug. Producing a flint from his pocket, the carpenter quickly fashioned a fire and set it to the kindling. All the men present realised that their friend was trying to give them the best possible chance of avoiding the terrible sickness by purifying the air with fire.

Taking one last look at the two most precious people in his life, Mathieu Charpentier raised his hand in farewell and disappeared from their lives.

Carefully, he made his way through the deserted streets of the city. For the first time, the magnificent papal palace failed to move him as he quickly made his way to his workshop. Hundreds of the Pope's staff had perished as the terrible disease took an iron grip on the city. Townspeople spoke in awed tones as they wondered why Clement VI had not fled. They reasoned that as God's messenger on Earth, he must have been protected by divine intervention.

In truth, the Pope surrounded himself by fire. Everywhere he went within the palace he was accompanied by servants carrying braziers of burning logs. Physicians had agreed that this was one of the best ways to ward off the foul air that seemed to spread the pestilence so quickly.

Mathieu was relieved to find the huge workshop empty. He knew that the fear of the plague had driven people in their thousands to flee Avignon and other major cities. In a blind panic to escape, not many of them had realised that there was quite simply nowhere to run to. Quickly walking to his work area, he withdrew a sack of tools from beneath the bench and planned in his mind exactly what he would do.

He worked steadily, enjoying the feel of the timber in his fingers as he created something beautiful from the plain-looking wood. Finally the small decorated plaque was finished. He breathed a sigh of relief as he set the beautiful carving on the bench. He cleaned away all the evidence of his labours and with a last tear-filled gaze around the workshop, he made his way through the great hall, and outside to the garden that had been started by order of Pope Benedict VII, and was a work in progress.

Mathieu worked for another two hours, remembering the little tricks of other tradesmen that he had watched and questioned over the years. Now he applied some of the things he had learned as he finished his task before making sure that all signs of his being there had been cleared away. The strain of being the willing custodian of the family secret lifted from his shoulders as surely as it must have been lifted from the countless generations of his family who had, like him, taken great pride in keeping this secret safe.

Finally, with dusk beginning to fall, he made his way by a back door from the great building. Once he deemed himself to be a safe distance from the palace, he slowly lowered his bag of tools into the River Rhone. Now he was ready to face death, either by the pestilence that he knew was travelling relentlessly through his body, or at the hands of the men who he suspected meant him harm.

Mathieu delighted in the sounds of the river, the bullfrogs croaking as they tried to catch their last meal of the day, and the birds singing their peculiar collective song as they settled into their nests. As he did from time to time, Mathieu gazed to the west and muttered, 'Look ever homewards.'

The young man was feeling tired now, from a combination of his day's labour and the dreadful illness that was killing him. A strong arm snaked around his neck and Mathieu was dragged to the ground. Kicks and punches rained down on him, until almost unconscious he felt himself being dragged back towards the Palais des Papes.

*

Sebastien de Beziers strode imperiously through the hallways of the palace. Completely unmoved by the works of art and the beautiful craftsmanship that surrounded him, he wondered where his trusted bodyguards had gone. For a moment he wondered if they had fled the city like the countless hordes of hysterical citizens who were trying to escape the dying all around them. He smiled evilly as he thought his men were probably more afraid of him than they were of the pestilence.

Although Pope Clement VI was regarded as God's emissary on Earth, his chamberlain was the most powerful man in the palace. As the secretary to the chamberlain Sebastien enjoyed the power that spread down to him. For centuries his ancestors had aligned themselves to the church, always working in the background, they had proved to be ruthless in their pursuit of the one thing that would give them absolute power across the whole of France and indeed the rest of Europe. De Beziers was a quite brilliant man. His command of languages ensured that he was privy to the most secret documents to come before the Pope and his chamberlain. Sebastien would either steal or memorise some of the important papers that he worked on and secret them away for future use as his family had done for centuries. The one lesson that every male member of his family had strove to impart on their children was that knowledge is power.

Like the incumbent Pope, the secretary commanded men to accompany him everywhere carrying the braziers filled with burning wood that afforded him the best protection from this terrible disease that was decimating the population of Avignon.

As he passed his private chambers, he was gratified to hear his three sons reciting their lessons. He felt no love for the boys and he would not allow them to harbour any emotional attachment to him, or indeed to any living soul. The boys all had different mothers, young women who he had had killed as soon as they had produced his children. The same fate had befallen any baby girls unlucky enough to be sired by him. For centuries the men of his family had acted exactly the same way, never allowing anyone to get close to them as they strove to achieve their sole objective.

Angrily he almost ran into the chambers of his personal bodyguards, determined to find out why they had left him unprotected. As he opened his mouth to admonish his usually trustworthy men, he was stopped short at the sight of a man, dressed in rough workman's clothes, lying on the floor.

As he stared at his men, the man who was clearly a

captive began to stir. Sebastien's most trusted guard pulled the man's hair back, forcing his face upwards. Both Sebastien de Beziers and Mathieu Charpentier stared at each other in amazement. The two men bore such a strong resemblance to each other that they were rendered speechless. Mathieu stared at the other man who was perhaps around ten years older than himself. Looking closer he noticed that his captor had unusually black eyes. The whole part of his eyes, not just his pupils, were as black as night. There seemed something so evil about the man's gaze that the carpenter recoiled in horror as if he faced the Devil.

The papal secretary laughed humourlessly as he enjoyed the dread on people's faces as they looked at him. Sebastien was exultant; this man was so like him that the two of them must surely share the same genetic background.

Like his father before him, de Beziers had often cursed the memory of the ancestor who had denied his family access to the everlasting search for what was rightfully his. He knew that with that most powerful symbol in his grasp, the de Beziers could ensure that the papacy would stay in France forever. Centuries of fruitless searches, meticulously recorded, disappeared from the mind of de Beziers as he realised that finally the treasured family heirloom was so close. That his captive could lead him to it, he had no doubt.

As if he could read the other man's thoughts, a shiver of fear ran through Mathieu's body. He knew that in his weakened state and with two strong men holding him, he wouldn't be able to withstand torture for very long. He knew that very soon he would be forced to tell his captors everything. The prisoner slumped over as if his fear was forcing him back towards the floor.

'Hold him firmly, you dogs!' Sebastien shouted. 'I will beat the truth out of him.'

Mathieu knew that if the two men grasped him beneath his armpits, they would all know of his condition. Summoning his last vestiges of strength, the sick man propelled his head backwards into the face of one of his captors. The man turned away, his shattered nose streaming blood and momentarily blinded as his eyes filled with tears. In almost the same movement, Mathieu raised his arm shoulder high and struck backwards with his elbow. The effect on the other man was devastating; the blow caught him squarely on the temple. Death was instantaneous.

With a savage grin, Mathieu propelled himself forward and catching his undoubted relative by the hair, he mustered as much phlegm from the back of his throat as he could and propelled the great gout of mucous and blood into the terrified man's face.

Sebastien knew instantly that he was doomed. In a state of panic he withdrew a dagger from his robes and thrust it straight into his exhausted adversary's stomach. Savagely he struck again and again. With his dying breath, Mathieu laughed and whispered the words that countless generations of de Beziers' family had strove to hear. Knowing that the secret would do him no good at all drove Sebastien de Beziers into an uncontrollable rage and he stabbed repeatedly at the dead man's body.

Ten days later.

A mile from the city, the small party of people took one last look at Avignon. The huge papal palace dominated the skyline. Each of them felt a whole gamut of emotions course through their bodies as they thought of their past life. The small forest-dwelling community had shrunk quite alarmingly as they had left family members behind, victims of the pestilence, and friends who preferred to take their chance in the great city.

Eleanor's eyes filled with tears as she watched the small group of children playing happily. She thought that all children should be like this, oblivious to the problems that life would burden them with as they reached maturity. Her tears flowed unchecked as she thought of her little boy's cold and lifeless body as he had been buried along with three children from the family of her great friends; the Welsh mason Simon and his wife Gwyneth. She looked at Simon; his strong shoulders slumped as grief revisited him and the remains of his family. Sadness would come back to them all many times until they managed to bravely carry on living.

Apart from losing her husband and their son, Eleanor knew that the quest that had been entrusted to the countless generations of her husband's family was finally over. She recalled the last time that she had seen her beloved husband, if only they had known what was to be, he could have stayed and she would have buried father and son together.

She knew that it had been Mathieu's dearest wish

to return to his ancestor's place of birth, so despite being alone she decided that she would go there and live out her life with these good people who had all lost so much.

One month later.

Simon was concerned for Eleanor. Ever since he had started working on the Palais des Papes, Mathieu had welcomed the stranger. He had helped him to get to grips with another language, smoothed the friction that invariably occurred when problems arose, and the local builders looked to blame the strangers amongst them. In short, Mathieu and Eleanor embraced the Welsh couple and their family.

That fateful day in the forest when Mathieu had bade farewell to his friends, Simon had promised to care for Eleanor, but neither he nor his wife could seem to lift her from her depression. She never complained, but simply walked in their wake. She ate very little and even though they had travelled a good part of their journey, she remained very depressed.

Gwyneth clapped her hand to her forehead and declared to her husband that she must be either blind or foolish. Simon looked at his wife thinking that perhaps she had had too much sun. She ran back to Eleanor and took hold of her hands. 'We will stop soon my dear, and eat and you can get some rest.' Eleanor looked at her friend with a dumb expression on her face. The expression changed to one of joy as her friend declared that she thought Eleanor was with child. She cried long and happily as she realised that her husband's family quest could continue.

Eleanor had never allowed Mathieu to tell her or anyone of the hiding place of that most precious object that his family had undertaken to keep hidden until such a time as it could be given to a greater authority. Now she questioned her decision as she realised that not a living soul knew of the location. She remembered that Mathieu had taught her two sentences of a strange tongue. During the long walk, she had taught Simon the mason and his wife these same two sentences. She could never explain why she had done that but had felt compelled to do so.

Holding her hand to her stomach as if to reassure the seed growing in her, she looked heavenward and declared to Mathieu that one day a descendant of his would finish the family task.

Eight months later.

Gwyneth carefully cut the umbilical cord, trying not to hurry but knowing that she didn't have much time. Without wiping the baby down she passed the infant to his dying mother. Eleanor had almost slipped away, when some primitive instinct opened her eyes. She looked tenderly at Mathieu's son who was showing his disapproval of this bright new world by yelling lustily.

A knocking at the door turned both women's heads towards the noise. Gwyneth looked inquiringly at her greatest friend, who simply smiled and nodded her head.

Simon the mason had been fishing for their evening meal when the small boy ran along the river bank, shouting that the outsider must return home. Both he and his wife loved this area, with the rivers and mountains that reminded them so much of Wales. His building skills had quickly been recognised and he had never been short of work since their arrival. Gwyneth had told him that Eleanor didn't have much time left and they had both prayed to God that Mathieu's child would be delivered safely.

At his wife's command, Simon the mason entered. He smiled through his tears as he repeated his promise made to Mathieu Charpentier that he would care for any member of his great friend's family.

Her voice little more than a whisper, Eleanor thanked the Welsh couple for getting her to the homeland of her late husband. During the long journey from Avignon, Eleanor had often amused her greatest friends by wishing that their two families were one; now, as her eyes dimmed with the onset of death, she repeated those words with an insistence that it would come to pass. The Welsh couple looked in awe at their dying friend.

'I know that the two of you will envelop my child in the love that you have in abundance. Instruct him well in the ways of the world and never let him forget his family. When the time comes for Mathieu to spread his wings, remind him that wherever his feet take him, he should look ever homewards.'

Gwyneth took the now sleeping infant from his dead mother's arms. Turning to her husband, she bade him take the child and declared that she would ready Eleanor's body for burial. The Welshwoman cried as she thought of the great circle of life that brought a new life into the world while strangely taking one out.

Simon took the child from the small cottage that he had built and gave the news to the waiting villagers that they should welcome the latest arrival, but also say farewell to the infant's mother.

Chapter 3

Southern France, 2014.

Jean-Luc Morrisson ached in every part of his body. Over the last few weeks he had been soaked often by heavy rains, burnt by the punishing sun and buffeted by the winds that prevailed in this part of France. He felt dirty, his clothes stuck to him and he yearned for the luxury of a long bath. A contented smile lit up his face as he realised that he had never been happier. He thought how different his life had been just two years ago.

Jean-Luc had had an office in the city of London, indeed he had had access to offices in all the great cities of the world. An award-winning architect of international renown, he had been admired by his colleagues and envied by his rivals.

He accepted the wealth that came to him as a reward for making unbelievable amounts of money for his employers, but in truth his life had never been motivated by the desire to acquire riches.

Finally Jean-Luc had tendered his resignation. His employers and his girlfriend had been shook rigid. They had all begged him to take a long holiday and reconsider his decision. The young man had been adamant that he was finally doing something for himself. He had known for some time that the relationship with Susan Travers had run its course. The pair rarely enjoyed the short times that they spent together. As a very successful magazine editor, Susan was almost never at the apartment they shared. They both knew that they had been growing apart for some time.

Despite this the young woman had pleaded with him not to walk out on his life. 'What on earth will you do?' she had asked repeatedly. Jean-Luc had known exactly what he would do, a few days before resigning he had seen an advertisement for tour guides to accompany coach parties around Europe. He knew that he had no other skills, but as a fluent French speaker, he saw the opportunity to escape from a suffocating industry and to build his social skills by helping people from all walks of life enjoy their well-earned holidays.

The work had proved to be exactly what he had needed. He had often been teamed up with a driver called Ted Green. Ted was a cheerful cockney, always with a smile and a joke. The two men were poles apart but became good friends. Jean-Luc admired the older man's ability to put people at their ease with a cheery smile, and a witty remark. After thirty years of driving the roads of Europe, Ted had a legendary knowledge of routes, and a knack of knowing exactly which diversion to take should the need arise.

Jean-Luc had given his apartment to Susan and had moved into a much smaller place in London's east end. Ted, a widower, had often invited the younger man to his home for a meal. On one such occasion, he had been introduced to a woman around his own age. Sally Roberts was a specialist nurse who cared for terminally ill people, helping them keep their dignity as they approached the end of their lives.

Sally had cared for Ted's wife in her final months, but she had also helped him to face life without his much-loved wife. The two had become great friends as Ted grieved for his late partner, and the young woman would often call to check that Ted was doing well. Jean-Luc came to look forward to the dinner invitations that became more frequent, and as Ted was quite an accomplished cook, he began to feel that his desire for a normal life was finally happening. Sally would always be accompanied by her teenage daughter Molly. Molly blushed a lot when spoken to and rarely answered. Jean-Luc put this down to the fact that as children entered their teenage years, they lost the childhood exuberance when they were entering the transitory period before reaching maturity.

'Come on Granddad, get a move on, or we will be as old as you before we reach Spain.'

Jean-Luc laughed as he was shaken from his reverie by one of the theology students. Despite being only thirty-two years of age, his hair was snow white. Both he and his two sisters had inherited that particular gene from their mother whose hair had gone white in her early twenties. As a child, Jean-Luc had been teased that he had sent his mother's hair that colour. His eyes sparkled with joy as he thought of his parents and he promised himself that when this trip was over, he would spend some time with them.

There was furious activity round the campsite as the small group of people made ready to continue their journey. A few months earlier Jean-Luc had been asked by his employer if he would escort a small group of theology students from America on a pilgrimage to Santiago de Compostela. Like millions of pilgrims before them, the small group wanted to make the pilgrimage the traditional way, on foot. Jean-Luc gazed ruefully at his trainers as he pulled them on. His trusty walking boots had fallen apart a few days earlier and he hoped that the only footwear he had left would last out for the remainder of the journey. His trainers had been well worn before the start of his trek as the young man was a very keen runner. Indeed he had often stated that running allowed him to escape from the pressures of his work.

With a start he realised that he had never given a thought to his past life or indeed to the eight-year relationship that he had shared with Susan.

The first greetings of the day were offered and returned around the campsite as the party prepared to leave. Jean-Luc smiled at the woman around his own age as she looked up at the sky before pulling on her waterproof coat.

Amandine Dubois returned the smile offered by the pleasant man before her. She had told herself many times how lucky she had been the day he rescued her from, what was to her mind, a veiled threat to her well-being.

Some months earlier, Amandine had successfully applied for a job in Avignon translating and collating some very old diaries written in both old French and Latin. A brilliant scholar specialising in French medieval history, she had been both fascinated and horrified as her body of research revealed right from the start, a place that was so dear to her. It was a stipulation of her contract that she must always be accompanied by a security guard as she studied the old manuscripts. She was never to take any work away from its safekeeping, nor should she ever discuss her work with anyone.

The young woman had been frightened of the guard who always stood behind her. The man never spoke to her but simply handed her written instructions from an unknown employer.

On the day that Amandine felt that her work was drawing to a close, she received a handwritten letter from her employer telling her that he was delighted with her work and he wanted all her private details for future reference. As she read the letter, the hairs on the back of her neck had stood up and the woman had been terrified for her life.

As soon as she had finished her work that evening, Amandine had driven to the airport and taken a flight to London. She had found a small bedsit in the great metropolis and for a week she had hardly moved from her refuge. As she had never received her last month's wages, she had needed to find a job in order to send money home to her family. Armed with a very impressive CV, she had found a post at an internationally known library. It had pleased her that most of her work was in the offices away from the general public. One day, she had been asked to help a gentleman who was researching the various routes through France and Spain to Santiago de Compostela. A rapport had quickly been established between the couple. An avid walker back in her homeland, Amandine envied this opportunity to make the celebrated walk that Jean-Luc Morrison and his American group were planning.

After all the details had been finalised, Jean-Luc had invited Amandine Dubois to meet the small party of theological students so they could thank her for her invaluable help. Amandine had been about to refuse politely when she saw that they were being observed by a rather mysterious-looking man at the back of the room. The young woman couldn't tear her gaze away from the man, who although wearing dark sunglasses seemed to be staring straight at her. Suddenly he took off his glasses and she found herself looking into eyes that were completely black and with a fathomless expression.

Scared beyond belief, she had immediately offered her services as a guide to the party. Jean-Luc had been intrigued by the offer, but as he saw the look of desperation on the woman's face, he told her that he would be delighted to have her as their guide. An observant man, he had thought that the woman was possibly struggling financially. He had insisted that she accept a payment for her services that was breathtakingly generous. Despite her fear of the stranger, who had disappeared, Amandine and Jean-Luc had both laughed as she asked him who she needed to kill for such a large amount of money.

The six young Americans were keen to get underway, but waited in a good humour while the two older people checked that the campsite had been left tidy, ready for the next group of people. They had all endured rather Spartan living conditions during their long journey and they wanted nothing more than a long relaxing bath and some clean clothes to put on.

Jean-Luc had seen that Amandine, who was always rather quiet, seemed quite upset. A caring man, he immediately asked if she was okay. After the weeks of travelling together, the young woman reasoned that she could trust Jean-Luc. Over the next twenty minutes she gave him a concise report of the events that had led up to her joining forces with him on this pilgrimage. Although he had not understood the significance of her research, Jean-Luc could see that she had been frightened at the thought of the mysterious man with the black eyes.

Once she had started talking about recent events, the young woman told her new friend about her past life. Jean-Luc endeared himself to Amandine as he made a snap decision. He quickly explained to the students that their guide was very close to her home. With the promise of a hot shower, a home-cooked meal, and a chance to rest for a while, the cheerful group of young people agreed that it would be good for Amandine to see her family.

The anticipation of soon being with her loved ones put a spring in her step as the young woman led the group on a different route. She smiled as the students started to sing the by now familiar hymn, 'To be a Pilgrim'.

Sunlight reflected in the lens of the binoculars held by the man stood in a distant copse of trees. A thoughtful expression filled his face as he watched the group divert from their path. Turning to his companion, Hugo de Beziers hid his loathing well as he told the hired killer that it would be soon.

As they got into the stolen van, de Beziers told himself that the minor problem of the Dubois woman and her companions would soon be dealt with and he could go back to that interminably long search for the object that had meant so much, albeit in very different ways, to two branches of a family for nearly two thousand years.

Hugo de Beziers had been struck rigid a few months earlier as he had sifted through the applications for the researcher needed to translate the very old, meticulously recorded documents. Despite there having been at least two applicants better qualified than the Dubois woman, when he had seen her address details, there had only been one choice.

Dougeres, Pays-Basques, 2014.

In a tableau that had probably not changed for hundreds of years, the two elderly women, clad from head to foot in black, sat on the wall of the small well in the centre of one of the town's few streets. Usually part of a trio, the two women smiled as their knitting needles moved faster than the eye could see. They were making tiny woollen clothes for the new addition to the family of their great friend, the other member of their group.

The two cast experienced eyes over the rich array of luscious-looking fruit and vegetables as the market traders set up their stalls. Soon the tiny village would be full of people from all around the region as the weekly market got underway.

The van pulled up at the side of the well. The

driver cursed as he saw the black-clad women sat before him, they looked as if they would be there all day. One of the occupants of the van got from behind the wheel and made a big show of lifting a heavy sack from the back of the van.

The strange-sounding voice bothered the man as one of the old women repeated a question that he couldn't understand. Glaring at the woman who was now looking at him suspiciously, he cursed under his breath as he thought that his cover was about to be blown.

Walking the short distance to the pair, Hugo de Beziers pulled the sunglasses from his face and throwing a bundle of letters in front of the old women, snarled that they could read them in hell. As one the elderly ladies recoiled in horror as they looked into black bottomless pools of hatred.

Crossing themselves, the old ladies moved with a speed that belied their years and made for one of the tiny dwellings where they quickly bolted the door. With a smile of satisfaction, de Beziers made sure that he wasn't observed and bent quickly at the back of the well. A few minutes later the van pulled away and the elderly ladies returned to the places by the well that they had used for many years, and picked up the balls of white wool and their needles. They talked about the devil incarnate they had just seen as they resumed their knitting.

Just two miles from the village where Amandine Dubois had grown up, the young woman chatted excitedly to the group of theological students. She told them about growing up in this most beautiful of regions. Jean-Luc was only half listening as he studied the area all round him. A shiver ran through his body as he thought that he recognised certain features of the landscape. He told himself not to be stupid as he realised that he had experienced the feeling of déjà vu that most people experience at least once in their lives, that feeling of certainty that one has visited a place before, whilst knowing that they had never been anywhere near it.

His mobile phone rang loudly. He smiled as he saw that the caller was Ted Green. He had received quite a lot of calls from Ted during this journey and he was touched that the older man was making sure that all was well with Jean-Luc and his pilgrims. Ted had given notice of his plans to retire, but a few days later had offered his services to his supervisor, stating that nobody knew this run like he did.

His friend was taking a coachload of terminally ill people and their carers to the shrine of Bernadette Soubirous at Lourdes. The two men chatted for a few minutes. When Jean-Luc was about to explain about the unplanned diversion, Ted told him that he could be at their destination in around one hour. The older man added that he knew that it was market day in the village of Dougeres, and they were sure of a good lunch. Jean-Luc shook his head at his friend's encyclopaedic knowledge of the byways and villages of Europe.

The two men agreed that the two parties should have lunch together and made their goodbyes. Jean-Luc smiled as the older man shouted that the last one there could buy the sandwiches. The young man turned back towards the group of pilgrims and laughingly explained that they had just received an invitation to lunch. Something that Ted had said was niggling at the back of Jean-Luc's mind, however hard he tried he couldn't think what it was. He smiled as he thought that probably it would come back to him during the early hours of the morning.

*

On a mountain road high above the village, Hugo de Beziers looked with disgust at his psychotic companion. The hired killer paced up and down, waiting for the explosion that would signal that their intended prey had been eliminated.

Expertly focusing his binoculars on different parts of the region, de Beziers saw that there were two scenes of activity in this most difficult of terrains that could only be his two targets. As he saw the dust cloud created by the coach, he calculated which party would arrive at the intended destination first. Cold-bloodedly, he thought that it didn't really matter as the outcome would be just the same. Making sure that his back was never turned towards his accomplice, he knew that the killer had passed the sell-by date.

He had killed many times himself over the years, but he told himself that it had always been for a reason. The lunatic before him derived a sickening pleasure from killing that made Hugo's blood run cold.

Turning the high-powered binoculars to the signs of life in the small village, de Beziers saw that the two old women were still sat by the well. 'So be it,' he muttered, 'you can stay there for eternity.'

Dougeres, Pays-Basques, 2014.

Jean-Luc smiled as he saw the coach parked between the well and a small church. The tiny village was a hive of activity as people came from the communes for miles around. It gave them a chance to catch up on all the news of their friends and relatives.

The market was in full flow as trestle tables groaned under the weight of the abundant produce. There were several types of fish, freshly caught that morning with eyes so bright and skin so lustrous that one could almost think that they were still alive. Every kind of fresh vegetable was there as elderly women haggled and made disparaging remarks about the food, in a ritual that was as old as the commune.

Bottles of different strengths of locally made cider were covertly passed to men who tried unsuccessfully to hide them from the prying eyes of their womenfolk. The wives berated them publically, but everyone present knew that the women would enjoy the refreshing cider just as much as their husbands.

Amandine Dubois made her way towards the market. She shouted greetings to some and kissed other people as they stopped the good-natured young woman, remonstrating with her for being away too long. Introductions were made; the group of young theology students was almost drowned under the sea of humanity as the locals rushed forward to greet the friends of Amandine. Jean-Luc received more than a few appreciative looks from the young, and not so young women who gazed at the tall, slim stranger thinking that his snow-white hair and the dark grey eyes made for a very handsome man.

Jean-Luc made his way to the coach. As he shook hands with Ted Green, the older man introduced the carers of some of the terminally ill people aboard the coach. Coach was perhaps the wrong word as it resembled a mobile hospital. Most of the seats had been taken out to make room for beds along with all the equipment necessary to keep the patients as comfortable as possible.

The young man felt a lump in his throat as he was introduced to first one patient and then another. A man who had forsaken religion, much to his mother's dismay, he marvelled at the faith that kept these desperately sick people going. As he looked at first one and then another, he couldn't see one expression of self-pity.

Jean-Luc heard the sound of many fans as carers tried to bring some cool relief to their patients. Looking through the window of the coach he turned and asked who was ready for an ice cream and a cold drink. Every hand shot skywards, so with a smile the young man asked his own group of pilgrims to help him with the order. The ice cream salesman had parked his van besides a long wooden trestle table filled with the most delicious array of fruit. Jean-Luc asked the vendor to cut him some big slices of melon and pineapple, his mouth watered as the fresh-smelling fruit was expertly sliced. Within twenty minutes the order had been filled and there were contented smiles within the coach as all those on board enjoyed the cooling ice cream and slices of fruit.

Jean-Luc wondered aloud where Ted had disappeared to. One of the young nurses on the coach, with ice cream round her mouth, told him that Ted had needed to walk down the street to get a signal for his phone. At that moment the ice cream seller shouted that Jean-Luc had left his wallet in the van. Laughing at himself, the young man left the coach and walked back across the square and round the back of the ice cream van.

As if a giant hand had picked him up, Jean-Luc was thrown through the air as the huge explosion ripped through the small mountain village.

*

From his vantage point high above the village, Hugo de Beziers gazed down with satisfaction at the scene that resembled a slaughter house. With a look of disgust that he couldn't hide, he looked at the maniac next to him who had made the bomb. He marvelled as to how someone who could barely string two sentences together, could construct the most sophisticated explosive devices.

He had found the killer living in the red light areas of Marseilles where decent people never went. Only five feet two in height, the killer had a stocky, powerful body. Repeated use of sunbeds had resulted in dried-up skin and had aged the killer by at least ten years. Incongruously, the short cropped hair was dyed a bright orange colour and the obscenely grinning mouth revealed a few blackened stumps that served as teeth.

L'Anglaise, as she was known, had turned up in France a few years earlier. Rumours abounded as to her origins, she rarely spoke, but she would knife anyone that displeased her. De Beziers had seen the streak of ruthlessness in her that he recognised in himself. He started to give her small amounts of money for the cocaine that he had introduced her to. The evil drug that she now craved. Occasionally, whilst in a drugged state, she would make little slips and reveal some of her history.

A man who knew the benefit of meticulous research, de Beziers spent a large amount of money to discover that she had served a prison sentence for what was jokingly called manslaughter. At the time she had served in the British armed forces. An NCO, she had shown a cruel streak on several occasions and inflicted serious injuries on the new recruits who couldn't manage the increasingly difficult tasks that she set them. All the complaints were brushed under the carpet by senior officers who while not liking the sadistic streak that she showed, secretly agreed that the recruits needed to be toughened up.

One day she went too far to be ignored. A young male recruit made the mistake of telling her to her face that he was going right to the top brass to get her thrown out of the army. The woman went berserk, punching the teenager so hard in the stomach that she ruptured his spleen. Her senior officers may have been able to hide this act, but not content with leaving the unfortunate recruit alone, she proceeded to punch and kick him so much that he died from his appalling injuries.

At her trial, her defence counsel excelled himself and got her the minimum possible sentence that she could expect and she went to prison. In an indictment of the judicial service, she was sent to an open prison to serve the second half of her sentence. She absconded the first night and somehow managed to get to Europe.

Hugo de Beziers looked covertly at the monster whose reputation he had helped to build and thought that thankfully she would soon be gone. Bizarrely, de Beziers had had the Englishwoman accompany him while he arranged his nefarious activities. Thinking that she wasn't right in the head, he had boasted of all his accomplishments and told her of his burgeoning criminal empire. Jumping up and down in delight, she punched the air in triumph. The woman was in a state of euphoria; pointing down to the village, she gestured to Hugo that they should go down. The instigator of the heinous crime nodded his head in agreement and the two of them got into their stolen vehicle.

Within minutes they had pulled up in the rubble-strewn street. With satisfaction they looked at the result of their handiwork. Body parts were lying all around; clothing that had been blown from the wearers' bodies blew down the street. The smell of burning flesh assaulted their nostrils. There was not a single movement as they looked carefully in turn at anything that resembled a human body.

Satisfied that there were no witnesses to their terrible crime, Hugo de Beziers signalled to his accomplice; the two got back into the stolen van and drove from the scene of destruction.

*

The pain was unbearable. He felt as if someone had taken an axe to his skull and repeatedly struck him. The bright sunlight assaulted the one eye that he could force open. He tried to open his mouth to call out, but his parched lips would not respond. His tortured body was breaking down, he felt wet warmth on his thigh as his bladder emptied and he knew that he was spiralling towards the death that his battered body craved.

A strong arm shook him, and a calm voice ordered him to open his eyes. He felt it again and again as he tried to embrace an eternal sleep. 'Jean-Luc, Jean-Luc open your eyes, it is not your time.'

The young man forced an eye to open. Through the tiny slit, a barely discernible shape enveloped in a bright light was revealed. Again, a disembodied voice wormed its way into the confused mind of Jean-Luc.

'You have much to do, my son, and a long, full life to live. Sleep now and we will talk again in due course.' The human-shaped shaft of light placed gentle hands on Jean-Luc, bringing an instant peace to the young man's battered body. For the second time that day, it felt as if an unseen force was picking him up, but this time he felt an incredible calmness wash over him.

*

Hugo de Beziers drove the stolen mail van some miles away from the apocalyptic scene and parked beside his own powerful car. He realised that his murderous accomplice was entering that state of depression that she always felt after the excitement of a killing spree had worn off. He knew that he had to act before she reached her own peculiar normality and became a very dangerous person to be with.

Alighting from the stolen vehicle, he turned to his companion.

'That went so well, I can't believe how you

managed to construct a bomb of such power. To show my gratitude, I have a little bonus for you.'

Her eyes filled with pleasure, the sociopathic killer knew that she was about to receive her second fix of the day. Her hands went to her mouth in an almost childlike expression of delight.

Hugo had known that his flattering remarks and the promise of cocaine would keep her calm for the next part of his plan. Quickly crossing to his car, he retrieved a small package from the glove compartment. Returning to the passenger door of the van, de Beziers nonchalantly threw the package to the killer. She tore at the wrapping, anxious to travel to that dreamlike state she craved. Her face was a study of concentration as she used a magazine and a credit card to expertly fashion the cocaine into a long narrow strip. Hugo quietly opened the back door of the van, as his employee started her trip. On his hands and knees, de Beziers crept forward; he thought that she would be too far gone to notice him, but nevertheless he wasn't about to take any stupid risks.

Earlier that day Hugo had given L'Anglaise her first snort. While she had been in a paroxysm of delight, he had carefully removed the head rest from the back of the passenger seat. This had been a calculated risk that had paid off as the diminutive woman liked to travel on the edge of her seat with her hands on the dashboard.

Swiftly, he pulled a small object from his pocket; passing his hands in front of the woman, he made a quick calculation as to the location of her windpipe. Involuntarily she jerked forward, which gave de Beziers the opportunity he needed. His eyes closed as he pulled on the two handles of the garrotte with all his strength. With a peculiar instinct, the woman had realised that her life was in danger. Quickly, she had raised her hand to avert the threatening constriction at her throat. De Beziers pulled and pulled as L'Anglaise struggled and twitched until finally she was still. De Beziers lay on the floor of the van. His whole body shook from the efforts of the last few minutes. He felt secure in the knowledge that nobody would miss L'Anglaise.

He looked with distaste at the body of the postman he had killed earlier. The flies were enjoying an unexpected meal on the bloated corpse. They buzzed in indignation as de Beziers, with a great physical effort, dragged the body into the back of the post van.

He knew that he still had much to do so reluctantly he walked on shaking legs to his car and removed a heavy petrol can from the boot. He could only just lift the large can. Deciding that it would be easier if he held the petrol can to his chest with both his arms beneath it, he removed the binoculars from round his neck and placed them on a flat stone nearby. Without another thought for his latest victims, de Beziers splashed fuel all over the van and threw a lighted match at it.

As he walked back to his car, he looked all around him. For some minutes he had had the feeling that he was being watched. He had relied on his instincts for many years and almost got out of his vehicle to explore the area for any threat to him. Looking at the burning van just a short distance away, he knew that as soon as the flames reached the petrol tank, it would become a bomb, capable of causing a lot more damage. With one more look around the area, he realised that he needed to leave immediately.

Quickly, he drove down the mountainside to the rear of the destroyed village. A man wandered aimlessly along the street, uninjured but in a complete state of shock. As the mass murderer stopped the car at the side of him, Ted Green stared with loathing at the monster before him.

'All those poor people, all my friends and the villagers, all dead. How could you do that? What kind of a man are you?'

De Beziers watched the man before him as he ranted and raved about the deaths of so many innocent people. Calmly, he walked towards Ted Green and offered him a bundle of money. Ted knocked the money from his hands and threatened that he would tell the police everything he knew.

'Which is exactly what? Can you tell them my name, where I live? What was my motive? I'm afraid, Ted, that you can't tell them anything. You were quick enough to accept the offer of a large amount of money when I approached you in London. Will you tell the police that you simply wanted to augment your pension? That you betrayed your friends for a few thousand pounds?'

Thinking back to the time when that accursed Dubois woman had fled from Avignon, de Beziers had quickly discovered that she had flown to London. It had taken him a week to find her. Relentlessly he had travelled from one library to another, knowing that the woman would have to work to support herself in this most expensive of cities. Finally he had struck lucky. As he had walked seemingly innocently around the library he had observed the Dubois woman deep in conversation with a white-haired stranger. That they were conversing in French had caused his breathing to quicken. He had heard enough to realise that the man was planning a pilgrimage through France to Spain. He had cursed as the woman looked at him, as her shoulders slumped with shock, he had made his escape.

Outside the library, he had waited until the tall white-haired man left and then simply followed him. For two days he had watched the stranger's every move. He wrote down descriptions of who he met, where he worked, and had even followed him to the house of an older man. The following night, he had returned to the small terraced house and had charmed his way inside. Ted Green was an affable fellow and always ready for a chat. He had told the Frenchman all about the job he had just retired from, and spoke in great detail of his friend Jean-Luc Morrisson.

Ted Green, his shoulders bowed in grief, looked at the man who had told him that he merely wanted to stop Amandine Dubois from finishing her journey to Santiago de Compostela. The man before him was right, what did he know and would the authorities listen to him?

As he looked at the beaten man before him, de Beziers played his trump card, one that would ensure that Ted Green would keep silent.

'If you intend to go to the police, Ted, you might like to know that right at this moment, some of my accomplices are making arrangements to escort Sally

Roberts and her daughter Molly to a place where you will never find them. At one word from me their throats will be slit and their bodies disposed of.'

He had lied of course, but the horrified expression on the face of his unwilling companion filled him with pleasure. He further twisted the knife by adding, 'Given that you will soon be officially declared dead, you can serve as my driver. With your experience of the roads of Europe, that will suit me very nicely.'

Dougeres, Pays-Basques, 2014.

White-faced with shock, the elderly man walked along the barely recognisable street. He looked at the burnt-out chassis of a coach and crossed himself as he thought that some poor tourists had perished along with the villagers. Names and faces of his friends and neighbours ran through his tortured mind. He could not comprehend what had happened, that such destruction had invaded this tiny community where he had lived most of his life.

Looking round, he noticed that most of the small cottages in the main street had been destroyed; cottages that had been constructed hundreds of years ago were now just piles of rubble, in the midst of which lay twisted and broken windows and doors. Remnants of flower pots that had earlier been filled with beautiful flowers by proud hands lay in the dust.

He looked sadly at the destroyed well. In his long life the well had been a meeting place for sweethearts, a play area for children, and a seat for all as they passed the time of day with their friends.

The elderly doctor knew that he too would have perished but for the arrival of a new baby just a few miles away. He had just handed the infant to her exhausted but delighted mother when he heard the terrific explosion. He had driven to the village as if the hounds of hell were after him.

His tear-filled eyes rested on small round objects lying forlornly in the dust. As his mind cleared he saw that they were two balls of blood-soaked wool. He remembered the elderly ladies proudly telling him that they would knit some woollens for the commune's latest citizen.

Dr Daniel Doissneau fell to his knees, his whole body convulsed as the shock finally took hold of him. He cried long and hard.

A faint noise jerked his head upwards. He listened carefully, there it was again. It sounded like a frightened kitten making little mewing noises. Looking in the direction of the sounds, the elderly doctor struggled to make sense of the scene before his eyes. Lying amongst the shattered fruit and vegetables was something that had once resembled a human being. Walking over, his eyes filled with compassion the doctor saw a man with terrible head injuries. His medical training told him that the poor wretch didn't have long to live, but he knew that he must do something.

*

Geographical borders were forgotten, long-held political arguments brushed aside and the forces for good descended on the tiny mountain community. Offers of help came from all corners of the continent as the news of the tragedy travelled quickly.

An American battleship had been on manoeuvres in the Bay of Biscay and had quickly dispatched a helicopter and a team of medics to the stricken village. There hadn't been much that the medical team could do apart from respectfully collect body parts and place them in bags away from prying eyes.

The world's media had descended like vultures on the tiny mountain community. All anxious for the exclusive that would lift them above their competitors; the reporters badgered the elderly doctor in a multitude of tongues.

The surgeon, who had examined the battered body of the one remaining survivor of the atrocity, roughly shouldered his way past the baying mass of media. Giving them all a look of contempt he gently led the elderly man to the helicopter, telling the pilot that the doctor must travel with the patient and be treated for the effects of shock at the nearest hospital.

The navy surgeon was a big man who had played football for his college in his younger days, and now he used his physical strength to good effect. One very keen photographer thrust the lens of his camera into the face of Howard Steinberg, his reward was to find himself lying in the dust with his nose pouring blood.

As he climbed aboard the helicopter, the navy surgeon told the pilot to make good speed, while to himself he muttered that no amount of speed could save the dying man lying in the back of the cabin.

Like baying hounds the assembled reporters got into their cars and made for the local hospitals, all anxious for that human interest story that would sell their papers.

High in the mountains a group of quiet men looked down on the village as the specialist forensic teams and the local police searched for clues to ascertain exactly what had happened.

*

The young woman, mindful of her charges in the back of the minibus, drove as fast as she possibly could towards the spiralling clouds of smoke.

Excitedly, the children gazed upwards at the huge military helicopter as it sped away from the scene. Children and adults alike looked at the convoy of cars that drove quickly in the direction of the helicopter. The woman's heart sank as she realised that they were heading away from her own village.

Cries of horror were followed by screams and tears as the children saw for the first time the carnage that had once been their home.

The smaller children cried for their parents, as the older children in the small group looked to the driver of the vehicle to make everything right as she had done so many times.

Her mind was in turmoil, she knew that she couldn't take the children any nearer. But what could she do with them?

Stopping the minibus, she looked back through tear-filled eyes at the bewildered faces behind her. She couldn't stop the tears as the grief shook her body. One by one the children came forward and hugged her and each other. The sounds of crying filled the vehicle for a long time. Finally knowing that her immediate concern was getting the children to safety, she started the vehicle and turning the minibus round, drove off in the direction of a nearby village, where she knew that her many friends would take these poor orphans in until a permanent solution could be found.

Bayonne Hospital.

Philip Morrisson strode into the reception area of the hospital. Closely followed by his son Vincent, worry and grief was etched on both their faces.

Like the rest of the world they had followed the events in the Pyrenees for three days until the older man received the phone call that every parent dreads.

The two men identified themselves to the receptionist and soon the director of the hospital and the chief surgeon arrived and introduced themselves. The chief surgeon wore a funereal expression on his face as he quietly explained the extensive head injuries that Jean-Luc had suffered, and despite him hanging on for three days, there was little hope for his survival. Bluntly, he added that if the young man did survive, he would in all probability need constant care for the rest of his life.

Vincent Morrisson was only half listening. He was watching the rather strange behaviour of a man dressed as a hospital porter. The man was pushing a trolley but seemed to be unsure as to his destination. In the muted illumination of the hospital corridors, Vincent wondered why the subject of his curiosity should be wearing dark glasses.

Alarm bells rang in the mind of the younger Morrisson as the porter disappeared into a room guarded by two police officers. Vincent raced down the corridor. The policemen, their minds and bodies numbed by the interminable hours spent outside the private room, were slow to react. One of them rose to his feet as Vincent reached the room. Knowing that he had no time for explanations, he simply shoulder charged the policeman who was propelled backwards into his colleague. The two fell in a confused melee of arms and legs.

Vincent pushed open the door to see the porter bent over Jean-Luc holding a rather vicious-looking knife. The killer, for that was what he obviously was, smiled evilly as he looked at Vincent Morrisson. Stood before him was a short, chunky individual. With a shaven head and wearing glasses, he had an almost owlish expression on his face. The porter advanced, holding the knife expertly. He was going to enjoy this. A few moments later he was lying on his back, stunned as to how this fat little man could have disarmed him. He couldn't have known that Vincent was a black belt in judo and indeed had represented France in international competitions.

Just as Vincent was about to demand answers from the intended killer, the door burst open and the two, by now, fully restored police officers raced in, revolvers ready and pointed at the young man. They screamed at him to lie down on the floor; knowing he had no other option, he quickly complied.

In the noise and confusion the porter made good his escape. As he slipped the dark glasses over his eyes, Vincent was shocked to see that the man's eyes were completely black.

Two hours later, explanations had been offered and accepted. Handshakes were made all round and the two officers of the law smiled ruefully, with one of them declaring that he would rather face a rampaging bull than tackle Vincent Morrisson.

Philip and his younger son gathered round the bedside of Jean-Luc. The older man's eyes filled with tears as he remembered his vibrant son and thought that the boy would not want to merely exist.

Vincent, a practising doctor, looked carefully at his brother and thought that there were some rather subtle movements that didn't usually occur with deeply comatose patients. Suddenly, his eyes opened and he struggled to focus as if trying to make sense of his surroundings. Jean-Luc tried to open his parched lips but to no avail. Vincent quickly lifted a water bottle from a trolley and pushing a straw into the top of the bottle, gently fed his brother a few drops of the liquid.

Jean-Luc looked for long moments at Vincent who waited, hardly daring to breathe. His face lit up with joy as his brother spoke.

'Now I know that I must have died and gone to hell, because God would never have an angel as ugly as you.' The words had a peculiar rasping quality and they had struggled out of the young man's mouth, but Vincent and his father Philip were overjoyed.

The chief surgeon shook his head in disbelief. He had been practising medicine for almost forty years, but if anyone had told him that the event he had just witnessed would have taken place, he would have laughed at them for a fool. He knew that now the patient was on the road to recovery, he would have to be given a thorough examination as soon as possible.

The elderly man walked into the hospital's reception area. He was stunned to see several members of staff stood in small groups, discussing in animated tones, the events of the day. A receptionist recognised the frequent visitor and told him of the miraculous recovery of the man from the village.

Daniel was astounded; surely she was confusing the man from the explosion with another patient. He had visited the hospital each day, fully expecting to be told that the grievously injured man had succumbed to his injuries and also to take his mind from his own grief that now had settled into a dull ache.

The receptionist escorted him to the private room and introduced him to the male members of the Morrisson family. Jean-Luc's father, although not quite sure who the elderly man was, came forward and shook his hand warmly.

'I am very pleased to meet you Dr Doissneau, do you know my son?'

Walking towards the bed, Dr Daniel ran a professional eye over the patient, all the while, shaking his head in disbelief.

'I found your son in the aftermath of the explosion. To be honest, I didn't dare hope for his survival; his head injuries were so terrible.' Turning to the patient, Daniel took one of the younger man's hands in his own.

'Jean-Luc, I am amazed but delighted at your recovery. Amandine, my daughter, sent me several texts, detailing your part in her escape from London; I want to thank you for the kindness that you showed to a very frightened woman.'

Jean-Luc's eyes filled with tears as he remembered the vivacious young woman whose company he had enjoyed immensely. As his thoughts went back to all of his group, and indeed the gravely ill patients on the coach and the warm, friendly villagers from that dreadful day, he cried. All the shock of the blast, the faces of the people he had known, and the ones he had met that fateful morning came back to haunt him. He cried for several minutes; the elderly man pulled Jean-Luc's head to his shoulder until the tears stopped.

As the tears subsided, Daniel ran his fingers gently over Jean-Luc's head. Most of the terrible swelling had gone down, and the surgeon had expertly stitched up the wounds received in the bomb blast and those caused by the operations that had been necessary to save the young man's life.

His face was a mass of stitches, caused by countless shattered windows sending slivers of glass in all directions. Jean-Luc would always wear the scars of that dreadful morning.

Still with the patient's head in his hands, the elderly doctor smiled as he remarked that Amandine had described Jean-Luc in her texts. He commented that it was a shock to discover that the mass of long white hair had gone.

'I can answer that Doctor, you see my elder brother has always admired me, wanting to model his life on my own so virtuous one, that he shaved off all of his hair in order to look like me.'

The four men laughed at Vincent Morrisson's remarks. Daniel thought that two brothers could not be so different. Nature had shown her bizarre sense of humour with the two men, giving Jean-Luc his English father's tall slim build and his French mother's colouring. Conversely Vincent was short and stocky like his mother's side, yet he had had the wispy fair hair like his father that he had shaved off at an early age.

At the unspoken question in Jean-Luc's eyes, Philip Morrisson reassured him that his mother was fine. Turning to Daniel he explained that his wife, Marie-Francoise, was looking after one of their two daughters who was going through a rather difficult pregnancy.

An air of despondency settled over Daniel as he thought sadly of his own grandchild. He smiled and waved his hand dismissively as Philip Morrisson apologised for his lack of sensitivity.

Petit Dougeres, Pays Basque, France.

For the last three days the young woman and her niece had existed in a state of shock. Numb with grief, they had, without protest, allowed themselves to be gently bullied into accepting refuge at the house of a dear family friend in a village just a few miles from their own.

They went through the motions of living, grateful for the tranquillity of their friend's quiet home.

Quite often, it is young children who show the

first signs of recovery from a great loss. The six-year-old girl shyly asked for permission to watch the television. Her hostess beamed with delight at the child, grateful that the youngster wanted some normality back in her life.

Sat on the floor in front of the television, the little girl prepared to press a button on the remote control to change to one of the channels dedicated to cartoons.

The two women were quietly drinking tea when the little girl raced over to them. The girl laughed and cried at the same time, as she uttered one word over and over. 'Look, look, look.'

Mystified, the two women allowed themselves to be led to the television. A special news bulletin was reporting on the events at a hospital in Bayonne, where an unknown man had tried to assassinate the sole survivor of the bombing of the mountain village.

Chapter 4

London, England.

Hundreds of miles away, Sally Roberts and her daughter Molly were watching the evening news on the television.

Even though they had only known Ted Green for a short while, the cheerful cockney had worked his way into their affections. Molly in particular, had idolised Ted. He had never been patronising with her and had always shown a genuine interest in her school work. Molly had confided in him that she dearly wanted one of the latest phones. Ted had known that the girl would never ask her mother for money as they were struggling financially as it was. Ted Green had suggested to Molly that if she was a good girl and continued to help her mother, who knew what may turn up on her birthday.

Her birthday had passed by almost unnoticed the previous day, as they were still saddened by the realisation that they would not see the cheerful man, who they had both come to regard as a great friend, again. Molly had cried when she had opened a present from Ted. Both she and her mother had been amazed at his generosity. The delivery driver had assured them that Mr Green had insisted that the shop set the phone up with the few of Molly's contacts that Ted knew on it so that she could use it right away. The phone, although never far from Molly's sight, was still unused.

Now as the mother and daughter watched the news on the television, they were astonished that not only was Jean-Luc Morrisson alive, but that someone had tried to kill him as he lay in his hospital bed.

Sally had always been quick witted. Turning to her daughter, she said, 'Molly, did Ted have Jean-Luc's number put on your phone?'

The girl quickly scrolled through the contacts and brandishing the phone excitedly, declared that there it was.

Sally took the phone and pressed the call button against Jean-Luc's name. Her heart sank as a voice answered and proceeded to speak rapidly in French. Quickly cutting in, Sally apologised for not knowing any French, and asked if by any chance the respondent spoke English.

On the other end of the line, a slightly amused Vincent Morrisson stated that yes, he knew a few words of English.

Vincent grinned at his father and brother as a torrent of words exploded from the phone. He listened patiently as the woman demanded to know how Jean-Luc was and if there was anything that she could do to help. Seeing the smile of recognition on his brother's face, Vincent thought that perhaps there was a romantic involvement there.

Impetuously, he asked if it would be possible for the woman to go to the airport the following morning and take the first available flight to Biarritz.

'I'm s-s-s-sorry,' the woman stammered, 'but I couldn't possibly afford two air tickets.'

Cursing at his assumption, Vincent apologised and told the by now thoroughly embarrassed woman that the flight would be arranged by him, and she had simply to turn up at the airport with her travelling companion. After names and details had been exchanged, the two people ended their conversation.

A red-faced Vincent squirmed as his brother teased him mercilessly that he had finally talked to a woman on a subject that wasn't medical.

Vincent Morrisson had always been rather shy where the opposite sex were concerned and had chosen to immerse himself in his work.

*

In his hotel room, Hugo de Beziers cursed for perhaps the twentieth time that day as he watched the news bulletin. He knew that he would have to be patient, but he was determined that he would destroy the man who could perhaps supply the police with information that may lead them to him.

He cursed as he recalled how that man in the hospital room had so expertly disarmed him. He remembered that the stranger had looked right at him as he replaced his dark sunglasses. Now there were two people that he needed to eliminate, and if there were any other people near them, well that would be unlucky for them.

He had organised a room for Ted Green in the same hotel, but was careful that the two men were rarely seen together. That wasn't difficult as the Londoner only left his room to eat.

His mind worked feverishly as he made plans for the destruction of Jean-Luc Morrisson.

Hopital de Bayonne.

Vincent Morrisson had enjoyed chatting to Sally during the short drive from the airport. He thought that she wasn't conventionally pretty but she had such strength of character about her that he thought his brother was a very lucky man.

Vincent had tried to involve Molly in their conversation, which had caused Sally to look at him gratefully, but the young girl seemed painfully shy.

At the hospital, introductions were quickly made. Philip Morrisson quickly put the Englishwoman and her daughter at their ease and the small group of people soon began to enjoy each other's company.

Sally looked at the sleeping Jean-Luc. Her face mirrored her concern as she noticed the numerous scars on his still-swollen face. She knew that the physical scars would fade but wondered what effect the terrible events of a few days ago would have on his mind, once he left the safety of the hospital.

The presence of so many people in the room jolted Jean-Luc from his sleep. His eyes crinkled with pleasure as they rested on Sally Roberts. Whooping with delight, she launched herself at the invalid. After a moment, Molly joined her mother in hugging the laughing man.

A mixture of laughter and tears caused the group round the bed to turn to the opened door. In seconds the elderly doctor was locked in an embrace with a young woman and a small girl. As the trio finally parted, the woman lifted her head. The blood drained from the face of Jean-Luc, as he stared at the woman.

'Amandine, how, how is that possible?'

The young woman turned her tear-stained face towards Jean-Luc. A chill seemed to settle over the room as she looked at him with something close to contempt in her eyes.

Her father quickly realised the reason for his daughter's attitude. With a slightly embarrassed shrug of his shoulders, he gathered the remains of his family to him and told Philip Morrisson that he would talk to them all later.

Dougeres, Pays-Basque, France.

The convoy of cars pulled up in front of the small church. It had been a hectic couple of days since the arrival at the Bayonne hospital of Dr Daniel's daughter. As she had introduced herself to the receptionist, the young man had told her that a courier had just delivered a letter for Jean-Luc. Gwenaelle Doissneau had dropped the letter into her handbag and simply forgotten about it in her desire to be with her father.

Later that evening, Jean-Luc had ordered his family and newfound friends to go and have a meal and let him have some peace and quiet. The meal had lasted long into the night as the group of people, thrown together by tragedy, had made the first tentative steps towards friendship.

The following morning, the whole group had gathered round Jean-Luc's bed as Dr Daniel handed him the letter. They all assumed that it was a get well message from a stranger. The few typed words conveyed a threat that if a certain long sought-after object wasn't delivered to a place of the author's choosing, the family and friends of Jean-Luc would die, one by one. Shock filled all their faces. Nobody could understand what the letter meant. Slowly, Jean-Luc and his brother Vincent began to piece together the few things that they did know following the inclusion into the pilgrimage of Amandine Dubois.

It had been the elderly doctor from the bombed village who had provided the most logical solution to their problem. He had quietly reasoned that the maniac responsible for the heinous act would not be content with killing just Jean-Luc's family; he would feel that he must destroy anybody close to the Morrissons. Before any objections could be raised, he had quickly taken a mobile phone from his pocket and held a short conversation in the Basque language.

Within hours a convoy of cars had pulled up at the hospital. The chief surgeon had protested that he couldn't allow his patient to be moved as there were concerns over Jean-Luc's ability to walk. Vincent Morrisson had effortlessly lifted his brother from the bed and a group of quiet, yet capable-looking men had quickly ushered the whole group into the cars and driven out of Bayonne. As they had arrived in Dougeres, the doctor had explained that their protectors were friends and relatives of all the villagers who had perished in the bombing.

The short journey from Bayonne had proved exhausting for Jean-Luc. The elderly doctor had quickly made a phone call to a family friend in a nearby village who, just as Daniel had expected, promised to find accommodation for the entire group. He quickly explained to the grateful strangers that for centuries the Basque peoples of France and Spain had welcomed people from all over the world into their homes.

Daniel Doissneau had not exaggerated, all the members of the tiny commune had indeed welcomed their guests with smiles and handshakes, declaring that any friends of the doctor were their friends also. A bed had been moved onto the ground floor of one of the houses and a grateful Jean-Luc allowed his brother Vincent to help him get undressed and into bed.

Philip Morrisson realised that Alais, the granddaughter of the old doctor, was in deep shock at hearing of her mother's death. The little girl had withdrawn into her own private world. Gwenaelle, the girl's aunt, had explained to Philip that the child's father had died in a road accident just eighteen months before and now she had been orphaned like all the children from the village.

The young woman explained that on the day of the bombing she, as the teacher of the local school, had decided to take the children on a field trip. It had been a spur of the moment decision that mercifully had stopped another thirteen names being added to the list of the dead.

Avignon, France.

Hugo de Beziers gazed from the window of his luxury apartment. The views of the beautiful medieval city failed to move him. He was busy planning his next move to obtain the one thing that would give him the power that he craved above anything.

He had instructed one of his trusted henchmen to find a room for Ted Green and to guard him night and day, until Hugo needed the Englishman. Gazing at Ted's phone, which he had taken from the distraught coach driver, he carefully planned his next move.

Three times he had driven into the area of the bombed village. Each time he had been followed by several quiet men. The men never spoke to him, he had found that very unnerving, but simply watched his every move. He had known that he had no chance of finding Jean-Luc Morrisson and his small group of friends.

Taking a new mobile phone from his pocket, he quickly typed in Jean-Luc's number and deliberated over the composition of the text he was about to send.

Dougeres, Pays Basque, France.

Jean-Luc had quietly insisted that his brother drive him over to the ruined village. His father had quieted Vincent's objections, telling him that perhaps his elder brother needed to see the place of so much destruction to try and piece together the events of that terrible day.

Effortlessly, Vincent lifted Jean-Luc from the passenger seat of the car and sat him in the wheelchair that their host had borrowed from a friend. All the villagers had rallied round to provide accommodation and a sense of belonging to the Morrisson and Roberts families.

The two men made several circuits of the deserted village. They looked at the shattered masonry of the well, the centrepiece of the main square. A few houses on the edge of the village remained; houses with soot-blackened blinds covering shattered window frames stood in silence as Jean-Luc and his brother walked slowly past. Thankfully all the signs that people had died had been removed. To the outside world, the lives of the survivors of Dougeres were like yesterday's newspapers.

The two men looked in amazement at the only building that remained on the main street, the small village church.

Vincent watched the brother that he knew and loved so much. He searched Jean-Luc's face for signs of depression. He was delighted to see the resolve and grim determination in the other man's face that augured well for the future.

The two men were startled to hear Jean-Luc's mobile phone ring. Jean-Luc's brow furrowed in disbelief as he stared at the text message displayed on his phone. After he had read it for perhaps the fifth time, he silently handed the phone to his brother.

In an unspoken agreement, Vincent loaded his brother and the wheelchair into his car and quickly drove back towards their temporary home.

*

Dr Daniel Doissneau and Philip Morrisson had quickly become friends and both men were delighted to discover that they shared a love of music and chess. Huddled over the chess board they would exchange stories of the families and of their hopes for the future. A future that just a short time ago had almost completely been destroyed.

'If you don't mind me asking, Daniel, do you know why Gwenaelle seems to hate Jean-Luc?'

Dr Daniel smiled. 'My daughter doesn't hate your son, Philip; she is grieving for her sister. My daughters were identical twins and as they grew up they shared so much together. It has often been recorded that one twin can feel the pain that the other is suffering. That was certainly the case with Amandine and Gwenaelle. They would often amaze people round them by knowing just what the other was thinking or about to say. I think that when Gwenaelle looks at Jean-Luc she thinks that he is responsible for her sister's death. In time reason will prevail and she will learn that your son was just another victim of that terrible tragedy.'

The two men sat in a comfortable silence. The calm was disturbed as a rather excited Vincent burst through the door carrying his elder brother in his arms. The two older men thought that Jean-Luc and Vincent were about to explode, their eyes were wild as they looked all around them as if searching for some hidden threat.

Philip Morrisson, as he had done so many times in the boys' childhood, calmed them down with a few quiet words. Then he told them to explain the reason for their agitated state.

Pulling the mobile phone from his pocket, Jean-Luc selected the recently received text and simply handed it to his father. Philip's face turned white as he read the text. Silently, he handed it on to Daniel Doissneau. After reading it to himself, the doctor read the text aloud.

'By now you will probably be thinking that the letter you received a few days ago was just some kind of sick joke. I am about to disappoint you. You have luckily escaped death twice in a few days. You think that you are safe surrounded by your bodyguards, well there are several ways to get at you, as you are about to discover. I am sure that the Dubois woman would have told you of her work for me, so I have decided that you can help me find the object of my search. Then and only then will I disappear from your lives.

'Do not think of bringing the police in on this as it will cause me to inflict even more suffering on you and those close to you.'

The four men stared at one another. A complete lack of understanding at the text message covered their faces.

As one, the men heard a car pulling up outside. Knowing that Gwenaelle and her niece Alais would soon enter they forced themselves to chat about mundane subjects to avoid spreading the distress that the text message had brought.

London, England, two days later.

Susan Travers cursed under her breath as her managing director's voice droned on. Looking round the table, she saw several pairs of eyes with the same glazed expression that she was wearing.

She glanced at her watch and cursed again as she realised that she wouldn't have time to go home and change, she would just have to head straight to Covent Garden. She didn't want to miss the opening night of the opera that had just enjoyed a sensational twelve-month run on Broadway.

After what seemed like an eternity, the talkative man started to tidy the pile of papers that he had been reading extracts from. As one, his staff rose to their feet and started to make for the door. Susan Travers cursed again as her boss held her back for a few moments to ask her to be in his office early the following morning.

Susan was the last one out and watched in frustration as her colleagues filled the lift. Despite their assurances that there was room for one more, the young woman shouted goodnight and made for the staircase. The door was slowly closing shut. Something at the back of Susan's mind told her that someone must have just gone down the stairs.

As she peered over the railing, Susan was relieved that she couldn't see or hear anyone. Thankful that she was alone, the young woman took a compact and some lipstick from her handbag and decided to make a few running repairs.

Her heart skipped a beat as she looked in the

mirror of the compact. She froze in terror as she gazed into a pair of completely black eyes. The compact and lipstick fell from her hands and shattered on the concrete staircase.

Unable to even turn round or cry out, the petrified young woman felt an indescribable pain as the stiletto blade severed her spinal column. Her lifeless body tumbled down the staircase.

A smile of satisfaction covered the face of Hugo de Beziers. After savouring his act for a few moments, he carefully checked his clothing for any drops of blood, although he knew that cutting someone's spinal cord allowed very little blood to escape. Despite that, he took an overcoat from his holdall and quickly put it on. Placing the stiletto into his bag, to be disposed of at the earliest opportunity, the killer donned a pair of dark sunglasses and without another glance at his latest victim, made his way quickly down the staircase.

Exiting the building, de Beziers hailed a taxi and directed the driver to Heathrow Airport. He removed a newspaper from his bag to deter the cab driver from striking up a conversation.

As the cab came to a halt at a red traffic light, the taxi driver engaged in some cheerful banter with a fellow cab driver alongside him. Hugo de Beziers quickly pulled back the carpet on the floor of the cab and placed the knife beneath the carpet and as close to the seat as he could.

As he stepped from the taxi at the airport, de Beziers paid his fare and gave the driver a small tip, reasoning that the man would be more likely to remember him if he didn't leave a gratuity.

As he waited to board his flight, de Beziers played back the day's events in his mind.

He knew much of Jean-Luc Morrisson's life in London from Ted Green. It had been a simple task to contact the managing director of the popular women's magazine. He had convinced the man that he wanted to publish a series of true life tales on that most topical of subjects, the Great War. He had produced false documentation showing his credentials as a respected publisher in France. Seeing the hesitation on the other man's face, de Beziers had hinted at a vacancy in his organisations head office in Paris.

It had been simple from then and over a first class meal, at de Beziers' expense, the Englishman had proved to be very talkative, telling his newfound friend details of his staff, in particular, the editor of the magazine, Susan Travers.

Dougeres, Pays Basque, France.

Vincent Morrisson looked carefully at his brother as he helped him from the car. Placing Jean-Luc in the wheelchair he pushed him to the opening in the church wall where the door had been before the explosion. Vincent was concerned for his brother. The news of Susan Travers' brutal murder had shaken her ex-boyfriend to his core.

Two detectives from London had travelled to France to interview Jean-Luc but had quickly realised that the man was so badly traumatised by his own near-death experience that he couldn't possibly help them with their inquiry.

Jean-Luc had asked for time alone to think and this was the only place that he could get the solitude that he craved.

The two men were startled as Vincent's mobile phone rang. He smiled as he saw that the caller was Sally Roberts.

Jean-Luc listened to the one-sided conversation then nodded his head as his younger brother explained that Doctor Doissneau needed some help with several casualties following a farming accident just a few miles away. He added that Sally, as a trained nurse, had insisted on helping.

Jean-Luc told his brother that he would be perfectly fine and looking at Vincent's animated expression, added that he mustn't keep Sally waiting. He laughed aloud as the other man blushed furiously.

Jean-Luc propelled his wheelchair up and down the aisles of the small church, marvelling that it had only received superficial damage. A thick layer of dust covered every part of the church interior. Absent-minded, the young man drew designs in the dust. Looking at one design in particular, he laughed at himself for being a fool and with the palm of his hand wiped the evidence of his work from the pew.

He looked at the rows of well-worn pews on each side of the aisle and noticed that there were beautifully carved designs on the ends of each one. With the sleeve of his coat he wiped the dust from the nearest one and saw the name of Doissneau carved into the wood. Excitedly he moved from pew to pew, seeing the name again and again with dates recording the passage of time.

Suddenly the family name changed. His forehead furrowed in concentration, Jean-Luc rolled himself back to the previous pew. Although the surname had changed, the same design adorned each pew down one side of the aisle. It was a mallet and a chisel suspended above a block of stone. Jean-Luc wondered at the significance and determined to ask Doctor Doissneau at the earliest opportunity.

Tired from his exertions, he laughed at himself for being as weak as a newborn kitten. The silence of the church brought great comfort to Jean-Luc and he settled back into the wheelchair to wait for his brother.

Moments later he sat bolt upright. The sound of running water had disturbed his daydreams. Looking all around the church, he could see no sign of water. Perplexed, he wheeled himself over to the doorway and gazed at the ruined well. He listened to the almost musical sound of the water, a sound that had enchanted men for centuries. In his work as an architect he had often used water to great effect, mostly for an aesthetic aid, but now he reasoned that water brought life and so a germ of an idea was implanted in his mind.

*

A torrent of emotions raced through the mind of Gwenaelle Doissneau as she ran through her beloved hills. It had been the first time since the explosion that the young woman had put on her running shoes and shorts. Running had always comforted her in times of stress, but now she couldn't seem to rid herself of her mixed-up thoughts. So much had happened in the few weeks since the explosion, they had had to cope with the massive upheaval of finding homes for all the orphaned children. In itself that hadn't been a great problem as the close-knit communities in the area had rallied round and distant relatives had stepped forward to welcome the still-grieving children into a loving embrace.

The Morrisson family had also been welcomed. Vincent in particular had proved a great help to her elderly father who really should have retired by now. The young doctor had soon become a firm favourite with the Basques; his quiet ways and his great physical strength had endeared him to the people. Often accompanied by Sally Roberts as his nurse, the two had worked alongside her father and quietly insisted on doing the lion's share of any medical work that was needed.

Gwenaelle worried constantly about her niece's state of mind. In the immediate aftermath of the explosion, Alais hadn't been told of her mother's death. Just the thought of losing her grandfather had left her distraught. That happy outcome had been overshadowed by the deaths of most of the villagers along with the pilgrims and of course, Amandine Dubois.

As she ran, Gwenaelle cried for her dead sister, thinking that she would never recover from the shock, but she cried more for Alais who had retreated into her own little world. She ate and drank and carried out any task given to her, but she did things without enthusiasm.

The young woman's thoughts turned to Jean-Luc Morrisson. She knew that she didn't hate him as she had declared in the days following the explosion, but she couldn't make conversation with him. If ever she came upon him alone she would always leave the room.

From her late sister's daily texts, she wondered, rather unkindly, where this wonderful man was. She had seen no trace of the caring, gentle man that Amandine had enthused about.

Dougeres, Pays Basque.

Jean-Luc worked like a man possessed, he wheeled himself along first one pew then another. He drew feverishly, finishing one design then starting another.

Suddenly, the young man felt a presence behind him. He felt no fear as he slowly turned round. In a calm reassuring voice, the stranger spoke. Jean-Luc felt as though an electric shock had passed through his body; he had heard that voice before, but where?

'Hello Jean-Luc, it is good to see you so well.'

'I'm sorry, do we know one another?'

The man seemed to be a few years older than Jean-Luc. His forehead was lined and his eyes narrowed like someone who had spent many years under an unrelenting sun. As his eyes travelled down the man's body, Jean-Luc had the impression that the man had great physical strength. His upper arms and shoulders rippled with muscle. Strangely, his forearms carried numerous scars. Jean-Luc didn't know why but he immediately thought that perhaps the stranger had been or was a fisherman. As he looked at the other man, Jean-Luc wondered why the man seemed so familiar.

The stranger smiled kindly as his wheelchair-bound companion finished his appraisal.

'What can I do for you?' Jean-Luc asked.

The stranger looked first at one of the designs etched in the dust, then another. He walked slowly along each pew. As he came to the first pew that the younger man had drawn on, he turned and smiled kindly. Jean-Luc blushed as he realised what the man was looking at, although he was sure that he had wiped the evidence of that particular drawing away.

'These sketches are quite beautiful, my son. They convey great strength and practicality yet are so simple. You have set your dreams on the path of giving them a physical existence. Now what are you going to do about it?'

*

The sky had been a vast expanse of clear unbroken blue when Gwenaelle had started her run. She, more than most, should have known how quickly the weather in the mountains could change. Within seconds the sky had turned black. Freezing cold rain took her breath away. The raindrops were like stair rods as they exploded onto her head and body. Desperately she looked for shelter. She knew that her home village was nearby, but she had resolved never to set foot in Dougeres again.

Gwenaelle raced towards a copse of trees. A lightning bolt beat her to it and crashed into the trees, severing branches in its wake.

Raising her fist to the sky, the young woman cursed as she realised that she would die without shelter and dry clothes. Already a chill was coursing through her body. With a heavy heart, she turned towards the village that she still cried for at night.

Dougeres, Pays Basque.

'What can I do about it?' Jean-Luc asked. 'Most of the villagers are dead, who would want to help me?'

'My son, people are drawn to you like moths to a flame. You can make your dreams a reality. A community has existed here for centuries, it must not be allowed to die through the acts of one madman. Jean-Luc, you must bring the people back.'

'But they all perished in the explosion,' Jean-Luc insisted.

'The children must return, then others will follow. Dougeres will grow again into a place ready for the descendants of my descendants.'

Jean-Luc was much too polite to remark on this passionate man's slip of the tongue. As he gazed at the other man, he saw the intensity in his eyes and despite his misgivings, felt his own excitement mounting.

'This church, built with loving hands, has for hundreds of years been the heart of the village.' He grasped Jean-Luc's hands fiercely. 'Make it so again.'

The priest, as Jean-Luc had decided he was,

suddenly raised his eyes as if he was looking into the far distance. 'The first of your assistants is about to arrive.'

*

Barely conscious, Gwenaelle Doissneau dragged herself up the church steps. She shivered uncontrollably. She was desperate to lie down in the dry warmth of the church. She was suddenly afraid as she heard a voice. *Who would be in here?* she thought.

Stepping through the doorway, she looked into the eyes of Jean-Luc Morrisson and collapsed at his feet.

The young man in the wheelchair looked in horror at the stricken young woman before him. Turning to his companion, his eyes pleaded for help.

'We must do something to help her, she is soaked through, and we have to act now.'

'Calm down, my son. Gwenaelle is not about to die anytime soon, but you are right, you must help her.'

'Me? But I am a cripple, I can't help her.'

'Who said you are a cripple, Jean-Luc?'

'The doctors at the hospital said that I probably wouldn't walk again.'

'Ah probably, and were they the doctors who said that you would probably die? Listen to me, young man.' His eyes bored into Jean-Luc's brain. 'Many people need you, but Gwenaelle needs you to act now. You have everything around you to save her life but you don't have much time. Stand up, my son. I said stand up.'

Jean-Luc was scared of moving. Looking at the unconscious woman before him, he gritted his teeth and rose to his feet. Predictably with his first step, he fell to the floor. Beating his fist on the floor, he shouted at the older man, 'I can't do it, I am useless!'

Calmly, his companion told him that his muscles had gone lazy. 'Get up Jean-Luc, this young woman needs your help immediately.'

Gritting his teeth, he raised himself to his knees. Sweating profusely, he forced himself upright. He looked round for more reassurance. He was alone with the stricken Gwenaelle.

'Father, Father!' he cried desperately. 'Damn you, where are you?' The silence closed in on him.

Jean-Luc took a few tentative steps. The pain of the pins and needles as his blood coursed through his veins galvanised him. Draped over the pew before him were some clean clerical vestments. He assumed that the priest had fetched them and then gone for some more.

Quickly, he stripped the soaking clothes from the young woman's body. Vigorously, using some of the vestments, he rubbed her dry. He hoped for a quick response but there was only shallow breaths to indicate a sign of life.

Gwenaelle's hair was soaking wet and Jean-Luc rubbed and rubbed at it. He massaged her scalp, hoping it would help.

He remembered that Vincent had often told him that the body needs warmth. He looked around for something to provide that warmth, but there was only some more of the clerical vestments. He spread some out on the floor, marvelling that every time he made another layer on the floor, more of the vestments were draped over the pew.

His heart pounded and he felt as though he was burning up with his exertions. Jean-Luc stripped off his own clothes. He lay down at the side of Gwenaelle and draped his clothes and some more of the clerical vestments over the two of them. Wrapping his arms around the young woman, he pulled her into his embrace and gently rested her head on his shoulder.

Looking at her calm face before him, he was pleased to see that her lips had lost that blueness that often signals the onset of hypothermia. With the young woman in his arms, Jean-Luc Morrisson fell into an exhausted sleep.

*

Vincent Morrisson drove as fast as he could towards Dougeres. He had been so busy caring for the victims of the farming accident that he hadn't noticed how quickly the time had gone.

His clothes were stained with blood, as were those of his passenger in the car. He smiled as he thought what a great nurse Sally Roberts was. She had worked tirelessly alongside the two doctors as they fought successfully to save the lives of the two men that had been critically injured by the threshing machine's malfunction.

'We make a good team, Sally. Thank you so much for providing another pair of hands.'

'I am glad that I was able to help, Vincent. I think that Daniel would have really struggled on his own today. He is well past retirement age, he could perhaps do with a younger partner, but not many doctors would want to come to such a remote place.'

Vincent's thoughts had turned to his brother and he wondered how Jean-Luc had filled in the long hours alone in the church.

Dougeres, Pays Basque.

Jean-Luc had been awake for a while. Resting the palm of his hand beneath his chin, he had carefully watched for signs of distress on the face of Gwenaelle Doissneau. The young woman looked peaceful as she slept deeply. Vincent had often told his brother that sleep was nature's way of ensuring that the body had time to recover from many problems.

Suddenly alarmed, he looked at his watch. He had been here for seven hours. Surely his brother would come for him soon. He carefully retrieved his clothes that were draped over his and Gwenaelle's bodies. Covering her up with the vestments that had been left for him, he quickly dressed and went to the young woman's running shorts and shirt that he had earlier draped over one of the pews. He said a silent prayer of thanks as he saw that the clothes were perfectly dry.

Jean-Luc was all fingers and thumbs as he sat the young woman up and dressed her. He prayed that she wouldn't wake as he struggled to hook her brassiere up and slipped her shirt over her head. Thankfully there was not even a murmur from the young woman as Jean-Luc continued with his task. He carefully lay Gwenaelle on her back and pulled her underwear up her thighs followed by her running shorts.

Grateful that he had been able to dress her without waking the young woman, he covered her again and thoroughly wiped all the pews that he had drawn on. He looked curiously at his first rather childish sketch, he could have sworn that he had wiped the evidence of that particular drawing away. Laughing at his foolish behaviour, he stooped over and used the whole length of his forearm to obliterate the drawing.

A few moments later he heard a car drawing to a halt outside the church.

Vincent Morrisson ran into the church, closely followed by Sally Roberts. Vincent started to offer an apology, then stared in amazement at the empty wheelchair and then at Jean-Luc stood at the other side of the church. The doctor in him quickly surfaced as he noticed the still sleeping young woman covered by a pile of surplices.

Crossing over to Gwenaelle, Vincent placed his hand on her forehead and looked enquiringly at his brother. Jean-Luc gave a very brief explanation of the day's events, leaving out the part he had played other than telling how he had covered the young woman in the clerical vestments.

Gently Vincent examined the sleeping Gwenaelle. He proclaimed that she seemed fine, but she needed to be in her own bed.

Placing his hand on her shoulder, Vincent shook her repeatedly and told her to wake up.

Gwenaelle smiled in her sleep, she was having a lovely dream. For the first time in weeks she felt safe. She murmured pleasurably as she dreamed of being held in a strong embrace. She felt strong arms holding her, but no matter how hard she tried, she could not see the face of her lover.

Lover? Why had that thought invaded her mind?

'Gwenaelle, Gwenaelle, wake up, we need to get you home.'

The young woman didn't want to wake up. She grumbled as the intruding voice continued telling her to wake up. Finally she opened her eyes and stared at the concerned trio gazing down at her. She allowed Vincent and Sally to help her to her feet. As she took a tentative step, Sally Roberts's eyes narrowed and she looked accusingly at Jean-Luc. He flushed with embarrassment although he had no idea why his friend Sally should look at him that way.

Completely oblivious of the strained atmosphere, Vincent asked his brother when he had realised that he was able to walk.

Jean-Luc started to tell them all about the day's happenings and how the priest of the little church had convinced him that he must walk. His voice tailed off as one of the trio stared at him.

Gwenaelle looked at him, disbelief covering her face.

'Our priest died in the bombing, and as we have no village now, the powers that be have probably decided that we have no need of spiritual guidance. It is clear to me that you have pretended to lose the use of your legs in order to gain sympathy.'

As soon as she had uttered the scathing remark, Gwenaelle could have bitten her tongue off. She flushed as she looked at the hurt expression on Jean-

Luc's face. Vincent stepped forward as if to defend his brother. Before he could speak, Sally Roberts placed her hand on his arm and put her finger to her lips.

It was a very subdued quartet that made the journey to their temporary lodgings in a nearby village. Vincent stopped the car outside the home of Gwenaelle's best friend. The young woman alighted from the car and after a very brief thank you and goodnight, she disappeared into the house.

Vincent allowed the car to roll down the steep slope to the house where he and Jean-Luc were staying with their father. The thoroughly miserable man made his way inside and shocked his father rigid by walking in.

Molly Roberts danced round Jean-Luc, her pleasure at seeing him walking was palpable. Philip Morrisson apologised that there wasn't a lot of food in the house as they had shared a meal earlier with Doctor Doissneau.

Quickly, Sally Roberts insisted that she would make a meal for herself and Vincent. The woman refused to listen to Vincent's protest that she must be dog tired and taking hold of Molly's hand, she made for the door. Vincent followed meekly after checking that his elder brother was okay. Jean-Luc smiled weakly and told them that he would like to go to bed.

An hour later, Vincent thanked Sally for a lovely supper and suggested that he would wash the dishes. The two worked together in silence, comfortable in each other's company. Molly announced that she was off to bed; shyly, the teenage girl kissed Vincent's cheek and walked from the room, humming happily.

Her mother thought that the shy young girl was finally coming out of her shell.

As Sally helped Vincent on with his coat, he smiled and hurriedly kissed her cheek. The Englishwoman looked at him for a few moments, then putting her hands to his face, kissed him on the lips.

The next moment the two were in each other's arms.

St Malo, Brittany, France.

Marie-Francoise Morrisson smiled at the shop assistant who had opened the door for her as she left the shop laden with baby clothes.

Although middle aged and with snow-white hair, the woman was very beautiful and attracted many admiring glances as she loaded her parcels into the boot of her car.

A long phone call with her husband Philip that morning had allayed her fears about their eldest son. Jean-Luc seemed to be well on the road to recovery, thanks to the care that he was receiving from his family and some newfound friends. She was anxious to hold her husband and sons in her arms just as soon as Sophie had her baby.

Automatically, Marie-Francoise crossed herself as the police cars, fire engine and ambulance, with sirens wailing and lights flashing drove past her at high speed.

Train Station, St Malo, Brittany, France.

Hugo de Beziers breathed a sigh of relief as the Paris-bound TGV pulled into the small station. He had been on edge since he had fled the scene of his latest crime just a short while ago.

Although he had arranged the deaths of countless numbers of people over the years, he had very rarely carried out the killings himself. The actual act of murder didn't bother him in the least, it was just the thought of being apprehended that made him nervous.

Earlier he had watched in frustration as the Morrisson woman had left her daughter's house and driven away. Forcing open the back door to the small cottage in the quiet avenue, he had listened intently for any sounds of alarm from upstairs. Satisfied that the young couple were still asleep, he smiled evilly as he took the parcel from his backpack. He congratulated himself at the masterstroke of wrapping the parcel in paper with the name of a well-known supplier of baby clothes.

Placing the parcel on the living room table, he was sure that with its brightly coloured paper it would be seen by the first person to open the door.

Although not as talented with explosives as L'Anglaise had undoubtedly been, he had watched her often enough to be sure that the bomb on the table would have the desired effect.

Leaving the house by the back door, he walked to the main road and flagged down a taxi, requesting that he be dropped off at the train station in St Malo.

*

The first signs of unease filtered through the mind of Marie-Francoise Morrisson as she waited in the traffic jam on the quiet country lane. In the distance she saw a column of black smoke spiralling upwards.

Slowly the traffic problems eased and impatient drivers sped on their way. Madame Morrisson turned her car into the quiet avenue where Sophie and Jerome had made their first home.

The first thought that crossed her mind was that she had taken the wrong road. Her brain refused to accept the scene of utter desolation before her eyes. The three small cottages at the end of the avenue had ceased to exist. A few buildings still stood but only as shells. Thick black smoke pervaded her eyes and nostrils as the grief-stricken woman realised that her daughter was gone.

It had all been too much for the young police officer. Fresh from his training, he had not been prepared for the horrors that were unfolding before his eyes. Inevitably, the young man was unable to control his bodily functions and he vomited several times.

As he tried to restore himself, he noticed the middle-aged lady walking round as if in a dream. Wiping his arm across his mouth he walked towards the woman, glad of something practical to do.

Marie-Francoise looked down into the crater that had once been three homes. Although it looked as if it had been steamrollered, she recognised immediately the pram that she and Philip had bought for their first grandchild.

The stricken woman looked round as if searching

for her lost child. The police officer reacted quickly as her legs gave way and she collapsed into his arms.

Petit Dougeres, Pays Basque, France.

Gwenaelle Doissneau had endured a white night. Her guilt at the way she had spoken to Jean-Luc weighed heavily on her mind. Refusing breakfast, she explained to her father exactly how she had behaved the previous night.

Doctor Daniel smiled as his daughter insisted that she go and apologise to Jean-Luc Morrisson. She looked so animated that her father thought that perhaps her life was returning to something like the time before Amandine's death.

As Gwenaelle closed the front door behind her, she saw an obviously distressed Vincent Morrisson being comforted by Sally Roberts. Feeling like a voyeur, she turned and went back into her own dwelling.

Moments later a knock sounded at the door. As Daniel invited Sally in, the young woman blurted out the news of the terrible accident in Brittany.

Daniel Doissneau knew that he must act quickly. He made four quick calls and each time repeated the short message. Putting on his coat, he hurried from the house just as the three Morrisson men were making for Vincent's car, Daniel begged that Philip should listen to him for a few minutes. He gently ushered the grief-stricken men back into the house. Twenty minutes later two cars arrived with four quiet yet tough-looking Basques. The men were invited in by Doctor Daniel and emerged thirty minutes later accompanied by Vincent Morrisson.

Petit Dougeres, Pays Basque, France.

Three days later the small convoy of cars pulled up outside the house. Jean-Luc and his father rushed to help Marie-Francoise from the car. Holding her eldest son, she looked anxiously at his badly scarred face. Fresh tears covered her face.

'The scars will fade, Mother. I am fine, I promise.'

Philip Morrisson embraced his wife. As the family walked slowly into the house, one of the Basques spoke softly to Daniel Doissneau, who looked thoughtfully at the back of Marie-Francoise Morrisson.

The Morrisson family had reeled from one great shock to another. As the tragedy of the deaths of Sophie, Jerome, and their unborn child was settling into a dull ache, the news was brought to them that it had been murder that had robbed them of a much-loved daughter.

Daniel Doissneau acted quickly. He asked Philip Morrisson to phone his youngest daughter, Amelie. He explained that the girl, who was a student in Paris, was in mortal danger. Daniel explained that two of his friends would accompany Vincent and bring Amelie to the relative safety of this small community.

The thought of losing another member of his family galvanised Philip into action. Quickly conferring with Vincent, they agreed that the young doctor would leave immediately for Paris.

Apart from the practical help of preparing meals and washing clothes for the Morrissons, Sally Roberts had kept her distance from the grieving family. Now as Vincent explained that he was preparing to bring his young sister here, Sally embraced him and told him to be careful.

*

Jean-Luc couldn't believe how quickly the last three weeks had gone. With the arrival of his youngest sister Amelie, the family had travelled to Brittany together, as usual accompanied by a group of bodyguards. The funeral service had been a harrowing affair for all concerned. The priest had tried his best to invoke the spirits of all the dead, but how could that be done without bodies to provide tangible evidence.

After a few days with her parents and brothers, Amelie Morrisson announced that she must return to her studies in Paris. Despite all her family's protestations, the strong-willed young woman was adamant. As a concession to allay her parents' fears, Amelie allowed Daniel Doissneau to arrange for the girl to be protected by two of the elderly doctor's friends. Jean-Luc marvelled at the affection the people of this area had for Daniel.

Marie-Francoise Morrisson found it particularly hard to share her grief, even with her family. She had invested so much love and care in Sophie and Jerome during a most difficult pregnancy that she found it hard to come to terms with the savagery of their murder.

The time came for Amelie to leave. Despite his sadness and his fears for his wife's state of mind, Philip

Morrisson was immensely proud of his youngest daughter. She had set her mind on a path of her own choosing and nothing could shake her resolve.

The members of the small commune had come to wish farewell to a young woman that they had come to respect. Some had brought presents for Amelie. She thanked them all profusely as she received their gifts gracefully.

Finally, just the family of the elderly doctor remained. Gwenaelle and Amelie embraced and exchanged mobile numbers. Even though there was a strained atmosphere between Gwenaelle and Jean-Luc, the young woman cared deeply for the rest of his family.

Little Alais, who was still traumatised from the death of her mother, looked closely at Marie-Francoise. Without prompting, the girl walked across the room to the quiet woman.

'Is your little girl in heaven?'

Marie-Francoise smiled through her tears at Alais.

'Yes my dear, she is.'

'Do you think she knows my mummy?'

For the first time in days, Marie-Francoise looked beyond her own grief. She realised that the scared little girl before her had lost so much in such a short space of time, with the death of both her parents in such tragic circumstances.

Taking hold of the girl's hands, the older woman smiled.

'Alais, I am sure that your mummy and my Sophie are the best of friends.'

The floodgates opened for both Marie-Francoise Morrisson and Alais Dubois. The two clung to each other and cried for a long time. Finally, the little girl slept, content in the arms of the older woman.

Everybody present had tears in their eyes as they witnessed the sad, yet joyful occasion.

Amelie Morrisson kissed her mother, father, and brothers in turn and left quietly.

Jean-Luc picked up his drawing pads and pencils and after kissing his mother tenderly, bade farewell to all those present.

At his departure, Philip Morrisson looked at the unspoken question in Gwenaelle's eyes and simply declared that his son was a man on a mission.

Chapter 5

Dougeres, Pays Basque, France.

Madame Casillas walked down the ruined street. All the rubble had long been removed but as she stared at the ruined buildings she saw the faces of friends long gone and those of the recently departed.

Her lips trembled and the tears flowed as she stood by the destroyed well. It had been there all her life and she expected it to be there long after she had gone.

Although she loved her granddaughter dearly and adored the little baby boy whose birth she had attended on the day of the blast, a part of her wondered why God had spared her but taken into his care her two childhood friends.

The three had been inseparable. They had never left the village, nor ever wanted to, they had gone to the small school together, supported each other through the many sad times that women endure. They had laughed at each other's wedding ceremonies and acted as midwives as each other's children were born. This microcosm of life had been conducted in the presence of the well.

A shadow crossed in front of her and she looked up in alarm.

'I am sorry to startle you, Madame. I wondered if you were okay.'

'You must excuse an old lady's tears, Jean-Luc.'

'You know who I am?'

The old lady smiled. 'It's a very small community, young man, and we all know the miracle of your survival. It sounds easy to say, Jean-Luc, but we are all so sorry at your family's losses.'

Jean-Luc felt the tears stinging the backs of his eyes. He smiled at the old lady.

Madame Casillas looked closely at the young man. She clutched her chest, causing her companion to enquire as to her health.

'I am fine. Tell me young man, what is your mother's forename?'

'Marie-Francoise,' a puzzled Jean-Luc replied.

The old lady smiled enigmatically and declared that she looked forward to meeting Marie-Francoise when the time was right. Changing the subject, she declared that when one was as old as she, people should forgive her curiosity.

At Jean-Luc's puzzled look, she pointed to his sketch pad and asked him what he had been drawing.

His face burning with embarrassment, Jean-Luc carefully turned over the first two pages of his pad and told his amused companion that he had just been making some rough sketches following a rather fanciful idea that he had had.

Madame Casillas looked open-mouthed at first one sketch, then another. 'These are beautiful my boy, and so practical. Do you think it would be possible to bring these plans to fruition? Bearing in mind that I am very old and I don't know how much longer God will spare me.'

A faraway look came into Jean-Luc's eyes as he declared that if it was the last thing that he did, he would bring the sketches to life.

The young man hadn't seen that a gust of wind had blown the pages of the sketch pad back to the first one. The elderly lady smiled as she looked at the quite beautiful and lifelike drawing.

Petit Dougeres, Pays Basque, France.

Daniel Doissneau had listened with great interest to Jean-Luc's passionate speech. The older man's eyes sparkled as he looked at the fervour in his young friend's face. He tried to instil a note of caution into the proceedings, but it was difficult as he was so enthusiastic about the whole idea.

'Jean-Luc, where will we start? This venture will cost a great deal of money I think.'

'Not at first Daniel, because we have all that we need for the centre of our operation. I wanted to approach you first because you can provide me with enough information to set the scheme in place.'

The older man smiled and said that he would call a meeting for that very afternoon. Although he knew the answer to his next question, he looked enquiringly at the younger man.

As if Jean-Luc had read Daniel's mind, he smiled and said, 'Where else?'

Dougeres.

All her fears about coming back to her home village had disappeared, but nevertheless Gwenaelle experienced a moment of great sadness as she looked at the empty street.

Lots of voices clamoured to be heard as the young woman walked into the church. She smiled as she thought that it sounded like a class full of children.

She stopped in surprise as she saw the packed church. Her father beamed as he came towards her. Taking her hand, he declared that now the meeting could start.

Gwenaelle looked round with interest at friends and neighbours. Along with the residents of Petit Dougeres, there were all the relatives and guardians of the orphaned children of her own village.

Daniel Doissneau opened the discussion. He asked that people simply listen as he outlined the plan that had been conceived by Jean-Luc. The young man in question reddened as all eyes turned towards him.

'Although I am in full agreement with my young friend, I think as it was his idea, he should be the one to explain it in greater detail.'

Nervously, Jean-Luc looked at the assembly before him. His first thought was that now he knew how the gladiators of Ancient Rome must have felt.

'To the outside world, Dougeres has ceased to exist. They should realise that it is not bricks and mortar that make a home, it is the beating hearts of the people who occupy that home. I, along with my family, owe a debt of gratitude to the people of Petit Dougeres and indeed everybody who has looked out for us in these most difficult of times.

'The legacy that we leave is quite simply the children. The children will take Dougeres forward and in turn leave it to their children. That has happened for all time and must continue to happen. The alternative, quite simply, doesn't bear thinking about.'

Applause rang round the old church. Daniel implored his friends and neighbours to ask questions to try and settle all the salient points in that one afternoon.

Of course there were dissenters. The most asked question was how much it would cost. Jean-Luc rose to his feet.

'At first it will cost nothing. Someone told me recently that this church has been at the heart of this community for around seven hundred years. I would like to suggest that it can be so again. Firstly I think that you, the people of this community, should use the church as a community hall for regular meetings and to have your say in how best we can rebuild Dougeres. Secondly, and in my mind the most important, is to bring the children back.'

There were gasps of amazement round the room, with more than one person asking what effect that would have on the children.

'Both Daniel and Vincent, my brother, as doctors have impressed on me how resilient children are. I am not a parent, but I think that children have two constants in their young lives. The first is the love and support of their parents, which in this case was cruelly taken away from them. The second constant is quite simply their school. At the moment they can only dwell on what they have lost. They need an education to take their rightful place in the world.'

Jean-Luc's gaze swept the room, finally stopping at the young teacher.

'Gwenaelle, it is you who can help these children to start living again.'

The young woman's eyes filled with tears as she thought how much she had missed the children, she knew then that no matter where the classes were conducted, that they would be was of prime importance.

Jean-Luc held his hand up. Immediately the excited chatter stopped.

'I hope that sooner rather than later, the church will be used for what it was intended. With that in mind I have drawn a few sketches to illustrate what I hope will be the rebirth of Dougeres. As I said earlier, everything must revolve around you, the people of all the small communities in this beautiful region. On that fateful day, most of you lost someone close. You have shown by taking in the orphans of Dougeres that you have good hearts. I would like to build a community hall that during the day will function as a school for all the children of Dougeres. I know it will be a difficult road, but will you allow me to give something back to you for the kindness that you have extended to my family and friends?'

The applause reverberated round the small church. Daniel Doissneau took the opportunity to pass a series of plans round. As people craned to see them, there were gasps of amazement at the superbly detailed drawings before them. Along with the drawings for the community hall, Jean-Luc had designed an open grassed area with trees and benches and a simple yet beautiful fountain.

Madame Casillas stepped forward to examine this last drawing and declared that she wanted just one opportunity to sit there with her knitting before the good lord claimed her.

Everybody laughed as an elderly man exclaimed that as everybody knew, only the good died young, so Madame Casillas would be sitting there for a long time to come.

People clamoured to know how soon the work could start. Daniel stated that he would make an appointment to see the local mayor the very next day.

A young man stepped forward and suggested that they were being a little hasty. As one, the audience glared at him with more than one of them muttering that a kanpotek should not tell them how to conduct their business.

The young stranger smiled engagingly and held his hands up.

'It's true that I am indeed an outsider, but my mother was born in this village.'

As he uttered his mother's maiden name, there

were smiles all round as people remembered one of their own. The stranger introduced himself as Damien Gaulthier. Turning to face Daniel Doissneau and Jean-Luc, he explained the reason for his interruption.

'I work as a reporter in Bayonne and when I heard of this meeting, I thought that there could be a nice human interest story here. The mayor of this small collection of communes is a politically ambitious man. After he reads the next edition of our newspaper, I think that he will view your project very favourably.'

All those present smiled as they realised that the reporter was correct in his opinion of their mayor and they cheered as Daniel agreed to wait for a few days.

The reporter held his hands up for silence. The audience waited with bated breath.

'The most important reason for my visit is to give to you, the people of these small communities, a cheque to help with the rebuilding program. I wanted to see if you were determined to see this project through. I can see the resolve in the eyes of each one of you. My editor approached a few of the leading citizens of Bayonne, each one of them willingly dug deep into their pockets and this cheque is the result. Obviously you will need more money for a task of such magnitude, but I have a good feeling that it will come.'

Loud cheers rang round the church for several minutes as the whole congregation rushed forward to shake the reporter's hand.

Daniel Doissneau and Jean-Luc grinned at each other as they realised that the much needed building work could be started sooner than they had hoped.

Gwenaelle's heart sank as her father asked Jean-Luc to join them in their car for the journey to their temporary home. Quickly, the young woman declared that she was exhausted and she would lie down on the back seat. Daniel smiled as he realised that his daughter was doing her best to avoid this young man.

The following car was that of Vincent. He had persuaded his mother to come to the meeting. Marie-Francoise was pleased that he had. She thought that she would burst with pride as people admired Jean-Luc's beautiful plans. As she replayed her eldest son's impassioned speech in her mind, her thoughts were interrupted by Sally Roberts. The Englishwoman declared that when people worked as one unit they could accomplish a great deal. Madame Morrisson agreed wholeheartedly with the sentiment. Looking at Sally, she saw that the younger woman's gaze was firmly fixed on her son Vincent.

As the cars came to a stop in Petit Dougeres, Vincent told them he would go and rescue his father from his babysitting duties. Sally mentioned that Philip seemed in his element looking after children.

Marie-Francoise smiled and told the younger woman, that was what had made her fall in love with the father of her children. At Sally's curious look, she enlarged her statement.

'As a young teacher, I took the opportunity to improve my English by accepting an exchange position at a boarding school for boys in England. I was one of only three women on the staff there. You would have thought that some of the male teachers were like the young boys there in the way that they mooned after the three of us.'

Sally thought that Marie-Francoise would have turned most heads as she was still a very beautiful woman.

Marie-Francoise continued, 'I had, and still have, a great love of music. The headmaster agreed that I could help the music teacher who was interested in putting on a musical evening for the boys and their families. The music teacher was a very shy confirmed bachelor. He had cared for his elderly parents for a long time and dressed like a man twenty years older than he actually was. An accomplished musician himself, the man was transformed when he listened to his charges as they attempted to carry out his instructions. He never shouted at them or bullied them in any way. By quiet encouragement and gentle persuasion he brought out the very best in his young charges. He was so passionate about all kinds of music, that he carried us all along on this wave of euphoria.

'Sadly, my exchange year soon came to an end and I reluctantly made plans to return to my home in Brittany. The head booked a restaurant for my last evening and all the staff came, with one exception. As you can probably guess, the music teacher. Early the next morning, I slipped a note under his door with just my home address on it.'

Looking directly into Sally's eyes, Marie-Francoise said that there are some men who need a little push.

'I knew that my instincts had been right when that music teacher turned up at my parents' house one month later. Philip and I were married within six weeks and I love him as much today as I did then.'

Sally Roberts told the older woman how much Philip had helped Molly become a much more confident girl. 'I hope that you and your husband won't mind, but my daughter refers to him as Granddad.'

Marie-Francoise laughed out loud and declared that Philip would be delighted.

'Does Molly not have grandparents of her own, Sally?'

'My parents both died of cancer when I was quite small. I was taken into care by the local authority. I know that children's homes have a bad press, and in lots of cases rightly so. But I grew up with a large group of children from different backgrounds and we looked out for one another. I was very happy until it came time for me to leave and make my own way in the world. Scared out of my wits, I got involved with an older man. As soon as he knew that I was expecting his baby, he was off. I had nobody to care for me, so I knew that if we were to survive it was down to me. With the help of different agencies and more important, kind neighbours and friends, I managed to complete my studies and eventually qualified as a nurse.'

Marie-Francoise looked with respect at the younger woman. In just a short time they had become the best of friends. She realised that through hard work and an unshakeable desire to care for her daughter, a woman of great strength had emerged from the frightened little girl who had been left alone at such a tender age.

The two women smiled as Vincent appeared in the

doorway and handed a sleeping Alais to Gwenaelle Doissneau. Both Vincent and Philip Morrisson were embraced by Molly Roberts. Sally gasped with delight, she had never seen her daughter so animated. The teenager skipped over to the car and kissed her mother and Madame Morrisson in turn.

Dougeres, Pays Basque.

People from all over the area poured into the small church. Their excitement was tangible as they waited to hear news of the meeting between their mayor and the action committee.

Two days earlier, Daniel Doissneau, accompanied by his daughter Gwenaelle and Jean-Luc Morrisson, had endured a long meeting with a man who thought more of himself than of the people he served.

Jean-Luc had fumed inwardly as the officious man had undressed Gwenaelle with his eyes. He had further gone down in the young man's opinion as he placed a proprietary hand around her waist as he led her to a chair.

The small party from Dougeres all thought that the reporter Damien Gaulthier had been right with his summary of the politician's character.

He had feigned interest as he looked at the plans for the community hall, drawn up by Jean-Luc. The politician was busy working out how much publicity he could glean as the man who rebuilt Dougeres. He had been even happier when after apologetically stating that he didn't think there would be much that he could offer in the way of financial help, Jean-Luc had stated firmly that the people of the local communities would finance it as it would be their centre.

As the Dougeres action committee left the town hall, they looked at one another and laughed. Daniel Doissneau stated that the mayor was a consummate politician who would milk the project for all that it was worth.

Gwenaelle said rather feelingly that she had felt dirty at the way that the mayor had looked at her. Jean-Luc was secretly pleased that the young woman was so indignant.

The small church rocked as people cheered when they learned that planning permission for their community hall had been given.

The following three weeks passed in a blur as Jean-Luc and Gwenaelle Doissneau discussed what exactly the young woman wanted for her pupils. Damien Gaulthier's help proved invaluable. Besides acting as an intermediary for the residents of the commune and the mayor, the reporter introduced Jean-Luc and Gwenaelle to heads of construction firms who were willing to help the battered community get some purpose back into their lives.

Soon, earth moving machines descended on Dougeres and foundations were quickly dug to Jean-Luc's exact specifications.

Daniel Doissneau smiled as his daughter wondered why the base appeared to be so big.

'Surely, thirteen children will not need a classroom that big. I will need a loudhailer just to take assembly,' Gwenaelle said to her best friend Elixabete Dicharry.

Her friend smiled enigmatically. As assistant to the lecherous mayor, she had seen all the plans for the proposed school and community hall. Her breath had been taken away at the sheer magnitude of Jean-Luc's vision.

As Gwenaelle's closest friend, and indeed as her temporary landlady, Elixabete had noticed the sparkle in her friend's eyes and thought that it wasn't just the thought of teaching her beloved students again that had caused her friend to appear so animated. Known for her blunt speaking, Elixabete turned to her friend.

'I can arrange to be out for an evening if you would like to invite your Jean-Luc over, Gwenaelle.' As she spoke she pointed to the object of their discussion as he watched the concrete for the foundations being poured.

Gwenaelle Doissneau blushed to the roots of her hair.

'I, I, I don't know what you mean, he is most certainly not my Jean-Luc. Why, I don't even like him.'

Elixabete looked at her best friend, disbelief written on her face, but wisely she didn't press the point.

A rather relieved Gwenaelle changed the subject to that of the mayor.

'How on earth do you cope with that lecherous man?'

'Oh you mean Mayor Octopus? Actually it's easy. I remind him that I quite often have lunch with his wife, or if that doesn't work I tell him that my invented boyfriend, the rugby player with the short temper, will be calling for me after work. That always does the trick.'

The two women watched the work progressing for a few minutes then decided that they would go and make some lunch for the workmen. As they got into Elixabete's car, she noticed that Gwenaelle looked several times in the direction of Jean-Luc Morrisson. The man was completely oblivious to everything but the concrete being laid and levelled skilfully.

As they left, neither of the women noticed Philip Morrisson and Daniel Doissneau. The two men laughed together like a couple of schoolboys sharing a smutty joke. All the residents of the local communes, although pleased, were mystified as to why the two elderly men volunteered to spend so much time with the orphans of Dougeres.

*

The small church was filled to capacity once more as people came anxious to hear how their community hall was progressing.

Daniel Doissneau smiled as he struggled to be heard above the excited chatter.

'My friends, I am pleased to announce that stage one of this exciting project will be completed by the end of the month. The builders have told me that they are prepared to work night and day to stop Jean-Luc bullying them.'

Everybody smiled at the thought of this most pleasant young man being a hard taskmaster.

'I have two things that I would like you all to think about. The second one is really quite easy and I am sure what your reaction will be. I would like to propose that we have a party in one week's time to celebrate the opening of our new building.'

There were cries of approval from all corners of the church with women discussing each other's culinary specialities. Daniel allowed the chatter to die down. His face was serious as he looked at the people of the area that he had been so delighted to serve for a great number of years.

'Following that dreadful day that will live long in all our memories, you, the wonderful people of this area, took into your houses and indeed into your hearts a small group of people who like you lost loved ones that day and in the days that followed. We were never fortunate enough to know Sophie and Jerome, but I am sure that they would have been as well received here as the thousands of people over the years who have come to share your homeland.

'I hope that next Sunday morning, we will all gather here in our church to hold a memorial service for our loved ones. I think the time is right to say our goodbyes. In the absence of a priest, I think that we can have a service that will be personal to each one of us. We can laugh, cry, and sing in the way that Basque people have always done.'

Applause rang round the church as Daniel made his way back to his seat. Philip Morrisson winked at his friend and gave him a thumbs up sign. Leaning across the pew, Philip whispered, 'And now for stage two.'

*

The following seven days passed in a blur of activity. Jean-Luc, always accompanied by a bodyguard, travelled the length and breadth of the Pays Basque. Some of his journeys were of his own making, others were errands run on behalf of his father. Each morning he was out at first light and his returns were always late at night.

Gwenaelle was consumed by curiosity. Her best friend Elixabete smiled enigmatically as the young woman wondered aloud why all this fuss for a one-room school was necessary.

A mist hung over the picturesque valley as groups of people converged on Dougeres from all directions. Adults told their children that the mist promised a beautiful day.

Friends greeted one another with hugs, kisses, and handshakes. The orphans of Dougeres were rather apprehensive about their particular place in the day's proceedings. They needn't have worried. A smiling Daniel Doissneau hugged each of them, bringing instant reassurance.

A delighted Marie-Francoise and Philip Morrisson were greeted by their daughter Amelie who explained that Im, as she referred to her bodyguard, had driven through the night to get them here for the memorial service.

'I could have killed him when he told me that we would want to be here. On top of that I didn't sleep because he wanted the company.'

As Madame Morrisson listened to her daughter's babbling, she thought that Amelie had always tried to hide her innermost thoughts by talking about anything. She looked carefully at the quiet young man whose eyes never strayed far from her daughter.

The following three hours passed in a blur as all those present were encouraged to speak openly about their loved parents, relatives and friends who had lost their lives on that terrible day.

Jean-Luc had started the proceedings by telling the congregation of the American students who had insisted on calling him Grandpa. He endeared himself to all those present by crying unashamedly as he recalled moments of the long pilgrimage made easier by Amandine Dubois's great knowledge and her love for her homeland.

The pride shone from the eyes of Daniel Doissneau as he spoke of his daughter's life from her childhood through to motherhood.

Gwenaelle spoke in hushed tones of the sister that she had often argued and fought with as they were growing up, knowing all the time that they shared an incredible bond as identical twins.

The orphans of Dougeres remembered their parents and whispered their gratitude for the start in life that each of them had received.

At Daniel Doissneau's insistence, Philip Morrisson told the congregation of his daughter Sophie and her husband Jerome who had had such great plans for the future. A future that had been cruelly denied them by a madman whose motives were still unknown.

He also paid tribute to the people of Petit Dougeres and the communes in the area for taking a grieving family and helping them face life without a much-loved daughter.

Philip smiled as he added that Daniel and the orphans had given him a sense of purpose and he hoped to show his gratitude later.

Sally Roberts and Jean-Luc told the assembly of their friend, the coach driver Ted Green. Of his insistence at taking the sick pilgrims to Lourdes, and of the tragic deaths of them all.

Alais Dubois ran to the doorway on hearing a loud noise.

'They are taking the fence down!' she shouted excitedly. All the children raced to follow her into the sunshine to discover exactly what lay beyond the hoarding at the edge of the village.

And so the memorial service came to an end. People filed out and smiled as they looked at their esteemed mayor. Fast asleep, saliva dribbled from his slack mouth. Daniel held a finger to his lips and the whole assembly left the church, the silence broken intermittently by the tuneless snoring.

The crowd stood at a safe distance as the hoardings were removed one by one. There were gasps of amazement as the new school was revealed. It was a single-storey structure but so big that eyes bulged as people tried to see what had been in Jean-Luc's mind.

Gwenaelle Doissneau stared in disbelief at the building before her. She turned to her father who asked her to be patient for a few minutes more as the opening ceremony was about to take place. At his daughter's puzzled look, he assured her that he didn't know any more than she did.

Jean-Luc stood self-consciously before a stone-built structure about as tall as himself. The top of the edifice was covered by a large cloth. As the crowd of people gathered before him, the young man cleared his throat and looked to his parents for reassurance.

'A few weeks ago I asked for your permission to give something back to this community. With lots of help from both the local population and outside forces, we have managed to erect a school just in time for the new school year.' There were mock groans of disappointment from the older children.

Jean-Luc continued, 'What you see before you is a work in progress. One that I hope will continue to grow through the years. Originally, I envisaged a building that would serve a dual purpose, a school by day and a community hall by night. Then I realised that people will need their community hall at all times of the day. The three buildings that share this complex are separated from each other and soundproofed so one group will not disturb the other.'

'Three buildings?' a mystified crowd shouted.

'All will become clear when we go inside. The construction firm have wisely given all their attention to the interior as that is the most important part. What you see before you is a prefabricated structure which over the coming weeks will be clad in local stone so that the appearance is in keeping with the locale. I know you must be tired of my voice droning on, so without further ado I would like to ask Alais to perform the opening ceremony.'

As the little girl stepped forward, Jean-Luc held his hands up.

'I was not sure if my next point would meet with your approval, but I wanted a name that would immediately bring to mind a much-loved place that the rest of the world seems to have forgotten. We have a lot of work before us but I swear that the people of this area will proudly say, look at what we have achieved.'

Everybody smiled at this humble man who had endeared himself to all of the people there. Alais Dubois took hold of the drawstring and slowly drew the curtain from the plaque.

There was a burst of applause as the plaque was revealed. The legend inscribed simply stated that this building was: THE DOUGERES MEMORIAL CENTRE.

Daniel Doissneau and Philip Morrisson were deep in conversation but every time they were approached the two laughed like overgrown schoolboys and changed the subject. As folks waited patiently at the door of this newly built centre, nobody seemed to see the orphans of Dougeres gathering round Philip as if he was their protector.

Jean-Luc unlocked the door and without ceremony stood aside as the peoples of the local community filed in. Their eyes darted everywhere, anxious to take in what they had dreamt and talked about for the last few weeks.

Daniel saw that people were surprised by the sterility of the centre. Quickly walking to the front of the hall, he held his hands up for silence.

'I know that the walls are bare, but we wanted you to decorate the community centre in any way that you like. You can hang pictures or photographs, or simply draw on the walls. In short this is your community centre and we want you to think of it as such right from the start.'

There was loud applause as Daniel added that he too was mystified by the mention of three buildings in one and the whole assembly laughed as he asked Jean-Luc to put them all out of their misery.

A fervent light shone from the young man's eyes as he reminded them that it was necessary to rebuild not just Dougeres, but to show the world that this small community would not simply roll over and die.

'I wanted a sense of normalcy to get back to all our lives, obviously we needed to start with the school as children need their education. As important was the need for somewhere for all of us to meet and exchange views, hence the community centre. The third yet equally necessary building was the doctor's surgery. From talking to my brother Vincent, himself a doctor, and Sally Roberts who has acted as nurse and confidante for both doctors, it is clear that while Daniel has performed admirably without a permanent base, it is a situation that cannot continue for long. The builders, who I cannot praise highly enough, have worked tirelessly to construct a modern surgery complete with a waiting room for those of you who just want to put the world to rights.'

There was a burst of laughter as people looked at one another, wondering how this young man had summed them all up so correctly.

Jean-Luc smiled as he gave the keys of the surgery to an emotional Daniel Doissneau. As the older man unlocked the door, Jean-Luc told him that there were two entrances to the waiting room, the one that was being opened and another one on the outside of the building that would be in use during school times.

'I know that Sally and Vincent are itching to show Daniel his new surgery and I would like to thank Gwenaelle for her patience.'

The schoolteacher was indeed eager to see the classroom but at the back of her mind were the texts that she had received from her late sister extolling the virtues of Jean-Luc Morrisson. She had noticed how animated he was when he was able to do something that would benefit others, but also that he was reluctant to receive gratitude from his beneficiaries.

'All my children are like that Gwenaelle, it is a quality that they have received from their father.'

Gwenaelle turned to face a smiling Marie-Francoise.

'How did you know what I was thinking?'

The younger woman was amazed that she was obviously so transparent.

'It's not really so difficult, given the circumstances, my dear. This whole community has endured so much together and my son feels that you need to get your lives back on track. Jean-Luc is a born organiser, but he would insist that he is just helping people realise how much they can do for themselves.'

The two women followed the subject of their conversation into the school.

Gwenaelle felt unable to breathe as she saw her new workplace. Light shone into every part of the school from the huge windows that dominated the roof. The huge area had been partitioned into four rooms, each of them bigger than her old single-storey hut. The bottom half of the partitions were of timber and plasterboard construction, giving way to glass at the top thereby ensuring that the sunlight would reach every part of the school. Jean-Luc pointed out that all the partitioned walls were built into tracking on the floor and ceiling so that they could be rolled back to create one huge space. He also showed the two women that the low stage had doors that opened to provide a storage area for any equipment that needed to be put away in storage.

A puzzled Gwenaelle finally asked Jean-Luc why there were so many classrooms when she only had thirteen students.

She shivered as Jean-Luc's eyes pierced her own.

'My parents advised me that as the children grow and prepare for their examinations that will shape their future, you will need quiet areas where they can study and receive individual help from you or any other teacher. The fourth classroom is the one that I think will indicate to the world that Dougeres has been reborn.'

At the young woman's mystified expression, Jean-Luc smiled and added that the fourth room would be used as a crèche and a nursery class.

'My parents love music passionately, and they would like to offer the school some musical instruments and more importantly, their services as teachers to you while you are busy getting the school established.'

Gwenaelle turned to Marie-Francoise. Her eyes shone with tears as she embraced the older woman. Taking her young friend's hand, the mother of Jean-

Luc led her over to a brand new array of musical instruments, the centrepiece of which was a piano.

'We hoped that you would agree to take both Philip and myself as your assistants, but even should you decide not to, we would like to offer these musical instruments as our gift to this community.'

Gwenaelle told the older woman that she would be honoured and delighted to work alongside such good people. Turning to thank Jean-Luc, she saw that he had disappeared. Marie-Francoise smiled and explained that her son had an uncanny knack for leaving just as people were about to offer thanks. She added that he would be walking around planning the next stage of the rebuilding of Dougeres.

As the two women walked through each classroom, Madame Morrisson showed her young friend an amazing array of equipment designed to aid the children's education. Gwenaelle gasped as she saw for the first time that Jean-Luc had provided six computers for each of the three main classrooms.

'My son wanted the children to have all they need to enjoy their learning experience as he believes that education is the key that opens the door to the world.'

Daniel Doissneau, his face wreathed in smiles, entered the classroom. As his daughter told him of Marie-Francoise's amazing offer, he smiled knowingly. The residents of the local communities milled round excitedly as they discovered all that Jean-Luc had promised had come to fruition. As the classrooms filled up, Gwenaelle and Marie-Francoise easily rolled the partition walls back, revealing one huge space. Men rushed forward to assemble the chairs that Jean-Luc had hired for the evening.

Daniel ascended the small stage and clapped his hands for attention.

'I know that after such a long day you must all be ravenous. In fact I could eat a hog on a baguette.'

Laughter filled the room and died down as the elderly doctor asked his friends to be patient a while longer as there would be some entertainment provided by the children of Dougeres.

The curtains were pulled back to reveal the thirteen orphans, dressed in their best clothes, waiting apprehensively for the conversation to die down. Alais Dubois stepped forward and raised a recorder to her lips. Nobody minded as the little girl missed a note or two. Her tune, instantly familiar to most of those present, was quickly followed by the rest of the children singing a much-loved children's song. The small ensemble, expertly conducted by Philip Morrisson, played and sang the songs of the Pays Basque.

With a thoughtful expression on his face, Daniel Doissneau carefully watched as Marie-Francoise sang every song along with the children.

More than one adult cried as the children finished their recital.

Despite not understanding the words of the songs, Sally Roberts applauded as loud as anybody as the children stepped from the stage into their guardians' embraces. Puzzled, she asked Vincent if he had seen Molly. She was calmed when he told her that the youngster would be with his parents. She had felt guilty at leaving the girl to the care of others each time that she assisted either Vincent or Daniel in some medical matter. Molly had told her mother not to worry as the Morrissons were helping her to learn French.

As the talk of the children's recital died down, Philip Morrisson stepped forward.

'Finally, my friends, we have great pleasure in introducing to you someone who has struggled in a strange land and with a foreign tongue. That she has quickly made friends has been testament to her strength of character and will stand her in good stead over the many years of hard work that she has in front of her. The young woman that you are about to hear has a wonderful talent that I as a music teacher had only ever dreamt of meeting. I am sure that you will all be as enchanted as I was when I first heard her sing.'

Sally Roberts was concentrating so hard as Vincent translated his father's speech that she couldn't quite believe her eyes as her daughter walked shyly onto the stage. She hadn't really noticed the change in Molly over the last few weeks. The girl had lost that awkwardness that is the curse of every teenager as they make the transition to adulthood.

The youngster had such poise as she walked forward; her hair had been piled up, giving her added height. Her freshly made-up face had been done so skilfully that Sally struggled to see that it was indeed her own daughter.

For a brief moment the girl's resolve faltered. A quick smile from Philip and she bravely walked to the centre of the stage. Philip quickly pressed a button on his computer that was connected to two huge speakers at each side of the stage. The first few notes of a well-known song began, and Molly Roberts opened her mouth and sang.

The audience listened spellbound as she sang that most sacred of songs, 'Ave Maria'. Her beautiful soprano voice soared effortlessly through the notes as they reached their crescendo. People would swear later that the hairs on the backs of their necks had stood up. As the girl finished her song, the audience sat in a stunned silence. A few moments later, they erupted into a deafening applause.

This proved too much for Molly, who burst into tears. Sally, her own face wet with tears of joy, rushed forward to comfort her daughter. A torrent of questions burst from Sally's lips. Marie-Francoise stepped forward and quietly suggested that both Sally and her daughter should perhaps repair their make-up as Molly still had to finish her programme. Daniel Doissneau rubbed his hands in glee as he joked that the audience would turn nasty if they didn't hear any more songs; he added, 'The Basques love to sing, they also love to hear songs beautifully sung as indeed that one was. Perhaps we can all save our questions till later.'

Both Sally and Molly Roberts allowed Marie-Francoise to lead them from the stage as Philip told the audience that the young girl would return shortly.

Ten minutes later Molly returned to rapturous applause and for the next forty minutes treated the spellbound crowd to a selection of songs that she had practised for weeks under the patient tutelage of Marie-Francoise and Philip Morrisson.

Children sat on the floor with their legs crossed and adults craned forward in their chairs, determined not to miss a moment of the young girl's stunning performance. Molly did not disappoint any of those present as she finished with the much-loved aria 'Un Bel Di Vendremo' from Madame Butterfly.

Even though Philip Morrisson had worked with Molly for weeks, he thrilled at every note. Marie-Francoise clasped his hand and pointed to the audience. His eyes full with tears, he could only nod at his wife's gesture.

Molly Roberts stepped from the stage. Instantly she became a shy young girl again and giggled as Vincent and Jean-Luc Morrisson rushed forward to ask for her autograph. Sally clasped her daughter to her and asked why she had never sung before.

'I love singing, Mum, but when I was at school in London, I applied to join the choir. Before the auditions began, some of the students sneered that I had ideas of being the next Katherine Jenkins. I was so embarrassed that I didn't turn up for the audition.'

All the adults present shook their heads sadly at the cruelty that some children possess. Sally asked her daughter where she had heard such beautiful songs.

'Do you remember that Ted gave us a spare key for his house, and that he used to pay me to keep the house clean when he was away?'

At her mother's nod, the girl continued.

'Ted loved opera music and while I was cleaning, I would play some of his CDs. I used to pretend that I was a great singer on the stage.'

Both Jean-Luc and Vincent told the red-faced young girl that she soon would be.

Marie-Francoise told the still emotional Sally that one evening when Molly had come over for a French lesson, Philip had been listening to a song from his favourite musical, Carousel. Molly had been entranced by the song and fired questions at him as to its origins.

'Later we were making some refreshments when I heard two voices singing in harmony. Philip puzzled that he had never heard two females performing that particular song as a duet and walked into the living room. He dropped the tray in his astonishment.'

Philip continued with the tale.

'I couldn't believe my own ears, Molly was singing along with the soloist from the show. I realised that I was in the presence of a talent that comes along very rarely. Molly has a quite beautiful soprano voice, as we have all learned tonight. She also possesses perfect pitch and an uncanny ability to hear a song once or twice, and then she has mastered it. She is many years from being the finished article but I believe that with lots of hard work and dedication she will thrill audiences worldwide.'

Turning to Molly, Philip took her hands in his.

'Promise me one thing, my dear. Please don't enter one of those talent shows that dominate television channels everywhere. In my opinion they are simply entertainment vehicles where youngsters become overnight sensations and then are dropped by record companies after a year or so.'

Molly smiled and told him that she would be much too shy to perform in front of crowds of people. The girl then blushed as everybody laughed and reminded her that was exactly what she had done.

Alais Dubois came forward and told her grandfather that the food was being served. As the group walked towards the trestle tables piled with a delicious-looking array of food, Vincent asked Daniel Doissneau for some urgent medical treatment. Alarmed, his parents turned to him. Vincent held up a blood-stained hand and declared that during Molly's performance Sally had dug her fingers into his hand so hard, that he didn't think he would ever function as a doctor again.

Jean-Luc quickly retorted that it was lucky that Sally hadn't had her hands around his neck. Marie-Francoise beamed with delight as her shy son and the young Englishwoman blushed furiously at the unwanted attention.

Two figures emerged from the new building from different doors. Jean-Luc Morrisson was walking round, his professional mind on the task that still lay before the community, Gwenaelle marvelling at her new school. She cursed herself for not having the grace to thank the man who had made all of this possible.

Inevitably the two almost walked into one another. They each waited for the other to speak.

'Jean-Luc, I cannot find the words to express my feelings at what you have done for us. Thank you seems so little.'

He smiled kindly at the young woman. Gwenaelle was so disarmed at the gentle smile of the young man that she embraced him. For a moment, the two held each other, seeming to fit together perfectly. As if she had suffered an electric shock, Gwenaelle jumped back. As he looked at the woman's white face, Jean-Luc held his hands up.

'I'm sorry that I disgust you so much, Gwenaelle. Perhaps if we avoid one another until the work is finished then I can leave and you can resume your life as if I had never existed.'

As the young man walked away from her, Gwenaelle fell to her knees. Her mind went back to the evening in the church, for some strange reason she had blocked the events of that night from her memory. In the brief moment of their recent embrace she knew that she had been in those arms before. Her mind struggled to make sense of what had happened.

*

A shambling figure appeared at the window. Unnoticed by all the revellers, he glared through the window. The mayor had emerged from the church after sleeping through the afternoon performance. As the day began to shorten, bands of red streaked the sky promising another glorious day to come. He peered at the legend displayed before him. His shoulders slumped in disbelief that after everything that he had done for this community, he didn't get a mention on the plaque as the man who, single-handed, had rebuilt Dougeres.

The mayor walked back to his official car and banged loudly on the vehicle's roof, causing the sleeping chauffer to wake with a start. The driver quickly alighted from the car to carry out his duty of opening the rear door for his employer. Taking his place on the rear seat, the mayor ordered the chauffeur to go for a long cigarette break far from the car as he had some important phone calls to make.

The man was sweating as he took out his mobile phone. He was dreading this call. As the connection was made, the mayor cringed as he waited for his ex-employer to speak.

High above the village two figures stood in silence. Crouching down, one of the figures raised high-powered binoculars to disbelieving eyes.

'You have done very well for yourself Albert Jammot, or whatever you are calling yourself now. You must be a man of considerable importance to have a chauffeur-driven car. I wonder what these people would think if they knew your history.' Taking a mobile telephone from a coat pocket, the mysterious figure dialled a number from memory and smiled as the recipient said hello. After a long telephone call that was so much more for both correspondents, they grudgingly made their farewells. Slowly the speaker stood and after a last look at the community centre, the two figures walked from the mountain.

Petit Dougeres, Pays Basque, France.

A sigh of contentment escaped from the lips of Alan Munro as he finished setting up the one man tent for another night under the stars. For a brief moment his thoughts were tinged with sadness as he remembered how Jean had planned this trip for two years. They had laughed as they decided it would give them something to do after Alan's retirement. His wife had been a devout Christian and had convinced Alan that he would enjoy the long walk to Santiago de Compostela. He had indeed loved the walk. It had given him the chance to collect his thoughts. His three daughters and their families had tried to ensure that he wasn't lonely, but they had been over attentive as mourning families often are and he had had to insist that he make this walk to preserve his sanity.

Alan Munro smiled as he heard a long-forgotten sound. Peering through the advancing night he laughed out loud as he saw a motorbike and sidecar combination weaving erratically as it was ridden along the road.

He fondly remembered that before his three daughters had been born, how he and his late wife had done all their courting in his own bike and sidecar.

He was surprised to see a living soul in this area as he remembered that it was just near here that the small mountain village had been destroyed by that bomb. He shook his head as he thought how much wickedness there was in the world.

His mind turned to more pleasant thoughts as he anticipated his last part of his journey. He intended to end his trek in Bayonne, a city that he had never visited during numerous holidays in France and a place that he didn't know much about. Finally, he wanted to return to Avignon. That particular city evoked pleasant memories for him as he had proposed to Jean there.

Just a short distance away, Madame Casillas paced

round the bedroom. She cursed at this inability to sleep during the night hours that affects elderly people in particular. She smiled as she realised that when one sleeps most of the day, how can they expect to sleep at night?

For the fourth night in a row a familiar noise startled her. Clutching her heart, the shocked old lady peered through the blinds at the window and tried desperately to find whatever had made that noise that she remembered so well. The old lady made the sign of the cross as she begged her god to stop haunting her with sounds from the recent past. She had heard her friends talking of ghostly sounds that haunted the empty valley that surrounded Dougeres.

Chapter 6

Avignon, France.

In his hotel room, the dishevelled man clutched his third large whisky of the evening and thought how quickly his life had unravelled. Peering into the full-length mirror, he wondered where the smartly dressed politician had gone. He had a four-day growth on his face, his eyes were bloodshot from a lack of sleep and he hadn't changed his shirt in a week.

Just two weeks earlier, apart from the disappointment he had suffered in Dougeres, Mayor Charles Demoulier had been reaping the benefits of all his hard work in getting elected as the mayor of the small collection of communes in the Pays Basque. Despite being an outsider, Demoulier had wheedled his way into local politics with a combination of bribes and empty promises. Several years of hard work had paid off, along with his marriage of convenience to an older local woman until finally, he had achieved an air of respectability.

Everything that he had worked for had been destroyed by two phone calls. The evening before the opening of the community centre in Dougeres he had received a call that had turned his blood to ice water.

He had known instantly who the caller was. The disembodied voice had simply uttered the name that he thought had vanished along with his old life. He recalled the words as if they had been branded into his brain:

'Albert Jammot, I wonder what the good citizens of the Pay Basque would think of one of their mayors if they knew of his previous life.'

Jammot had desperately tried to convince his caller that he was mistaken. The voice at the other end of the phone calmly stated that he didn't make mistakes. He had offered Jammot the chance to write off the huge amount of money that the crooked accountant, which in reality had been Albert Jammot's profession, had embezzled from his ex-employer.

The mayor's blood had run cold as the caller told him that he simply had to find an opportunity whereby a bomb could be placed in the little church in Dougeres when it was full with all the peoples of the local community.

He had desperately wanted to please the other man but he explained that while those damned Basque shepherds patrolled the village and the nearby mountains no stranger would get near Dougeres.

The caller listened in silence then suddenly broke the connection, leaving a man part relieved and more than a little scared.

The second terrifying call had come a few days after the party in Dougeres. He had strained to hear a voice that was almost a whisper call out his real name. The caller had simply told him to listen to some precise instructions that needed to be carried out to the letter or a dossier on his drug dealing and money laundering would find its way into the offices of the leading newspapers in France.

This task had been ridiculously simple. His wife's family had a huge store in Bayonne where they sold office furniture. He had stolen the keys to one of the large vans and as instructed had driven to the outskirts of Petit Dougeres where he had parked the van and after lowering the tailboard as directed, he had walked a considerable distance from the van. He had almost been knocked down by some damn fool on a motorbike and sidecar that had appeared out of nowhere.

Returning thirty minutes later, he had found some written instructions that simply stated he must drive the van to Avignon and park it on an industrial estate on the outskirts of the city. Again he was told to walk away from the van to return in thirty minutes when he would find that his unknown passengers had disappeared.

A very relieved Albert Jammot had simply left the removal van there and taken a taxi to the centre of the city. Finding a low budget hotel, he had taken a room for a week where he could lie low and make plans for a new life.

He jumped as his mobile phone rang. Fear coursed through him as he thought that nobody could possibly know where he was. He ignored the ringing of the phone but was forced to listen to the voicemail as a sinister voice first admonished him for staying in such a disreputable hotel, then informed him that some old friends were on their way to see him.

Jammot was galvanised into action. He filled his glass with the remainder of the whisky and downed it in one huge gulp. Racing down to the lobby, he made for the hotel entrance. A plaintive voice behind him asked if monsieur would like to pay the money owed for the room. Jammot snarled at the man that he would be back shortly to settle his bill and strode through the door to where the hire car was parked.

Quickly negotiating his way through the evening traffic, he made for the A9 intending to drive back to the suburbs of Bayonne where he could collect the large amount of money that he had stashed in an apartment that he had managed to keep a secret.

The shock of the last two weeks was wearing off and Jammot visibly relaxed. His thoughts moved on to the problem of where he could settle, but he knew that he would never seek a life in the public eye again.

The mobile phone's ringing startled him. Desperately afraid, he tore the device from his shirt pocket and threw it across to the passenger seat. Automatically his eyes followed it and he swerved across the busy AutoRoute. The bottle of whisky that he had consumed during the evening dulled his reflexes and unable to react quickly enough, he watched in horror as a motorway bridge loomed out of the darkness. The speeding vehicle met the concrete pillar of the bridge and rebounded back into the busy traffic. Cars collided as their drivers tried to escape the inevitable carnage. Albert Jammot never saw the flames that began to lick at the underneath of the vehicle as the impact had killed him outright. Soon the flames found the petrol tank and the vehicle exploded.

Avignon, France.

He didn't want to be late for work, especially on his first day back from his leave. Even though his position would stop anyone from questioning him, he couldn't tear his eyes away from the newspaper. Hugo de Beziers smiled with satisfaction as he read for perhaps the third time of the horrific thirteen-car pileup and the seven fatalities on the A9 the previous evening. The three heavies that he had ordered to follow Jammot had given him a full report but his sadistic mind enjoyed reading about the horrific crash.

He still couldn't believe how that quite brilliant accountant Jammot had been so stupid as to leave a trail that a child could have followed. It had been a stroke of luck that de Beziers had found him. While searching the internet for as much information as to the hiding place of Jean-Luc Morrisson, his eyes had been drawn to a picture on the screen of Charles Demoulier, the mayor of the commune to which the village of Dougeres had belonged.

He had read everything available on the mayor as soon as he realised that the politician and Albert Jammot were one and the same. It had been quite simple to obtain the man's telephone number. He had enjoyed the fear in the other man's voice as he gave him instructions.

Strangely de Beziers didn't understand what had compelled the man to come to Avignon, knowing that he would be entering the territory of a man who had sworn to kill him. The fact that the fool had entered Avignon and then stupidly used his mayoral name to get a room and hire a car had made it easy for de Beziers to find him, as he had a legion of acolytes in his employ who reported anybody and anything suspicious back to the criminal mastermind through his trusted bodyguards.

Putting the paper down, de Beziers set his mind to the thorny problem of Jean-Luc Morrisson and how he could get into the well-guarded Basque country where the interfering do-gooder was living. The self-confidence possessed by de Beziers would never allow him to think that he had been too hasty in killing Amandine Dubois. He was sure that another window of opportunity would open soon that would allow him to realise his destiny as the man who finally achieved the centuries-old quest for the object that even now could be used to challenge beliefs that were set in stone.

Pays Basque, France.

The people of the region had for the last two weeks reeled from one shock to another. The story of Mayor Demoulier's disappearance had in turn mystified and enthralled them. Many of them had simply shaken their heads and muttered that kanpoteks were not to be trusted. Others loved the scandal as the story began to unfold.

The Avignon police had managed to obtain fingerprints from the badly burnt corpse that had been found in the hire car, and quickly established that it was one Albert Jammot, a crooked accountant who had fled Avignon with a large amount of money, the proceeds of drug and people trafficking and money laundering. Police informants told the investigating officers that it had been rumoured that Jammot had stolen the money from his employer, a shadowy figure without a name but reputed to be a man who would stop at nothing to revenge himself against those who crossed him.

The investigation could have stopped there, but the fact that the vehicle containing Jammot's body had been hired to a politician from the Pays Basque had forced the Avignon police to visit that region if only to determine why Mayor Demoulier had had his name used to hire a vehicle.

The mystery deepened when officers from two cities, many miles apart, began to compare notes.

Fingerprints from the mayoral office and Demoulier's home soon confirmed that the mayor and the crooked accountant from Avignon were one and the same.

The mayor's office was in turmoil. As the staff reeled from one shock to another it was Elixabete Dicharry who provided much-needed leadership. As the assistant to the mayor, she provided the stability that the small collection of communes needed.

Dougeres, Pays Basque, France.

Thirteen children chattered excitedly as they sat in the classroom of their new school. The normal routine that Jean-Luc had promised had quickly come to pass when the youngsters had taken their places on the new school bus that had generously been provided by Daniel Doissneau. He had explained to his daughter that the children would associate their old minibus with the events of that terrible day that had irrevocably changed all their lives.

Gwenaelle had been up late the previous night along with Marie-Francoise and Philip Morrisson, working out a program that would benefit the children. She had been glad of their collective experience and knew that now it would be possible for her to dedicate more time to the older pupils who would need to prepare for examinations.

The fourteenth pupil was understandably nervous about her new school. Molly Roberts, at fourteen years of age, knew that she had to continue her education but was scared that she would struggle to keep up.

She need not have worried. A smiling Marie-Francoise told her that she would be Molly's teacher for the morning lessons which would include French, and that her husband would continue the girl's musical education in the afternoons.

The day passed quickly as the children began to use the new computers, so thoughtfully provided by Jean-Luc. There was lots of laughter among all those present as even the youngest children quickly grasped what had taken the adults months to learn.

Philip smiled ruefully as he asked if Alais would change seats with him and he would be the pupil. Gwenaelle realised that working alongside the Morrissons would be an enriching experience for both her and the children.

As the first day of the new school year drew to a close, Gwenaelle Doissneau was surprised to see her best friend Elixabete, accompanied by Damien Gaulthier, walk through the front door.

Kisses and handshakes were exchanged before the acting mayor asked if she could call an extraordinary meeting of the recently formed Dougeres committee.

A puzzled Gwenaelle took out her mobile to phone her father and asked Marie-Francoise if she would telephone her son. The older woman smiled and waited patiently as Gwenaelle chatted to her father. Madame Morrisson had been saddened to see that a wall existed between Jean-Luc and the beautiful young woman next to her, so as Gwenaelle finished her conversation, she told her young friend that her throat was hoarse from shouting at the children all day and sweetly asked if Gwenaelle would speak to her eldest son.

The young principal of the school looked at the older woman in disbelief. She couldn't imagine her friend ever shouting at any pupil. In her subconscious desire to talk to Jean-Luc she had missed the irony in the statement by Marie-Francoise.

'But I don't have his number,' the blushing woman stuttered.

Marie-Francoise quickly found Jean-Luc's number on her own phone. As the connection was made, she handed the phone to the younger woman and told her that she would have to speak to Jean-Luc sometime.

As she turned away, Elixabete winked at her and gave a thumbs up sign.

Not wanting to embarrass the blushing Gwenaelle further, Marie-Francoise led the others from the room.

Dougeres Memorial Community Centre.

Later that evening, a convoy of cars pulled up outside the new building. Quickly seating themselves, the committee looked enquiringly at Elixabete Dicharry and Damien Gaulthier. Elixabete seemed to all her friends to have grown in stature with the acceptance of her new responsibilities. Now she stepped forward.

'Thank you all for agreeing to this meeting. After the shocking events of the last two weeks concerning our not so illustrious mayor,' she paused as the laughter subsided, 'both Damien and I realise that we need to give not just our own community, but the whole of the Pays Basque something to take their minds off the quite shocking events that have reverberated round the whole of France.

'I have taken the liberty of inviting our new friends Marie-Francoise and Philip Morrisson. I hope that the rest of you will add them to your committee as Gwenaelle has told me that in the short time that they have lived among us they have become much loved and well respected by our small community.'

As she spoke, Elixabete noticed that Jean-Luc's eyes never left the back of Gwenaelle's head.

There was a quick proposal from Daniel Doissneau to formally invite the Morrissons onto the action committee, this was seconded by his daughter and ratified by the other members.

Once the audience had quietened down, Elixabete announced that she would leave it to Damien Gaulthier to explain his quite brilliant idea.

Avignon, France.

His mind reeling from the shock of yet another of his warehouses being destroyed by fire had left Hugo de Beziers wondering who would dare to challenge his position of authority as the criminal mastermind of Avignon.

One after another, the minions who he paid to act as the owners of his warehouses reported to him how they had been summoned by the police to explain the nature of the businesses that had been destroyed.

That there had been no loss of life didn't matter one iota to de Beziers. On the contrary, he was furious that the captives that he had had in one of the warehouses were now running around loose. It was a small consolation that even if found they could never be traced back to him.

The loss of millions of euros in the form of illegal alcohol, cigarettes, and the more lucrative quantities of cocaine had shaken him to the core.

He tried to think of any of the criminal gangs in the south of France that would presume to try and encroach upon his territory. He tried in vain as he thought that for the most part, as ruthless as they were, his rivals would not want to start a gang war that would only draw unwanted attention to them.

De Beziers wondered who among his own employees would have the courage to try and cheat him. Thinking of the value of the illegal haul, he was sure that whoever had torched his properties would have emptied them first.

He looked in contempt at the man shaking before him. He had very rarely allowed anyone to see him, but the severity of this issue had demanded that he deal with it personally.

Forcing a smile to his lips, he placed his arm around the visibly calmed man and told him that he would be in touch as soon as the insurance assessors had done their work and they could recommence their illegal operations.

As he escorted the man to the door, he looked pointedly at one of his hired thugs and simply drew a finger across his own throat. The heavy nodded imperceptibly.

Bayonne, France.

Alan Munro shook his head at the cacophony of noise that enveloped him as he walked through the medieval quarter of Bayonne. The noise of people cheering and clapping seemed to bounce from the walls of buildings that had stood for centuries.

A man who had never been much of a drinker, much to the chagrin of his past colleagues, Alan decided that he would like a long, cold beer. Crossing the road, he stopped at the nearest bar. With a heartfelt sigh he set his large backpack on the floor, making sure that it would not cause an obstruction. Despite not wishing to eavesdrop on a private conversation, Alan found himself staring at two men who were talking in a language that Alan Munro had never heard.

A big man in a white apron saw the stranger and approached him with a genuine smile on his lips.

'There is something you would like, monsieur?'

Alan Munro smiled and told the barman that he could drink the River Adour dry but he supposed that he should start with a beer.

The man disappeared and returned a few moments later with a long, cold glass of draught beer. As Alan's hand dipped into his pocket, the other man smiled and asked him to accept the beer from him.

'I have not had a customer all day, so why should I take money now? By the way my friend, I would like to praise your command of French.'

The two men had each been making a quick appraisal of the other and liked what they saw.

'It is kind of you to say so, and I accept the beer on the condition that I buy one for you in return. I am surprised at your lack of customers on such a pleasant day. Are your prices so expensive?'

The big man roared with delight at the stranger's humorous comment. He turned to his previous companion and repeated the funny remark. The elderly man shook with laughter. Alan was mystified as again the two men had spoken in another language.

As his host turned to face Alan he smiled at the

look of surprise on his guest's face.

'Excuse me for being so bold, but that language is nothing like French.'

The big man's chest puffed out with pride as he declared that his native tongue was like no other language on Earth.

'Euskara, which we call our language, is like no other European language as it was here before the arrival of the Indo-European language groups from which most of the modern languages are derived. Some learned men think that we, the Basques, originate from Neanderthal man, and when you see my son you will believe it. But seriously, Euskara, which sadly is not the language of choice for so many of our young, who only speak French or Spanish, is a quite beautiful language which our poets and modern troubadours are determined to preserve.'

Alan Munro recognised the strong sense of nationalism that he too possessed.

Although he had spent most of his career in London, he had never lost his highland burr and as soon as he had retired he had bought a cottage back among the mountains and rivers of his youth.

Rather belatedly, the two men introduced themselves.

'Alan I would like you to share a meal with me, my wife and son will be home soon and I would dearly like them to meet you. Bihote, my wife, is a wonderful cook and I am sure that you will not be disappointed.'

Alan accepted graciously, all the while thinking that his daughters and their families would be amazed at his willingness to spend time with total strangers.

A short while later, Iker Aroztegi's wife and son appeared, buzzing with excitement as they enthused at the concert that had lasted most of the day.

Iker had not exaggerated about his son. Xavi was just short of seven feet tall with huge shoulders and arms. He had a large skull which was entirely in keeping with his body, long ears, and thick eyebrows that covered twinkling brown eyes surrounded by laughter lines. As the two men shook hands, Alan was pleased that the younger man didn't try to display his undoubted physical strength.

Bihote reminded Alan of his late wife the way she bustled round the kitchen. She laughed a lot and made their guest very welcome.

'Alan if you would like to take a shower and change before we eat, I have prepared the guest room for you.'

Alan Munro was overcome, that these people would invite a complete stranger into their home without a thought.

Iker placed a hand on his guest's shoulder and repeated his wife's insistence that he should stay.

*

Jean-Luc Morrisson shook his head in disbelief. The whole community from around Dougeres had been invited to Bayonne. Damien Gaulthier had introduced him to the mayor of the city and a few of the leading citizens. Damien, as a reporter, had helped to publicise an open air concert outside the town hall. Despite the concert being used to promote the

Basque culture, the organisers had willingly agreed to Damien's request that the orphans of Dougeres be allowed to perform a couple of numbers. He had added that a rather special guest should also perform. He had laughed as he told the intrigued organisers that they must not miss this golden opportunity to put Bayonne on the map.

It had been a fantastic day. One of Bayonne's favourite sons had acted as the master of ceremonies. He had sung, recited poetry, and reminded his audience of their history. He had astounded youngsters in the audience with tales of how Basques had helped to shape the world. He reminded them that famous Basques, of which there were many, didn't stop at footballers and cyclists. The crowd cheered as the poet recited the names of each of the modern icons of the Basque regions of both France and Spain. The crowd listened, spellbound, as he told them of their brave countrymen who had dared to sail uncharted waters, men like Lope de Aguirre and Martin de Goiti. Of composers of considerable renown like Maurice Ravel. The list went on, including people from every sphere of public life. Finally the master of ceremonies spoke of a man who had helped to push the boundaries of exploration into space. The audience cheered as the name of Leopold Eyharts, an astronaut who had worked on the space shuttle, was announced.

Huge screens around the stage displayed translations of the Basque language into French, Spanish, and even English for those members of the audience unable to speak Basque. The huge crowd, which had grown as the day progressed, applauded each act as they were introduced and listened appreciatively.

The Basque poet's final speech reduced more than one member of the audience to tears as he asked them to remember that when they climbed into bed that night they would do so in the knowledge that they were surrounded by their loved ones. He added that the next act had had their loved ones taken from them in a most barbaric way. As the orphans of Dougeres filed onto the stage, he reminded the audience that they had been privileged to enjoy a free concert, and he told them that he would like them to make any donation that they could afford to help with the rebuilding of Dougeres.

Volunteers passed among the crowds with buckets and quickly staggered to the stage to replace full buckets with empty ones.

The children, expertly conducted by Philip Morrisson, sang and played instantly recognisable songs that touched the hearts of all those present. After their performance, the master of ceremonies told his audience that if they wanted to get the rotten fruit ready, they were going to hear an English girl sing. As the laughter died down, Molly Roberts walked serenely onto the stage. Again beautifully coiffured and dressed in a simple but stunning gown, she calmly faced her audience. They waited with bated breath. The young girl didn't disappoint as she sang with a self-assurance that belied her years. After her first song, the audience clamoured for more. Ninety minutes later, the youngster was finally allowed to leave the stage.

Jean-Luc was overjoyed as he realised that thanks

to the generosity of these warm people, the rebuilding of Dougeres would be completed a lot sooner than he could have hoped.

Damien Gaulthier brushed all the thanks aside as he stated that he had the easiest review to write for tomorrow's edition. Everybody laughed as he solemnly took a blushing Molly's hands in his and asked her if he could be her agent.

As the group of young children were ushered uncomplainingly into vehicles, Gwenaelle told them there would be a special class the next day. As one, the orphans looked at her in disbelief, then laughed as she told them that they must stay in bed and dream about homework.

*

Alan Munro knew that Iker hadn't exaggerated his wife's culinary expertise. He had just enjoyed a most wonderful meal. Bihote blushed as he thanked her profusely. She ushered them from the dining room, declaring that men were only good for one thing, and that was getting under a woman's feet. The three men sat in a comfortable silence until Xavi told them that the local news should be on the television.

The presenter quickly worked her way through the region's news and ended the bulletin with coverage of the concert outside Bayonne's town hall. Xavi explained that the few minutes' coverage didn't do justice to the concert and pointed excitedly as Molly Robert's face appeared on the screen.

'Listen to this girl sing,' he stated emphatically. His father and Alan Munro both agreed that the young girl had a very special talent.

For the next hour, Alan listened as his hosts explained the circumstances leading up to the inclusion of Molly and the rest of the children into the concert. As Iker mentioned the man who had shouldered the responsibility of rebuilding the destroyed village, Alan frowned in concentration at the mention of the name Jean-Luc Morrisson.

'Do you know this man, Alan?'

'No Iker, I never met him but some of my colleagues interviewed him following the brutal slaying of his ex-girlfriend. It was my last case before I retired and it has stuck in my throat that we never apprehended the monster who murdered Susan Travers.'

Iker and his son stared in amazement as Alan Munro told them he had been a chief inspector in the serious crimes squad. The three men laughed together as Iker told their guest that he too was a retired police officer and that Xavi worked on the local constabulary.

Alan gave the two men a concise report of the brutal slaying of the young woman and declared that even though the case was an ongoing investigation, the British police had very little new information.

'I would like to talk to this Jean-Luc to see if there is anything buried in his subconscious that could help solve this case.' The two Basques nodded their heads as they thought that sometimes people knew more than they thought of traumatic events.

'Now Alan, I must work at the bar to try and make some money to feed this human dustbin that I have for a son.'

While Iker made ready to start his working day, his son and their guest talked about the horrific murder of a young woman in London and her association with Jean-Luc Morrisson. Xavi was very impressed as he listened to the older man laying out the facts of the murder in a clear, concise manner. He thought then that he would study hard and try to attain a place working with the serious crimes division of his own police force.

Avignon, France.

Generally speaking regional news is just that. It rarely has any interest to people who live outside the area that the local news covers.

Thanks to the internet and various forms of social media, the open air concert in Bayonne the previous night had become a very newsworthy item. In particular, the performance of a young English girl that had enthralled the citizens of Bayonne spread like wildfire all over France and beyond her shores.

Hugo de Beziers only paid the news a fleeting glance. A man devoid of emotion, he had no interest in some squawking adolescent.

De Beziers was a worried man. For two weeks he had watched as his criminal empire continued to crumble. Some of his most loyal of underlings had decided to search for pastures new and they had left Avignon, wisely without telling their employer. News continually reached him of first one and then another of his warehouses, filled with contraband, had been burnt to the ground. He had thought of putting armed guards in the warehouses, but quickly realised that would draw unwanted attention from the local police force.

He had searched through his extensive files trying to find a clue as to the perpetrator of this assault on his empire. No matter how hard he tried, he couldn't think of one person or organisation who would dare to challenge him.

Lifting up his mobile phone he dialled a trusted employee and ordered him to move every article of contraband, human and otherwise, into the safest place that he could think of. He listened quietly as his minion raised objections as to the wisdom of such a move. Although he agreed in part with what the man was saying, he would not be challenged by anyone. Finally, he ordered the man to do as he had requested or come and explain to him in person why he was unable to do so. De Beziers smiled evilly as he heard the fear in the other man's voice. He knew that the allotted task would be done that evening.

Dougeres, Pays Basque, France.

Jean-Luc Morrisson had been up at the crack of dawn and had crept out from his lodgings so as not to wake anyone. As he arrived in Dougeres, he telephoned the building contractor who had exceeded all his expectations by building the wonderful community centre. The builder had grumbled in disbelief that he had been at a concert the previous night that had gone on a long time. He shook his head as Jean-Luc told him that he too had been there and wanted to discuss with the contractor how best they could start to spend some of the money so generously donated by the people of Bayonne.

The builder told Jean-Luc that he would be there in one hour and grumbled again as his young friend insisted that he bring the equipment needed for setting out foundations.

After terminating the call Jean-Luc unpacked his drawing pads and pencils from his briefcase and walked up and down the main street, stopping frequently to draw a particular detail.

Bayonne, Pays Basque, France.

Alan Munro and his newfound friend Iker enjoyed a cup of coffee together as the morning began to unfold. They talked passionately of the Camino. Iker had done the celebrated walk three times but never the distance that Alan had covered as the Scotsman had started the long walk in Arles.

As ex-members of their respective countries' police forces, Iker and Alan found much to talk about as they reminisced about their gradual climb up the ranks from idealistic police constables to their lofty positions as chief inspectors.

At first the two men merely generalised about police work. Slowly their conversation came back to the bombing of Dougeres and the brutal murder of Susan Travers in London. Cynical in the ways of the world, both men felt that Jean-Luc Morrisson was the unwitting denominator that linked the two heinous crimes. Together, they pieced what little facts there were into something resembling a dossier.

Alan Munro declared that he would contact an ex-colleague who had worked on the Susan Travers murder while Iker said that he would make a few tentative enquiries as to matters relating to the bombing. Both men knew that they would have to be careful not to upset their respective countries' police forces by interfering in investigations that no longer concerned them.

Dougeres, Pays Basque, France.

Like a small boy, Jean-Luc ran up the road excitedly as the low-loader discharged the excavators that were ready to start work digging out the foundations for the first of the buildings envisaged by Jean-Luc Morrisson.

Hands were shaken all round as the builders became caught up in the excitement that exuded from the young architect. They nodded appreciatively as Jean-Luc quickly explained his plans. Knowing full well that builders everywhere enjoyed an early morning coffee and a bite to eat, he led them to the community centre where Elixabete Dicharry had left a basket of croissants and assorted jams.

Thirty minutes passed agonisingly slowly for Jean-Luc before the builders lowered their coffee cups. Seeing how anxious their friend was for the work to commence, the builders joked that the weather didn't look promising and that they would soon be rained off. Jean-Luc stared unbelievingly at a clear blue sky then as laughter rang out, knew that the men were enjoying his desire to start the excavations promptly. The builders liked him even more as he joined in the laughter.

Work progressed steadily through the day and as finishing time approached the group of men declared themselves very satisfied with their achievements and told a pleased Jean-Luc Morrisson that they would be ready to pour the concrete the following day.

As each of the workmen shook the young architect's hand, they smiled as they realised that his mind was already focusing on the next part of his dream. Alone at last, Jean-Luc was indeed setting his mind towards the next stage of the building, but first he needed to ask a certain lady for some help.

The sound of a car pulling up disturbed his musings and as he turned, a voice that he knew well scolded him.

'Jean-Luc, you have not changed one iota. Mum always complained that she could never get you to the dinner table as you were always drawing something, and here you are now, still with a pad and pencil in your hand.'

The brother and sister embraced each other, tears of happiness in both pairs of eyes.

'Amelie, that is so typical of you. Turning up for a free meal with the excuse that you are a starving student.'

The two held each other for a while, both thinking of the sister they had lost. Finally Jean-Luc turned to his sister's companion; shaking the young man's hand, he thanked him for taking such good care of the baby of the family.

'Don't you want to see the new school where our parents are working?'

His sister told him that they would be coming back after dinner as a rather extraordinary meeting had been called. She smiled as she saw the puzzled look on Jean-Luc's face, but refused to elaborate.

Petit Dougeres, Pays Basque, France.

It had been a noisy dinner with lots of laughter and dozens of questions fired back and forth. After the meal was finished, the house began to fill up with their friends. Kisses and handshakes were exchanged and even more questions were asked. Wryly, Daniel Doissneau declared that he thought it had been feeding time at the zoo, there had been so much noise.

Molly Roberts looked admiringly at the clothes of Amelie Morrisson. The young woman looked like a fashion model to the English girl. Amelie felt the girl looking at her and came across to talk to the youngster. She tried to keep her voice low as she told Molly how much she had enjoyed the concert. 'Molly, you have a wonderful gift. Everywhere I looked that night in Bayonne, there were people with tears of joy in their eyes.'

Molly went bright red as she thanked Amelie. A moment later Marie-Francoise tapped her daughter on the shoulder and simply uttered one word. 'Kitchen.' Amelie knew from the tone of her mother's voice that she didn't dare refuse and dutifully followed the older woman into the kitchen.

'Why didn't you tell me that you were going to Bayonne the evening of the concert?'

'I'm sorry Mum, but Im only told me at the last minute and to be fair, how would we have found you in such a huge crowd?'

'You could have come back here afterwards. Where did you stay? I hope you didn't hang round the streets. It's not safe for a young woman these days.'

Amelie took her mother's hands in her own and told the older woman that she had been perfectly safe as Im's mother had invited her back to stay with her. Exasperated beyond belief, Marie-Francoise reproached her daughter at her poor grammar and declared that if she wanted to call that young man Im, she should at least put the 'h' before the word as she had been taught by her English father.

Amelie exploded with laughter at her mother's anger.

'Mum, he is called Imanol. Some of my fellow students christened him Im and the name has stuck.'

Both women giggled helplessly at the simple mistake. As Amelie turned to enter the lounge, her mother looked at her thoughtfully as she joined Imanol Etcheverrie and the rest of the group. Marie-Francoise gazed at the young man who had been the subject of the recent discussion. Feeling the woman's eyes on him, Imanol walked over and kissed her cheek. 'Madame Morrisson, do not worry about Amelie, I will look after her for as long as she needs me.'

Daniel Doissneau clapped his hands and declared that they must leave soon as there were people waiting for them in Dougeres.

Dougeres, Pays Basque, France.

The two retired detectives sat in the back of Damien Gaulthier's car. The reporter and his front seat passenger chatted animatedly about any subject that came to mind. In comparison the two middle-aged men were alone with their thoughts.

Alan Munro and Iker had worked tirelessly for four days gathering every scrap of information about the murder of Susan Travers and the bombing of Dougeres. It had been the reporter Damien Gaulthier who had given them something of a breakthrough when he told them of the brutal slaying of a young couple and their unborn child in Brittany. The two men had looked at him in disbelief when he explained that the young woman was also a member of the Morrisson family.

At every opportunity, Damien had pored through newspaper files from the Pays Basque and Brittany areas of France, while Iker and Alan had called in every favour that they could think of to persuade past colleagues who had worked on the cases in question. The two men had built a large file of evidence but they both knew that it would not stand great scrutiny as it was all circumstantial. They hoped that a chat with Jean-Luc Morrisson and his family may just give them the spark their investigation needed.

Soon a rather noisy group of excited people exited

several cars and piled in through the doors of the community centre. Heating was turned on and blinds were drawn across windows as Marie-Francoise bustled around making huge jugs of coffee.

An intrigued Jean-Luc was introduced to Alan and Iker. He stepped back in alarm as he learnt that they were both retired policemen. Alan reassured him that this wasn't an official visit but just a chance for Iker and himself to draw a line under the investigation.

Although apprehensive, Jean-Luc sat down opposite the two men. The painful events of the last few months came flooding back for everybody in the room. Wisely, Daniel Doissneau told the young architect that they couldn't hide for the rest of their lives and that if the two retired policemen could help to bring some closure to the horrific events then surely that couldn't be a bad thing.

Like a well-rehearsed double act, first Alan Munro then Iker Aroztegi took Jean-Luc back to the events leading up to the bombing. Suppressed memories were coaxed from the young man's mind. Tears came easily as he recalled the pleasure that the walk had evoked and his growing friendship with Amandine Dubois. He told how both of them had known that their relationship would only be platonic, but they had enjoyed spending time together.

Taking a deserved break from the proceedings and with coffee cup in hand, Alan Munro joined Amelie Morrisson, and of course the ever watchful Imanol, as Molly proudly showed them round the school that as she informed them, Jean-Luc had built. Alan secretly took stock of the young Basque as he followed his charge everywhere. He saw a quite ordinary-looking man until he looked in his eyes. Imanol Etcheverrie shared the same watchful look that Alan saw in the eyes of the special breed of men and women that guard heads of state and other notable people.

After three hours had passed, Iker wisely decided that would be enough for the evening. With a promise from Jean-Luc that they could return the following night, the two men asked Damien Gaulthier if he was ready to go. The reporter had recorded the complete interview and promised that as soon as he had made his goodbyes he would join them in the car.

Damien shook hands and kissed his friends. Marie-Francoise smiled as he and Elixabete shared a long embrace.

At the door, the reporter turned and told the entourage almost as an afterthought that Molly had gone viral. The girl blushed as everybody laughed.

'Seriously folks, the phones at the newspaper have never stopped ringing with people wanting to interview the singing sensation. I think that soon television crews will be trying to gain access to our Molly so we need to decide what to do.

Petit Dougeres, Pays Basque, France.

Madame Casillas was bathing her great-grandson when the knock came at the door. Her granddaughter hurried to open the front door, wondering aloud who the caller could be. A smile of pleasure filled her face as she welcomed Jean-Luc into her home. The young man apologised for calling round uninvited but declared that he needed to talk to Madame Casillas on a matter of some importance.

'Grandmother you have a visitor.'

The old lady turned and smiled as she recognised the caller. Returning his greeting, she struggled from her chair, apologising for her arthritic knees slowing her progress.

'How is the work progressing, young man?'

'The builders are starting to lay bricks this morning and I wondered if you would like to see the rebirth of Dougeres from the ground up as it were, pardon the pun.'

At the indecision in the elderly lady's face, Jean-Luc explained that he had a favour to ask of Madame Casillas. As he made his request, she grew increasingly animated and told him that she would just comb her hair and get her coat, then they could be on their way. As the old lady hurried from the room, her granddaughter, with tears in her eyes, thanked the young man by telling him she and her husband were becoming increasingly worried as her grandmother seemed to have lost her spark.

As Jean-Luc and his passenger travelled towards Dougeres, he told her about the visit from the two retired policemen and how they wanted to question him again about the murders of Susan Travers, his sister Sophie, her husband Jerome and of course all the people killed on that terrible day a few months ago.

He explained how Damien Gaulthier had had the idea of bringing in a television crew to show the citizens of the Pays Basque how the builders were beginning to transform the derelict village into a place where people could live again very soon. As he stopped the car outside the new community hall, he told the old lady that her help would be invaluable.

Almost as a footnote he added that they needed to get Molly Roberts away from the village and its communes before the television crew arrived.

'We need to move her away from prying eyes, but to have her close enough for us to watch over Molly and her mother.'

Madame Casillas clutched Jean-Luc's arm and told him that she knew of just the place.

Avignon, France.

As he enjoyed a late breakfast, Hugo de Beziers realised that he hadn't slept so well in days. After his men had moved the still substantial amount of contraband, which included some wretched men, women, and children, he was delighted that the burning of his properties had stopped.

At a snap of his fingers, one of his bodyguards switched the television set on and with a sigh of relief, de Beziers settled down to watch the news programme.

His mind half on the news and half on how he could recoup some of his great financial losses, he was brought rudely back to attention as he heard the name Dougeres.

He cursed as he listened to the reporter talk of the strength of the human spirit. Of how these people who had lost great friends and relatives were helping with the rebuilding of the village that had been the centre of their small collection of communes. The cameras followed the reporter into the new building that housed a school, a doctor's surgery, and a community centre. They lingered over the building and all the new equipment. Elixabete Dicharry and Damien Gaulthier were interviewed in their positions as trustees of the Dougeres rebuilding fund. The couple spoke admiringly of the architect and driving force behind the operation. Typically, Jean-Luc Morrisson had declined to be interviewed as he was working alongside the builders as they started the next phase of the village rebuilding.

The cameras were allowed to film through a window as the children studied but not allowed to enter the classroom as the teacher didn't want her lesson interrupted.

Hugo de Beziers, his face white with shock, felt unable to breathe as he followed the television camera as it zoomed to the front of the classroom. There, her mouth opening and closing in unheard conversation, stood Amandine Dubois.

Above Dougeres, Pays Basque, France.

Molly Roberts was frozen with fear. Too scared to move, too terrified to cry out to her nearby mother and Vincent Morrisson. The morning had started so bright that she told her mum that she would take a sandwich and a bottle of water and go somewhere quiet to practise her scales. Molly had found a quiet spot just a few hundred yards from the isolated cabin and settled down to do the vocal exercises that the man that she liked to think of as her grandfather, Philip Morrisson, insisted that she do several times a day.

Both Sally and Molly Roberts had questioned the wisdom of moving so far from all their friends when they had discovered the nine small mounds of freshly dug earth that looked for all the world like tiny graves.

While all the women from the large group of friends made the cabin presentable, Vincent, Imanol and Jean-Luc, accompanied by Iker and Alan Munro, excavated one of the small mounds of soil. The looks on all their faces showed a mixture of relief and puzzlement. The mounds were indeed graves, but each one of them contained the body of a decomposing goat. Intrigued, the men had made a thorough search of the area and had been horrified to find, not only the remains of a burnt out van and a skeleton in the back of it and some obviously human bones in the passenger seat, but in a deep cleft, a skeleton that seemed to have been there a long time. Wisely deciding to keep this information from the women, Imanol declared that he would ask some of the local Basques to remove the horrible finds from the mountain that very day.

That had all taken place a few days ago, and now Sally Roberts, her daughter Molly and Vincent Morrisson were enjoying the solitude that the mountain provided. Marie-Francoise had insisted to her son that the two women could not be left alone and while Vincent was arranging bedding and provisions for the three of them, his mother smiled at Sally and repeated to her that men needed to be led.

Molly was convinced that she was either going

mad, or about to be murdered, or both. She was convinced that she hadn't eaten her sandwich, but it had disappeared. The next moment her blood froze as something rubbed at the back of her legs. The girl closed her eyes as if that would drive away the menace. A moment later, she almost jumped out of her skin as a plaintive bleating noise made her open her eyes. Rubbing itself up against the girl's knees, the young goat was desperate for attention. Laughing at her foolishness, Molly tentatively offered the back of her hand to the goat. Just as nervously the animal sniffed at the proffered hand and slowly licked the girl's fingers. She squealed with delight as the rough tongue touched her skin.

Molly wanted to run back to the cabin and tell her mother and Vincent about the goat. Although only fourteen years old, Molly was wise enough to recognise the bond that was developing between her mother and the doctor. She idolised Vincent and knew that her mum felt the same way. The last few days had given the three of them such a shock as they had had to adapt to a life without any of the modern comforts that people took for granted. The simple act of washing one's face became a momentous task as they had to get water from the stream and heat it over the log fire. Despite all this Vincent, Sally, and her daughter took it all in their stride and laughed a lot.

Chapter 7

Avignon, France.

Each step was agony as the middle-aged clerk ascended the four flights of stairs to his office in the town hall. Lionel Michelot had refused a place in the elevator as his journey would have lasted mere seconds instead of the ten minutes of indescribable pleasure as the recently made cuts in his back opened up with every movement. Michelot was relieved that his wife had insisted on separate bedrooms some years ago. The physical side of their marriage, such as it was, had stopped after a few years and neither of them had missed it. Lionel had always been rather fond of firm-bodied young women and delighted in the rough treatment that they handed out to him at his fervent requests. For that reason he had married a woman much older than himself, to give him much needed respectability, who was content with the company of a television set as she watched the numerous reality television shows that are thrust onto a worldwide audience.

Returning the greetings made to him as he entered the office that he shared with three other clerks, Michelot was careful not to remove his jacket. He had felt the blood running freely from some of the deeper cuts and while he delighted in the sensation, he didn't want to arouse his co-workers' suspicions. The clerk worked steadily through the morning and told his associates that he would have his sandwiches at his desk rather than joining them at a restaurant of their choice. Secretly pleased, his three fellow workers left him to it.

The telephone disturbed his reverie. A fussy man, Michelot couldn't ignore the incessant ringing. Snatching the receiver from its cradle, he almost shouted, 'Michelot.'

He strained to hear the whisper-like words as his caller enquired if it was indeed Lionel Michelot. As he affirmed that it was him in person, Lionel Michelot was stunned as the disembodied voice enquired if he had enjoyed his visit to the torture chamber the previous evening. He struggled to understand who could have known of his assignation the night before. At his stunned silence, his torturer told him that his secret life could remain so in return for a small favour. After the caller had informed him of the small favour, that he knew could sign his death warrant, the call was terminated abruptly.

Lionel Michelot sat, his head in his hands, wondering what on earth he could do. He knew that he was on the horns of a dilemma through his depraved sexual proclivities.

Just a few years earlier after one of his nocturnal visits to a massage parlour, two men had roughly bundled him into the front seat of a car. He was ordered not to turn round. A sinister voice had told him that all his little dalliances had been recorded and filmed and he had been threatened with exposure. The speaker had given him a chance to avoid the public disgrace that his scandalous behaviour would guarantee. Like a drowning man he had clutched at the straw that the mysterious speaker had offered him. As a senior clerk in the town hall, he saw all the applications that came in the building for rental of warehouses and indeed whole industrial estates. He simply had to ring a number and give the details of the buildings for rent and see that certain applicants were placed at the top of the list.

As a sweetener, he had been told that in return for his endeavours, he could visit as many brothels as he wanted free of charge. Lionel Michelet had been in seventh heaven. He knew that corruption went on in the corridors of power, and now he had been offered a chance to enjoy some of the same.

It had proved to be a very satisfactory arrangement for both parties, and as time passed, Lionel convinced himself that nobody was being harmed.

Now his whole world was about to come crashing down. His recent caller had told him that soon, someone he knew very well would give him a small list of demands and he would need to make the right decision.

On the other side of the city a young woman arrived at her place of work. The fact that she seemed in a cheerful mood caused one or two people to look at her rather strangely. The doorman of the club reached for his mobile phone, knowing that his boss would want to know about this as during the last three years the bouncer had never known this particular young woman to smile.

Noor Bishara was indeed happy, she had received a telephone call from the only person that she had ever loved. Her lover had disappeared a few months ago, that in itself wasn't strange as work that had to remain secret had often parted the two of them. Noor had had a strange feeling that something bad had happened and that it involved not only her sweetheart but the shadowy figure who employed both of them.

Noor Bishara, at twenty years of age, was a stunningly beautiful young woman. She dressed like a Parisian model and drew looks of both lust and envy in equal measure from the men and women she passed in the street. Born in Algeria to a very poor couple whose only ability seemed to be having one child after another, Noor soon realised that her looks were her passport out of Algeria and hopefully to a life of riches that she craved more than anything. The young woman used men and women as stepping stones as she began her ascent from the gutter. Completely devoid of emotion and lacking in morals, she soon had enough money to leave her place of birth. Without a backward glance she persuaded one of her rich friends to take her to the south of France on board his yacht, intending to set herself up with a little business among the rich and famous. During the crossing Noor was drugged and woke to find that she had been sold into prostitution in the red light district of Marseilles. A tenacious young woman, she knew that she had learned an expensive but worthwhile lesson. Vowing that she would never trust a living soul again she applied herself to making some more money with the only asset she had.

The ruthless men that she worked for saw that she

was a cut above the ordinary whore and introduced her to some very wealthy clients. One of these men had no interest in her special skills but persuaded her that her prospects would be better served if she went to work for him.

Petit Dougeres, Pays Basque, France.

Marie-Francoise smiled as she peeped through the curtains. She remembered both her mother and grandmother doing the same thing and now here she stood like some old busybody. The three objects of her curiosity were just getting out of her younger son's car. The woman beamed with happiness as Molly Roberts skipped along the small road. Molly's mother Sally looked all around then quickly kissed Vincent. The young Englishwoman and her daughter went into their lodgings as Vincent walked the few yards to where he was staying with his parents and brother. Marie-Francoise laughed out loud as several sets of curtains in the quiet hamlet twitched back into their rightful position.

Despite his mother's insistence that he tell her all about the two weeks in a mountain retreat, Vincent declared that he needed a shower and a good rest.

'A good rest?' his mother asked in frustration. 'You have just spent two weeks resting. That is if Sally allowed you to rest.'

At his mother's quite perceptive remark, Vincent blushed to the top of his shaven head and he quickly ran upstairs.

Not to be done out of something different to talk about, Marie-Francoise let herself out of the house and walked over to Sally's lodgings. Molly answered the door and embraced the woman that she would dearly love to call grandmother. A look of innocence passed across Molly's face as Marie-Francoise begged the girl to tell her of the happenings of the last two weeks.

'Mum told me that you would be over soon wanting to know all about our little break, and I can only tell you that it was wonderful.'

Madame Morrisson laughed despite her frustration. She realised that Sally Roberts could read her like a book and so she gave in gracefully. She asked if Molly had managed to keep up with her studies and practised what Marie-Francoise and Philip Morrisson had taught her; the youngster was able to answer yes to both questions.

Showered and dressed in clean clothes, Sally Roberts descended the staircase. After telling her daughter that she could shower she embraced her friend. One look at the glowing young woman left Marie-Francoise very satisfied.

Dougeres, Pays Basque, France.

Madame Casillas stared at the young man. She thought that there was something quite magical about him as his pencil flew across the page. Within seconds of listening to the elderly lady's descriptions of the layout of the village before the bomb, Jean-Luc had sketched her memories down. Generations apart, the two laughed often as the architect cleverly removed the recent depression that had made the family of Madame Casillas fear for her future.

So deep in thought were they that neither of them heard the door open. Dr Daniel Doissneau led a small party into the community centre. Gwenaelle Doissneau and her best friend Elixabete Dicharry both kissed the elderly lady and while Elixabete greeted Jean-Luc with a hug and kisses, both he and Gwenaelle shook hands formally as if they had just been introduced. Alan Munro and Iker Aroztegi were introduced to the elderly lady as the reporter Damien Gaulthier made an entrance. Gwenaelle looked from her best friend to Damien as the pair exchanged secretive smiles. She noticed that they took every opportunity to pass close to one another and that they were very tactile. Gwenaelle was so happy for her friend. Despite Elixabete's flirtatious behaviour, all her friends knew that more than anything she yearned for a husband and a family. She had recently complained that at thirty-five years of age she had missed her chance.

Madame Casillas smiled as both Vincent Morrisson and Sally Roberts thanked her for providing a safe haven for them to hide in safety while the fervent glare of publicity surrounding Molly Roberts had died down. Vincent told the old lady that he had been expecting the cabin to be nothing more than a hovel, but he had been pleasantly surprised to find a very clean dwelling. Sally added that although the conditions had been quite Spartan, the furniture had obviously been made with loving hands. The young Englishwoman added that with some renovation work and some womanly touches the cabin would make an ideal mountain retreat. The three had been delighted to find a small vegetable patch at the side of the dwelling that they had gratefully used to augment the supplies that they had taken with them.

Marie-Francoise Morrisson was still determined to know more. Quite innocently she asked Molly if there had been enough bedrooms for the three of them.

'Oh that was no problem. Vincent constructed privacy screens from some blankets, so we all had our own separate sleeping areas.' The girl didn't add that she had often heard her mother getting out of bed and the quiet whispers that followed as Sally made her way to Vincent's bed. Although only fourteen, Molly was adult enough to realise that her mother needed a life of her own. It had been hard for Sally, coping with her daughter and holding down a full-time job, but with good neighbours and lots of laughter Molly had developed into a well-adjusted teenager. She saw a contentment in herself and her mother that had been provided by the simple lifestyle of these wonderful people who had taken some complete strangers to their hearts. The youngster didn't know what the future had in store for her, but she knew that her mother would never want to live in London again.

Iker Aroztegi sat beside Madame Casillas. Taking the elderly lady's hands in his own he gently spoke to her in the Basque tongue. He told her of the shock that they had all received when they went to help clean the cabin up for Vincent, Sally, and her daughter. Tears filled the old lady's eyes as she learnt of the several graves that had been found close to her late sister's home. Marie-Francoise had found herself drawn to the elderly lady, and now she comforted her as the tears flowed unchecked. After her composure had been restored, the old lady told them that she had always known that the skeletons in her family's cupboard would one day have to surface.

'The cabin in the mountains belonged to my late sister Agathe, God rest her soul. She was a strange one. She never had or indeed wanted any friends. I lived in fear of her when she was alive and now that damned motorbike and sidecar that she rode haunt my nights.'

At the mention of a motorbike, Alan Munro turned to the elderly lady and asked if they were popular in the area.

'No, I have never seen another one in my life. Why do you ask, monsieur?'

The Scotsman told his hushed audience that just a few nights earlier, he had nearly been run down by such a vehicle as he set up his tent for the night.

People clamoured to insist that perhaps Agathe was still alive.

Madame Casillas shook her head sadly and declared that she had seen her sister bartering with one of the stallholders just before she went to help Dr Daniel with the delivery of her granddaughter's baby. Fresh tears covered her face as she told all her friends that she couldn't cry for Agathe, but for the loss of her sister's grandson Yannick.

Marie-Francoise Morrisson comforted the elderly lady and shook her head to signify that no more distressing questions should be asked that evening.

The rest of the group left the pair alone and talked among themselves. Elixabete, whispered something to Damien Gaulthier and pushed the reporter forward. As he faced several enquiring looks, Damien took a letter from his pocket and passed it to Vincent Morrisson, declaring that it mainly concerned the young songbird in their midst. Vincent read the letter three times before telling his friends that it was an invitation for the orphans of Dougeres, accompanied of course by Molly Roberts, to take part in a concert that would be televised. Before anyone could dismiss the idea, Damien added that the author of the letter had promised to provide hotel accommodation for the whole entourage and give the proceeds of the concert and the television recording rights to the rebuilding of Dougeres.

As one the group of people stared at the reporter. The incredibly generous offer had taken all their breath away. Finally Jean-Luc asked where this concert was to be held. Only Daniel Doissneau saw the two retired policemen look at one another as Damien Gaulthier uttered the name Avignon.

Avignon, France.

Lionel Michelot had never felt so close to death. He delighted in the agony as the expertly wielded whip flailed the flesh from his body. He looked down as his blood pooled round his bare feet. He screamed to his tormentor to continue as he saw the whip hanging. Barely conscious, Lionel felt the hot breath close to his ear as the dominatrix whispered that he must promise something before his punishment could continue. Desperate to return to the state of ecstasy of just a few minutes ago, he whimpered that he would do anything.

With a look of contempt at the pathetic wretch before her, the prostitute raised the whip and lashed Michelot so hard that he slumped into unconsciousness. Only the shackles that held his wrists stopped the man falling to the ground.

The young woman towelled the sweat from her face and arms before turning to face the large two-way mirror that she knew concealed a room full of recording equipment. Without any semblance of modesty, she removed all her clothing and lay beside the unconscious form of Lionel Michelot.

In the secret room three of the four men present stared at the naked woman beneath them. Their employer stood and told them to make several copies of the movie and have them delivered to him as soon as possible. As he opened the door to leave, Hugo de Beziers ordered one of his men to get a doctor, declaring that he didn't want the pathetic Michelot dying before he made good his promises.

One hour later, back in the safety of his luxurious apartment, de Beziers mulled over the events of the evening. He felt satisfied that his daring plan was approaching fruition. He had had no reply from the reporter in Bayonne yet but he was convinced that would arrive soon. Hugo de Beziers couldn't imagine that Jean-Luc Morrisson and his friends would turn down the prospect of what would seem to the peasants of the Pays Basque a small fortune. De Beziers regretted parting with the considerable amount of money but he felt sure that soon he would hold in his hands the object that would bring him the power that he craved more than anything.

Bayonne, Pays Basque, France.

Iker Aroztegi smiled as his son frowned in concentration. He and Alan Munro had bewildered Xavi as they had set before him their ideas. He knew that everything written down was purely circumstantial but he felt excited as his father and his Scots friend explained it all so logically.

The two retired policemen with the wealth of experience that they had accrued over many years had repeatedly gone over every scrap of evidence they could find relating to what seemed, at first glance, three unrelated but barbaric crimes that had led to the deaths of dozens of people.

The two men had first flown to London and unofficially interviewed a taxi driver who had found a stiletto knife hidden in his cab that had subsequently proved to be the weapon that had been used to murder Susan Travers.

Like most of his colleagues all over the world, the cabbie had proved to be a mine of information. After being congratulated on his prodigious memory, the cab driver, one Michael Wilson, had smiled and declared that people were his business. Over the years spent as a cabbie he had settled disputes, provided up to the minute political and sporting news and even acted as a marriage counsellor. He claimed that people were not so different wherever they came from. Mr Wilson had known that the strange-looking passenger had not wanted to join in idle conversation as he had spent the journey looking at a newspaper. When pressed, Michael Wilson told his questioners that the newspaper was foreign but he had seen three large letters which served as the paper's title.

Both Alan Munro and Iker Aroztegi could feel the excitement mounting as they travelled to St Malo in Brittany. After many seemingly casual questions among the taxi drivers of the picturesque coastal town, the two men found the taxi driver who had taken an odd passenger to the railway station on the day of the horrific explosion that had devastated a pretty little hamlet close to St Malo. When asked why his fare had seemed odd the taxi driver remembered that the man had acted oblivious of an event that was on everyone's lips. He had insisted that he needed to get the first Paris-bound train where he could take a connection to the south of France. To avoid any more conversation, the passenger had simply pulled a newspaper from his pocket. Both retired detectives had known that the taxi driver would tell them exactly where the newspaper had come from.

Michael Wilson, the London cabbie, and his French counterpart had remembered this particular passenger because of his desire to remain anonymous. Their description of him matched perfectly with the one that Vincent Morrisson had given them of his brother's assailant in the Bayonne clinic.

Xavi Aroztegi felt himself being drawn into this investigation as his father and Alan Munro pinned large sheets of paper on the wall. Xavi studied each piece of the jigsaw in great depth. The two older men had built up a dossier of seemingly unrelated facts and managed to collate them into one horrific crime. The young police officer marvelled at how the case had built from the mass murder of the people of Dougeres, the slaying of the ex-fiancé of Jean-Luc Morrisson, quickly followed by the death of his sister Sophie, her husband Jerome, and their unborn child.

Along with the mysterious story of the late unlamented Mayor Demouliers, also known as Albert Jammot, there had been several seemingly unrelated events that Alan Munro and Iker Aroztegi had skilfully drawn together. The two retired police officers had in their own minds built a very strong case against a still-shadowy figure who had appeared to orchestrate all of the barbaric crimes that had almost destroyed an entire community.

Bihote Aroztegi ushered an unexpected guest into her living room. She smiled as the elderly man accepted her offer of a long, cold beer. Daniel Doissneau apologised for calling unannounced. Iker smiled dismissively as he warmly shook Daniel's hand, an act that was repeated by Alan Munro and last, but not least, Xavier Aroztegi.

'We have been found out, Iker,' Alan Munro laughed as he watched the elderly doctor read the hand-drawn charts that adorned the walls of Iker's lounge. 'There are still several large gaps in our hypotheses Daniel, but we all feel that these sad events that have blighted so many lives have been done with one unknown intention.'

The elderly doctor smiled and told the three men that he had been afraid for his daughter Amandine when she had fled to London rather than coming home.

'Although she told us very little of the person that she was terrified of, I knew that she was scared not just for herself, but her family and friends in Dougeres. I believe that Jean-Luc unwittingly is the key to the whole business. It is almost as if he has been brought here for a reason that none of us can understand.' Daniel took a sip of the deliciously cold beer and asked what had led the two former police officers to their conclusions.

Xavier couldn't control himself any longer. Adopting an almost professorial air, the young man explained that following the bombing of Dougeres, a pattern had emerged that had pointed them towards the same person each time. 'After Dougeres there was the savage murder of Susan Travers, the former fiancé of Jean-Luc Morrisson. Then came the horrific slaughter of Jean-Luc's sister and her husband Jerome. Along with the text threats that Jean-Luc has received, everything seemed to indicate that the person behind the horrific murders wants to draw Jean-Luc away from the relative safety of the Pays Basque.'

Both Daniel Doissneau and Alan Munro smiled as Iker Aroztegi embraced his son and declared that for a long time he had wondered if Xavier was indeed his flesh and blood. 'He has never shown the razor-sharp mind that I possess, or the persistence to follow a lead no matter how tenuous. Why, he looks nothing like me, with my good looks I could have been a film star you know.'

Seeing that Iker was likely to continue for some time, Alan Munro wryly declared that Xavier didn't possess his father's modesty either. The four men laughed long and loud as they enjoyed these moments of humour.

Alan Munro explained to the elderly doctor that it was the small clues that had piqued both his and Iker's interest. Seeing the older man's curiosity, Alan explained that they had very little in the way of a description of the supposed perpetrator of these crimes, the rather shadowy suspect in both France and England had been reading a newspaper with the letters AVI emblazoned across the top of the newspaper.

Daniel Doissneau reminded them that his daughter Amandine had told him in a text that the man who had so terrified her, and indeed had prompted her to join Jean-Luc's pilgrimage, had had completely black eyes. He added that Vincent Morrisson had described his brothers would be murderer as having exactly the same appearance.

Alan Munro asked Daniel if, as a medical man, he had ever seen such eyes before.

'Personally no, but I have heard of this phenomenon and following Amandine's experience, I have done a little research. The white of the eye is called the sclera. The black pigmentation is usually caused by an underlying medical condition which can be very serious. Always there are different points of view propounded by learned men, so it is quite difficult to pin down the exact cause. I imagine that the initial reaction from someone seeing another person with completely black eyes would be one of horror and fear. I know that Vincent Morrisson was so shocked that he allowed the frustrated assassin to escape from the hospital here in Bayonne.'

The four men mused quietly for a few moments until Iker Aroztegi reminded them that all the pieces of the jigsaw led to one place. The city where an innocent Amandine Dubois had gone to work to provide for her daughter Alais.

Alan Munro told Daniel and Xavier that both he and Iker had been suspicious of the incredibly generous invitation for the orphans to perform in Avignon.

'We know that Molly Roberts has a quite beautiful voice, but neither she nor the orphaned children are what you would call polished performers and for someone to promise such a fabulous amount of money to see the children perform, well I'm sorry but philanthropy only goes so far in my opinion.'

Clapping his huge hands together, Xavier Aroztegi declared that he would go and fill his car up for the following morning, destination Avignon. He laughed at his father's look of surprise and told them that he couldn't allow two frail old men to go wandering round a strange city looking for a man with black eyes.

Dougeres, Pays Basque, France.

The sweat ran down his back as Jean-Luc expertly wielded the shovel. He smiled as he remembered his first attempts to master the ratio of sand, cement, water, and a plasticiser to achieve the right consistency of mortar for the very demanding bricklayers. They had snorted in derision at several of his early attempts and stated that his mortar was like concrete. As fast as he mixed the mortar, the bricklayers would be shouting for more. They teased the architect while at the same time admiring the man who was more than willing to help with the tasks at hand as walls began to grow as if by magic. It had been a painful time for the inhabitants of the small collection of communes that had been like a rudderless ship without Dougeres as their main village, but now thanks to their own hard work and the guidance of Jean-Luc Morrisson, there was light at the end of the tunnel. Any spare time that the men of the communes had they willingly gave up to act as unpaid labourers on the building site. Their wives, not to be outdone, provided welcome hot meals for all of the construction workers.

The repetitive nature of mixing mortar allowed Jean-Luc's mind to move to other subjects. He, like all the other people involved, had been staggered at the generous invitation for the orphans to perform in Avignon. Although no decision had been reached, the architect fervently hoped that the committee would agree to it. The driven man had so many ideas for the village's rebirth. Ideas that he had kept to himself as he knew better than most how much money would be needed to finance his plans. Jean-Luc felt his excitement grow as he saw that the roofers were setting up their machine that would carry the new tiles up to the roof of the row of three cottages. The outward appearance was strictly in keeping with many dwellings in the Pays Basque, but he had consulted with Daniel Doissneau for a long time over the internal design. His practised eyes swept the building site. He could see beyond the houses that were in various stages of completion and he visualised the day when the area was landscaped to match the surrounding area that men had lived and dreamt in since the dawn of time.

'Gwenaelle, try to keep your eyes off your young man or you will fall in one of the foundations. Mind you, he is gorgeous, your Jean-Luc.'

Elixabete Dicharry smiled as her friend blushed and declared that she had no idea what Elixabete was talking about. The two women had brought cups of delicious hot chocolate, closely followed by Alais carrying a plate of biscuits for the builders. The little girl giggled as each of the men bowed and thanked her profusely. Jean-Luc winked at Alais. The youngster tried to wink back but only succeeded in blinking rapidly. As Gwenaelle took her niece's hand and hurried back towards the school, Elixabete saw with satisfaction that Jean-Luc's eyes followed the young teacher's progress right to the door.

Elixabete returned to the site thirty minutes later and told Jean-Luc that as soon as Damien Gaulthier returned from Paris in one week, a meeting would be arranged for all the committee to discuss the invitation for Molly Roberts and the orphans to perform in Avignon. For perhaps the first time in her life, Elixabete Dicharry blushed as Jean-Luc observed that she seemed rather anxious for the reporter to return.

Avignon, France.

Lionel Michelot felt strangely uncomfortable as he walked up the stairs to his office. He had noticed people pointing in his direction and heard one or two sniggers of amusement. Uncharacteristically, he was late that morning; it had taken him a long time to shower and dress as the new scars on his back and buttocks protested at every movement. He smiled as he recalled every stroke of the whip from the previous night. He knew that his body would need a few days to recover from the terrible punishment he had endured, but already he was salivating at the thought of his next visit to the dominatrix that he adored.

As he walked through the office door, he saw his three colleagues huddled round a desk laughing at some photographs that the security guard from downstairs was handing round. Lionel clapped his hands officiously and in his high-pitched voice demanded to know why there was no work being done. The first feelings of unease began to filter through his brain as his underlings smiled at him rather insolently. As the security guard left the office he carelessly threw the envelope of photographs onto Lionel's desk. As the fussy man walked over to see what all the amusement had been about, one of his colleagues told him that it was the mayor's birthday and they were having a whip round. The emphasis on the word whip sent Michelot's world crashing down. Laughter deafened him as he stared at the photographs on his desk. The images seared through his brain as he saw pictures taken from every conceivable angle of the two entwined naked bodies of himself and his angel. His bloodied form left nothing to the imagination and he knew that he would soon be the talk of Avignon. Silently, he turned towards the door. Howls of derisive laughter followed him as he left his office. The beaten man walked slowly up the three flights of stairs, whispers and giggling awaited him at every turn until finally he reached the top floor. One clear-thinking person realised what was in Michelot's mind and he shouted for the clerk to stop. His misery was complete as he pushed open the door to the roof. Screams followed Lionel as he simply walked to the parapet wall around the building and stepped into space. Death came instantly as the concrete pavement rushed up to embrace him.

On the other side of Avignon, Hugo de Beziers smiled mirthlessly as he broke the connection on the mobile phone. He revelled in the thought that the fool Michelot with his perverted desires had died, taking what was only a tenuous link, but a link nevertheless, with him. De Beziers quickly calculated that all the people who had served him well over the last few years had gone from the face of the earth. He had two minor concerns at the moment, one being the whore who had driven Michelot to such paroxysms of delight. His men had reported that the prostitute had seemed to be very pleased about something. That started the alarm bells ringing in de Bezier's head as he knew that Noor Bishara rarely showed emotion. His other problem being the inquisitive assistant commissioner of the Avignon police. He took an unused mobile phone from his pocket and after bringing forth a telephone number from his prodigious memory he quickly pressed the buttons on the number pad. The conversation was all one way as he instructed the recipient as to his next task.

Elsewhere in the city, the Palais des Papes caused the two Basques to stare open-mouthed at the magnificent structure. Iker Aroztegi and his son Xavier had never left their own region before. They had often declared that the Pays Basque had enough beauty of its own to satisfy any man through his lifetime. Alan Munro smiled at his two friends' reaction. Both he and his late wife Jean had felt the same way on their first visit to Avignon. Indeed it had been in the shadows of the immense medieval structure that Alan had proposed to his wide-eyed girlfriend. Tears of happiness had filled their eyes as Jean had immediately said yes.

Xavier Aroztegi's was fascinated by the street performers as they circulated round the huge square that formed the main entrance to the Papal Palace. An avid fan of the series of Star Wars movies, Xavier's eyes were drawn in particular to a character dressed as Yoda, who appeared to be levitating as he leaned on his staff. The image had perplexed the young man for a few minutes until he realised that the staff was a rather clever step that the performance artist was stood on.

'I can see at a glance that you three are up to no good. What are you doing in my beautiful city?'

The three men turned as one. Iker Aroztegi's face was split by a huge smile as he recognised the friendly voice. The two men embraced, as old friends who have endured a long separation often do. Alan and Xavier laughed as Iker and the stranger fired questions at one another. Alan Munro couldn't understand a word as the two men conducted their conversation in the Basque language. After a few minutes, Iker introduced an old friend to a new one.

'Alan I would like you to meet Alesander Ibarague, a good friend of many years and an ex-colleague of mine from Bayonne.'

The two newly introduced men shook hands, liking the strong handshake that each of them offered. Alesander, like Iker Aroztegi before him saw so much more than a small neatly dressed Scotsman. He saw steel in the intelligent eyes and thought that he would have been more than a match for the numerous criminals that he would have dealt with during his career.

'Hello Uncle Ali.' The three simple words caused Alesander Ibarague to stare in amazement at Xavier Aroztegi. The simple childhood greeting that came from Xavier's lips left the Avignon policeman unable to take his eyes from the huge man before him.

'Gook grief Iker, what do you feed Xavier on? I thought my boss was a big man, but Xavi is a giant.' The three older men laughed as Xavier went red with embarrassment. Alan Munro laughed as the Avignon policeman looked at Xavier and declared that he used to bounce the baby Xavier on his knee. Iker was never one to miss an opportunity to enjoy a laugh, especially at Xavier's expense, and wondered aloud if Alesander would like to adopt his huge son.

'Quite honestly my friend, unless Bihote and I can find someone to take him off our hands, we will have to work while we drop. I was looking forward to enjoying my twilight years fishing and having an occasional beer with my friends but this thing stood before you is eating me out of house and home.'

All four men enjoyed their camaraderie so much that strangers stood and stared. Iker asked why Alesander, resplendent in his assistant commissioner's uniform, should be patrolling the streets of Avignon when he should be in his office.

'Over the last few months we have received numerous complaints from our citizens of some fool terrorising them by riding along pavements and through red lights with little regard for their own safety or that of the pedestrians. Earlier this morning one of my men found the vehicle that has caused us so much trouble. I had to come down for myself to see this, as the press have christened it, ghost machine. How anybody could ride that contraption is beyond belief.' As he finished speaking he pointed across the square to where a breakdown truck operative was just loading an old motorbike and sidecar onto a trailer.

Alesander Ibarague saw the look that passed between the three men and realised that they weren't in Avignon just as tourists. 'Iker, what do you know about this motorbike?'

Both Alan and Iker took turns explaining that it may be a coincidence, but that they had a story to tell that in part concerned an old motorbike and sidecar. Alesander was intrigued and insisted that the other three men must tell him more over a home cooked meal that evening. 'Ainhote would never forgive me if I didn't invite you. Mind you it will probably take three months' salary just to feed Xavier.' The four men shook hands as Alesander gave Iker his address for that evening. Almost as an aside, Alesander told the other three men that there had been two lots of excitement in Avignon that day. The first had concerned the motorbike and sidecar, and the second one had been a suicide from the roof of a building annexed to the town hall. The three visitors to Avignon shook their heads and for the moment forgot that piece of news.

Petit Dougeres, Pays Basque, France.

It was a rather special day for Jean-Luc Morrisson as he left his temporary accommodation in the tiny hamlet. That evening there would be the meeting that everybody had anticipated, but first there was a rather more pressing engagement uppermost in the architect's mind. It was a foul day in Petit Dougeres, it had rained constantly for several days. The sky was a heavy leaden colour that guaranteed there was a lot more rain to come. As Jean-Luc opened the car door, he took a moment to look up the valley. Something was niggling at the back of his mind that he just couldn't put his finger on. Shaking his head, he started his car and drove the few hundred yards to the home of the granddaughter of Madame Casillas. He smiled as he saw the old lady stood waiting for him in the open doorway. He had promised her that as she had given him so much invaluable advice relating to the layout of the cottages that had existed in Dougeres for hundreds of years, she should be the first person to see the newly built homes that would start the renaissance of Dougeres.

Bizarrely, the weather was glorious in Dougeres. As Jean-Luc helped the old lady from the car, he realised that the builders had never been stopped by inclement weather, a phenomenon that they had commented on more than once. A puzzled Madame Casillas looked at all her friends from the various hamlets that made up their commune and wondered why they should have all stopped their busy lives just to see Jean-Luc's new house.

Feeling tears at the back of her eyes, the old lady declared that at least Jean-Luc listened to elderly people as the cottages had been built just as she remembered them. Marie-Francoise and Gwenaelle Doissneau approached Madame Casillas and after kissing her cheeks, each of them fell into step beside her. Her heart skipped a beat as Jean-Luc handed her a front door key. She looked at the smiling faces around her as she realised that one of the cottages was for her. Her hands were shaking so much that Gwenaelle took the key from her and opened the front door. People surged forward to see inside the cottage. Everybody laughed as Jean-Luc told them all that Madame Casillas didn't let just anybody into her home and they would need an invitation.

The similarity with the old dwellings of Dougeres stopped as soon as the front door was opened. Mouths gaped as people saw that the house was bathed in light. The beautifully decorated living room led to a well-appointed kitchen. Under Jean-Luc's direction the builders had fixed handrails around the room to ease the old lady's passage. Jean-Luc gently guided Madame Casillas to the back of the living room. Tastefully concealed behind a partition was a state of the art electronic lift that would take the old lady upstairs. Her lip trembled as she realised that the young man had ensured that she could live as independently as possible. Her granddaughter told Madame Casillas that Jean-Luc had quietly given her keys to one of the adjoining cottages so they would be on hand if the elderly lady needed help.

As she looked round for the architect, Gwenaelle realised that true to form, he had disappeared rather than be embarrassed by the effusive gratitude that he deserved. In a moment of clarity, the young woman remembered all the texts that she had received from her late sister. Amandine had repeatedly told her that Jean-Luc was such a good man, who was happiest when he was helping people. She flushed as she remembered how distant she had been with him even though he had never done anything to harm her. She knew at that moment that she loved Jean-Luc with every fibre of her being. As her tears blinded her, she felt herself being guided outside and away from the crowds by Marie Francoise Morrisson. The older woman held her gently as she cried. Her body shook as the emotions took hold. Gwenaelle cried for her dead sister, the villagers that had perished, but most of all she cried as she thought that Jean-Luc would never hold her in his arms. Marie Francoise told her that it would all turn out right but the young woman could not believe her friend.

Three hours later, the newly built cottages had been inspected by just about everyone from the area and an emotional Madame Casillas had decided to go to bed in her new home. She told everybody that her two oldest friends would be in her heart as she slept. Before retiring she kissed Jean-Luc soundly and told him that words could not express her feelings of gratitude.

Avignon, France.

Ainhote Ibarague laughed and cried as she embraced Iker Aroztegi. Both of them declared that they should have done more to keep in touch. Like her husband Alesander, Ainhote marvelled at the size of Xavier. She fussed round him like a mother hen. She wished for a moment that her daughter Katallin had been here to see Xavier; as she looked at the polite young man Ainhote knew that he would turn a lot of heads and not just because of his size. She decided that as soon as she could, she would telephone Bihote Aroztegi to find out if Xavier was seeing a young woman. Like most mothers she dreamed of seeing her only child happily settled down and if she could help matters along, well that was what mothers were for. Refusing offers of help from the four men, the homely middle-aged woman headed for the kitchen and smiled as Xavier's nose twitched as he smelt the delicious odours through the open kitchen door. Almost as an aside, Ainhote told her husband that his boss, the police commissioner of Avignon, had called round earlier with some top secret documents for him to read. She added that he had only stayed long enough to put the files in Alesander's study. Ainhote laughed as she told her husband that his boss was a funny little man.

A frown covered Alesander Ibarague's forehead as he thought about the delivery. Iker asked if his friend was troubled that his boss should call round, to which the Avignon policeman told them it was completely out of character for Auguste Claudel, his superior, to make a personal call. Alesander told the other men that he would just take a look at this file.

Xavier Arotegi was galvanised into action; jumping up from his chair he raced into the kitchen and quickly turned off the gas supply to the oven. He took the hand of Ainhote and led the shocked woman from the kitchen. 'Get your coats and get out of the building.' Xavier repeated his demand with a raised voice. Both Alan and Iker reacted quickly to the urgency in the young man's voice and half pulled and half carried the shocked Ibaragues from their apartment. Outside the building, Xavier threw his car keys to his father, telling them all to get the hell away from the vicinity. The young police officer shouted that he would go and warn the rest of the residents. As he made for the communal entrance, a horrific explosion ripped the still night apart. The force of the blast threw Xavier to the ground. He had the presence of mind to pull his coat around his head as thousands of shards of glass from a dozen shattered windows rained down on him. Iker and Alesander raced to drag the younger man clear of the falling debris from the collapsing apartment block. As the three men joined Alan Munro and a hysterical Ainhote Ibarague in the station wagon, Alan quickly started the vehicle and the five severely shocked people sped from the scene.

Dougeres, Pays Basque, France.

The community hall was buzzing as a dozen tongues chattered about the excitement that had touched everyone in the area as the first new buildings in Dougeres received their first tenants. Always thinking three steps ahead, Jean-Luc had pushed himself to the limit in producing what he hoped would sway the dissenting voices regarding the invitation for the orphans of Dougeres to perform in Avignon. The young man listened patiently as the argument leant first one way and then the other. Realising that an impasse existed, he stood and quietly made his way to the front of the hall. Silence descended as the committee prepared to listen to this passionate young man who had given them so much in such a short space of time.

'My friends, the children have suffered so much and for a short while lost their reason for being through the deaths of their parents. Now I see happy children playing like any others, safe in the knowledge that you will protect them from harm. It is natural that you want to keep them before you all the time, but children need to express themselves to reach their full potential. We have managed to build a place of learning for them and a community hall that deservedly echoes to the sound of laughter and debate, such as the area surrounding the well has done for centuries. This building could so easily have just been a monument to those who perished on that dreadful day. Instead, you and the rest of the people who make up this community have turned it into a place that will be the focal point of a resurgent Dougeres. Madame Casillas has returned to the place of her birth, along with her granddaughter and great-grandson. I hope they will be the first of several families who either return or decide to live in this beautiful spot. This invitation for the children to perform in Avignon can hasten the day when the streets of Dougeres are busy with many residents going about their lives such as they were meant to do. I have taken the liberty of bringing along a few drawings that will better illustrate my ideas for Dougeres.'

Gasps of amazement filled the hall as Jean-Luc's superbly detailed drawings were passed around. He had obviously not wanted any kind of uniformity as each of the dwellings on the drawing pad was quite different from its neighbour. He had created a feeling of space around each house and drawn balconies from where the future occupants could either watch the welcoming mornings or say their goodnights beneath the stars. A man who had grown to love the solitude of the mountains, Jean-Luc had tried to imitate the surroundings as the intended buildings converged into the natural sweeps of the mountainside. The architect's voice rose above the excited chattering as he explained that he had more drawings that would show that Dougeres was in full occupancy again. 'We must show the world that the heart of this community is beating strongly and that we and the orphans have no intention of being driven from our beautiful home.'

Gwenaelle Doissneau's heart thrilled at Jean-Luc's speech as she realised that he wanted to put down roots here. She clasped the hand of Marie-Francoise tightly as the older woman smiled at her. Gwenaelle wanted to hold Jean-Luc just as tightly, but she sighed with disappointment as she saw him leaving the building. He had explained to her father that the committee should take their vote without feeling pressured by him.

Daniel Doissneau took his place before his friends. A man so loved by this community that his very presence earned their respect. Quietly, he outlined the arguments for and against accepting the invitation that meant more money than anyone there could have dreamt of. Daniel skilfully evaded questions as to his feelings but reminded them that their first duty as surrogate parents was to the children that had had their very worlds torn apart just a few months earlier.

Avignon, France.

Thankfully Ainhote Ibarague had fallen asleep in the back of the station wagon. The four men had talked through the night, carefully dissecting the moments that had led up to the bomb blast. Iker Aroztegi looked in admiration at his son Xavier. The young man had explained that when Ainhote had remarked that Alesander's boss was a funny little man, he remembered Alesander telling them that Auguste Claudel was a big man. Allied to the fact that it seemed a strange thing for the police commissioner to hand deliver confidential documents when they should have been securely locked in police headquarters, the two things together had aroused Xavier's suspicions.

Xavier Aroztegi blushed as Alan Munro told him sincerely that he had the makings of a fine police officer. Thankfully Iker saved his son from further embarrassment as he declared that he had taught his son everything that he knew. The humour was just what the four men needed and after Xavier had brought them all fresh coffee and warm croissants they compared notes with Alesander Ibarague as he informed them of his suspicions that there may be some collusion between serving police officers and council officials. As his friends looked at him, Alesander told them that when his superior had removed him from the Jammot investigation, although he had understood why, he wondered why Auguste Claudel should take charge.

'It seemed to me that the inquiry was concluded with almost indecent haste and I wondered what Claudel could have to hide. I started to make some inquiries of my own. I looked into Jammot's activities as an accountant and I found that he acted as the middleman in the arrangements to rent or purchase several warehouses on the edge of town. The same warehouses that have mysteriously burnt down. Over the last few years there has been talk of a criminal mastermind controlling the trafficking of hard drugs, prostitution, and illegal gambling in the south of France. The name of Albert Jammot cropped up time and time again. Going back to the rented buildings here in Avignon, I feel that if we were able to do some digging, we would find the hand of Lionel Michelot in every one of the agreements.'

The four men were quiet as they thought of the implications of this enquiry. Iker Aroztegi asked Alesander what the background of Auguste Claudel was. Before his friend could answer, Xavier had turned his laptop on for any news of the explosion at the home of the Ibaragues.

The screen filled with the image of commissioner of police, Auguste Claudel, as he stood before the smouldering rubble of the once luxurious apartment block. Four sets of eyes watched as the man repeatedly shook his head and rubbed at his eyes while he talked of the loss of his colleague and great friend Alesander Ibarague. He told the reporter of his great sadness that a man who had dedicated his life to law and order seemed to have died in an explosion caused by a faulty gas cooker.

The four men in Xavier's car looked at one another in disbelief as they watched the consummate performance. Xavier was insistent that he had turned the oven off as he led Ainhote to safety. Alan Munro ventured an opinion that with the police commissioner heading the inquiry, the post mortem would agree that a gas explosion had indeed cost the lives of so many people.

Alesander Ibarague watched anxiously as his wife started to stir. As remembrance came back to the women and she shuddered as the reality as the previous evening invaded her thoughts. Four pairs of eyes watched Ainhote as she stretched and yawned. Laughter filled the car as she grabbed the last remaining croissant from its bag and told Xavier that he would have to fight her for it. Alan Munro questioned Alesander as to how much he actually knew about his boss, the police commissioner of Avignon.

'I think it would be fair to say that nobody knows much about Auguste Claudel as he makes a point of never socialising with people that he works with. He came to Avignon around ten years ago, having been a police captain in Marseille. We were all surprised that he jumped from his position there to being the top man here and we just assumed that he had been a political appointee.'

Iker Aroztegi ventured that it seemed highly probable that Auguste Claudel was in the pay of the criminal mastermind who ruled the Avignon underworld. They all knew that human nature being what it is, corruption not only existed but flourished in public office. Xavier talked about the one thing that was uppermost in all their minds. The safety of the Ibaragues.

'I think that perhaps you should leave Avignon as soon as possible. Alesander, you need to rest for a few hours and then this evening you and Ainhote need to get away from here as Avignon will be a dangerous place for you both. Luckily the car has a tinted windscreen and I think that we can do some necessary shopping this afternoon to allow the two of you to leave Avignon until this sorry business is sorted out.'

The three older men with many years' experience of police work behind them looked admiringly at Xavier as he spoke of the problem facing the Ibaragues. Ainhote asked fearfully where they could go. Both Alan Munro and Iker Aroztegi looked at one another and smiled.

*

Blissfully unaware of the bomb blast and totally unsympathetic at the news of Lionel Michelot's demise, Noor Bishara made her way to the arranged spot where her lover had asked her to leave some food and clean clothing. The fact that she had been asked for male and female clothing didn't cause the young woman any concern as she knew that her long-time lover would never cheat on her. So happy was she that she had no idea that she was being followed. As the young woman turned into an empty street a powerful car screeched to a halt beside her. Before Noor could react, a man had jumped out and roughly bundled her into the car. As she lay on the floor of the car, a voice that she hadn't heard for some time told her that she must tell him all about her little trips with baskets of food to various parts of the city. Noor Bishara tried to collect her thoughts, to try to find a way to stop this monster from discovering the whereabouts of her only love. The next moment a wicked-looking knife was thrust in front of her eyes and the voice told her that her options were very limited.

'Tell me the truth Noor, or your own mother will not recognise you.'

At the end of the street two sets of eyes watched as Noor Bishara was bundled into the car. One of the watchers was blissfully unaware. Instead curious eyes travelled all around this strange place. The other watcher who was hidden from view observed the little tableau with a great deal of interest. A few minutes later Noor was thrown from the car and it sped away. The interested watcher waited while the young woman stood and dusted herself down. Satisfied that Noor Bishara had not been harmed, the watcher made a signal and the small vehicle moved away from the scene.

Chapter 8

Dougeres, Pays Basque, France.

The small hamlets in the commune had been a hive of activity in the seven days since all the people had voted overwhelmingly that the orphans should be allowed to perform in Avignon. Soon after the vote had been taken, Daniel Doissneau had received a telephone call from Iker Aroztegi. The two men had discussed the vote, before Iker had asked for Daniel's help. The elderly doctor hadn't given it a second thought. He told Iker that any friends of his would be very welcome and he was looking forward to meeting the Ibaragues.

The understandably anxious couple need not have worried as the whole community welcomed them. Lodgings were quickly found and Alesander and his wife were reassured that there were men in the hills who had carefully guarded Dougeres since the explosion. Alesander Ibarague gave Daniel a brief summary of the events leading up to their leaving Avignon so quickly. The elderly doctor shook his head as he heard of the deaths of yet more innocent souls in the apartment block and wondered aloud how long it would be before the monster responsible for causing so much grief would be caught. Alesander's eyes sparkled as Daniel suggested that the two men should go fishing while Ainhote Ibarague looked at the school that she had heard so much about. As a retired schoolteacher of children with special needs, Ainhote was delighted to cast a professional eye over the school and declared that it must be a delight to work in an environment so conducive to learning.

Two days later the orphans of Dougeres along with their guardians boarded the two coaches that would take them on the long journey to Avignon. The children were both excited and nervous at the prospect of appearing before strangers, but as usual Philip Morrisson allayed their fears with a few quiet words. Sally Roberts and her daughter Molly took their places next to Vincent Morrisson at the rear of the bus. Marie-Francoise happily told her husband and two sons that Amelie, the baby of the family, had promised to meet them in Avignon that evening. Gwenaelle Doissneau had worked closely with Jean-Luc while the travelling arrangements were being made and a warm friendship was developing between the two. People changed seats several times during the journey to exchange views with friends from the different hamlets that made up the commune of Dougeres.

On one such occasion as Vincent sat with Daniel Doissneau to talk over the latest medical treatments for various conditions, Marie-Francoise saw that Gwenaelle and Sally Roberts were deep in conversation. Sitting between the two younger women, the three women made small talk in both

English and French with Gwenaelle praising Sally's advances in another language. Seeing her cue, Marie-Francoise told Sally that she would need to learn Euskara next as some of the elderly people in the commune would only speak in their own tongue. Taking the hands of both the young women in her own, Marie-Francoise looked at them in turn. In a low voice she asked, 'I have told both of you of how Philip and I met?'

The two women each side of their great friend nodded their heads wondering what the older woman was leading up to.

'Both my sons are at the top of their respective professions, but they are so like their father.' She gripped the hands of both Gwenaelle and Sally and looked at the two women in turn.

'Some men need showing what they want from life.'

As Gwenaelle thrilled at the words of Marie-Francoise, she didn't hear Jean-Luc's mother suggest that Sally needed to act quickly, nor did she see the young Englishwoman redden with embarrassment. A moment later the three women were split up as some of the younger women of the commune wanted an opinion from Marie-Francoise Morrisson. Jean-Luc's mother had soon become a quite matriarchal figure in the community. Two rows in front, Daniel smiled as he listened to her conversation that was littered with words from the Basque language.

Avignon, France.

Hugo de Beziers smiled triumphantly as he made several telephone calls. Each of his most trusted men were primed and ready to spring the trap that he had spent many sleepless nights perfecting. As he prepared to travel to his office, he knew that soon he would hold an object in his hands that would give him unbelievable power. He thought back over the years to the time when he had started his criminal activities. He had soon realised that blackmail was a most powerful tool. He had been in a position to see how some of the most powerful men and women in society were reduced to helpless wrecks as they sought to satisfy their lusts. De Beziers realised how simple it was to play on their fears of their depravities being exposed. He had drawn into his web people from all walks of life as he built up dossiers on their particular predilections. The money had soon started to flow his way and he needed to spend more to accumulate even more. He had invested heavily in drugs and prostitution as he reeled in even more victims who were desperate for the pleasures that he could provide.

A man who had never had the slightest interest in the pleasures of the flesh, nor any intention of destroying his mind and body with drugs, de Beziers was contemptuous of the outwardly respectable men and women, whose destinies he held in his ruthless grip. He had either killed or publicly exposed those who had become too close for comfort. He thought about some of those who had served him so well, and he admitted to himself that he was rather intrigued by the prostitute Noor Bishara. He planned to have a long talk with the young woman that evening and if it didn't go the way that he wanted, well, she would not see another sunrise.

*

Noor Bishara was perplexed. She had received several telephone calls over the last few days from the only person that she had ever loved. The calls always asked her to leave provisions and clean clothing in different parts of the city, but the two lovers had still not come face to face. She had also wondered at some of the things that she had been asked to supply, but quickly dismissed the thought by telling herself that she would find out soon enough. A few nights earlier, she had been forced at knifepoint to tell the most terrifying man that she had ever met the truth about the little bundles that she had been seen leaving around Avignon. The man had smiled evilly as she had told him everything. He had promised that they would meet again soon and that she must call him as soon as she received another directive. She was scared as she left the small parcel in the doorway of a closed shop, but she was determined to see and warn her friend of the car that was parked at the end of the small deserted street.

Noor waited impatiently for around thirty minutes. Just as she decided to leave, an adolescent walked casually down the street pushing a battered old pram. Her mind so distracted by her predicament, Noor Bishara had failed to notice that the same pram had been pushed down that particular street at least three times. Suddenly, the youngster picked up the bundle and after throwing it into the pram, raced off down an alleyway. Both Noor and the man who had been watching her from the safety of his car were slow to react. As one they raced towards the dark alleyway, but there was no sign of the pram or the youngster.

*

As the three coaches parked up outside the city walls. The party from Dougeres dismounted each of the vehicles. Most of them had never left their rural homeland before and they walked round in a daze looking at all the buildings and more people than they had ever imagined in one place. Marie-Francoise Morrisson made a quick headcount and telling everybody to take the hand of their immediate neighbour, she consulted quickly with Daniel and set off in the direction of their hotel. She was puzzled as her son, Jean-Luc, led the party as if he knew exactly where they were going. She couldn't ever remember him visiting Avignon before. Her frown changed to a smile as she saw Alais Dubois holding hands with both her aunt Gwenaelle and Jean-Luc. Alais looked at Marie-Francoise and they shared a secretive smile. The hotel was the biggest building that most of the residents of the Dougeres communes had ever seen and their eyes grew increasingly wider as they stared at the luxurious surroundings. Daniel Doissneau introduced himself to the smiling receptionist who after verifying the reservations quickly called for several porters to help with luggage and show an extremely tired group to their rooms. The whole of one floor had been set aside for the party from Dougeres and despite the children's protesting voices, their guardians ushered them into showers and baths, followed by a clean change of clothes.

An hour later, the still-excited party rendezvoused in the hotel dining room where a magnificent buffet had been laid out on several tables. Plates were quickly emptied and as Daniel saw a few suppressed yawns he told them that there would be lots of time to see the sights the following morning before they needed to get ready for the concert.

*

Noor Bishara had never been so scared. Her eyes were downcast as the man raged at her and the driver of the surveillance car. He called the hapless man an imbecile, wondering how anybody with his background didn't suspect a child walking down the same street not once or twice but three times. Just as quickly as his rage developed, Hugo de Beziers quietened down. This was even scarier for Noor as she wondered what the man would do next. He told the driver to get out of his sight. As the frightened man made for the door, Noor happened to glance in a mirror on the wall. Her blood ran cold as she saw de Beziers look at one of his trusted henchmen and draw his finger across his throat. The young woman's mind went into overdrive as she realised that she was destined to share the same fate.

'Now Noor Bishara, you need to prioritise your options. If you have the intelligence that I credit you with, it will not take you long to make the right decision.'

The words, so calmly put, had the desired effect and the young woman told Hugo de Beziers everything.

*

Adults groaned in disbelief as children raced along the landing of the hotel. Caught up in the excitement, the grown-ups allowed themselves to be cajoled into getting showered and dressed. A sumptuous breakfast was quickly eaten and the group from Dougeres walked out into a glorious summer's day. Amelie Morrisson shuffled from one foot to the other as she tried to convince her mother that it had been late when she and Imanol Etcheverrie had arrived in Avignon the previous night. Marie-Francoise tried her best to appear angry, but as she looked at her daughter and the young man who had promised to protect her, her heart soared. Forming a protective cordon around the children, the happy group set off to explore Avignon. Alais Dubois had got herself between her aunt Gwenaelle and Jean-Luc and happily held both their hands. Unerringly, Jean-Luc set off down the steep backstreet, telling everybody that he would take them on a short cut to the famous pont d'Avignon. Gwenaelle immediately led the children in a rendition of an internationally known song about the famous bridge. Both Philip Morrisson and his wife were perplexed as Daniel Doissneau remarked that their son must know Avignon very well.

The tired but happy group made their way back to the hotel. Over the course of the morning the awestruck group had marvelled at the world famous palace of the popes, and the other attractions that Avignon offered for suitably impressed visitors. The children dutifully agreed that the palace was magnificent, although they were more attracted to the street entertainers who filled the square at the front of the palace. Several ice creams were purchased and gladly eaten. As they walked into the hotel's entrance, more than one adult protesting that Jean-Luc Morrisson had walked their feet off. The young man grinned as he was told off by his parents. His mother said that they all needed some rest before Philip Morrisson rehearsed the children for the evening concert. Both Amelie Morrisson and Gwenaelle Doissneau wanted to shop for some little souvenirs for friends.

As if it was the most natural thing in the world, Jean-Luc rose to accompany Gwenaelle. The young woman linked her arm in his as a smiling Amelie and Imanol followed them from the hotel foyer. The two happy couples walked casually down a small cobbled street without any apparent destination. The two young women stopped to admire the many gift shops that all sold more or less the same things. Jean-Luc found himself drawn to a little souvenir shop in an alleyway. His feet led him through the doorway where a smiling lady asked if he needed help. The architect chose several things from around the shop and took them to the counter to pay. The shopkeeper made polite conversation as she totted up the prices of his selections. Turning to a small hatchway in the wall behind her, the woman asked an unseen person to wrap the bars of lavender soap in some newspaper so they wouldn't taint the foodstuffs that Jean-Luc had bought. A few moments later, a pair of arms appeared from the hatch holding the freshly wrapped parcel. Jean-Luc stared in disbelief as he saw the very muscular forearms were covered in scars. As his mind tried to accept the massive shock, he only half heard the shopkeeper tell him that she had put a little present in the bag for his very beautiful wife. 'You have a woman who will stand shoulder to shoulder with you, together you will share a life full of joy.'

Gwenaelle's heart soared as the man she loved stood in the shop doorway. His snow-white hair, which had grown long again, shimmered in the afternoon sunlight. The light seemed to bathe him and for a brief moment Gwenaelle thought that she saw another figure stood beside Jean-Luc. The shadowy figure seemed very familiar to the young woman but she was not the least bit frightened. The spell was broken as Amelie implored her brother to return to the hotel at once as their mother would be sending for the police to find them.

Hugo de Beziers allowed a satisfied smile to escape from his lips as he savoured the fact that his meticulous plans were about to bear fruit. His bait had worked perfectly and the interfering Morrisson family would soon be destroyed along with all the brats who had come to Avignon to die. He had made arrangements with his newfound explosives expert to fix lethal bombs to each of the vehicles that had carried the party from Dougeres to his city. Once the interfering Jean-Luc had perished, there would be nothing to stop him taking the Basque village apart brick by brick. His mind could not accept the concept of failure. A quite brilliant man, de Beziers would stop at nothing to achieve his aims. His inability to understand love and compassion had made him into a ruthless machine. He wanted to savour these moments, but with a sigh he looked at his watch and knew that he would have to change from his public face into the man that had spread so much fear and destruction.

Petit Dougeres, Pays Basque, France.

Elixabete Dicharry hummed contentedly as she transferred her computer and several bundles of paper from her house into her car. She knew that friends and colleagues had planned a leaving party on this her last day at work. The council had held an election for the post of mayor and the incoming official was due to take over from Elixabete as soon as she arrived at the town hall. She had enjoyed performing the mayoral duties even though they had proved to be very demanding. Now it was time for someone else to dedicate the time and passion to a position that Elixabete no longer had. The young woman waved to that nice couple who had recently left Avignon in rather a hurry. She looked at her watch and decided that she was entitled to be late on her last day and walked the few dozen yards to chat to the Ibaragues.

Ainhote was jokingly scolding a bashful-looking Alesander. After the couple had kissed Elixabete, Ainhotz told her husband that if he thought more of fishing than he did of his wife, then he'd better be off. Her tone softened as she asked him to bring a nice fish home for their supper. Alesander Ibarague waved to his wife and set off to walk the two miles to the river where Daniel Doissneau had told him that the fish were so glad to see you that they almost jumped into your hands. The two women watched as the man strode off happily. They exchanged pleasantries for a few minutes then Ainhote told the younger woman that she was going to spend the day with Madame Casillas, who had promised to show her round the new school that the lovely Jean-Luc had built, even though she had seen it three times. Both women laughed as they remarked that to the elderly Madame Casillas, there was nobody quite like Jean-Luc Morrisson. Ainhote Ibarague looked skywards and declared that it hadn't stopped raining since they had arrived here, to which Elixabete added that it had rained constantly for the three weeks prior to that. As Ainhote drove off, Elixabete turned towards her own car. A roaring noise startled her and as the young woman looked towards the mountains she was rooted to the spot with fear.

Avignon, France.

Jean-Luc held the phone away from his ear as his rather cross mother harangued him for being late. He apologised and told Marie-Francoise that they were only ten minutes behind the main party and would probably catch them up before they reached the theatre. Marie-Francoise could not stay angry with her children for long and smiled as she knew that both Amelie and Jean-Luc could be forgiven, especially as they had spent the afternoon in good company. As she thought of Gwenaelle and Imanol, she crossed her fingers and offered a fervent prayer to God, hoping that he would grant her the secret wishes that she craved for her children. Her heart lifted as she realised that they had thankfully come out of the dark place that they had been forced to endure for so long.

Conscious that they needed to hurry, Jean-Luc felt rather cross as he watched police officers holding pedestrians up while cars were given priority to negotiate their exit from the city. The next moment Jean-Luc laughed at himself as he knew that most times he simply wouldn't have noticed people just doing their jobs. Gwenaelle Doissneau tried to find out what the gift for her was from Jean-Luc. The young man laughed as he told her that the shopkeeper had simply put it in the bottom of his bag and told him to give it to Gwenaelle. He was puzzled that the lady in the shop had thought that they were man and wife, but it gave him a warm feeling as he imagined they were.

Daniel Doissneau was very watchful as they neared the theatre. He slowed his pace so Imanol Etcheverrie would draw level with him.

'Imanol, have you seen that big chap who has followed us from the hotel?'

The young Basque replied in Euskara that he had and his friends who were spread all round the group had seen him also.

'I think, Daniel, that it will take more than the six of us to just get him down, have you seen the size of the man? He is huge.'

Daniel laughed as he told the young man that the subject of their discussion was a friend and that he was there merely as a precaution. Imanol looked at the huge stranger again and with a heartfelt sigh uttered, 'Praise the Lord, I wouldn't like to fight him.'

The happy group reached the theatre. Daniel, pleased at the obvious police presence around the building, introduced himself to a senior officer who was talking to someone via his mobile phone. The officer shook hands with Daniel and immediately asked two of the police constables to escort the group from the Pays Basque to the lounge for some refreshments.

Philip Morrisson had noticed that the children were nervous and drawing them to him, he reminded them of how many people they had performed before in Bayonne. He remarked that the theatre only held a small audience in comparison and they simply had to go on the stage and enjoy themselves. He looked in amazement at Molly Roberts and thought how much the girl had grown up. The serene teenager kept her mother calm. A female police officer approached the group and told them that she would be pleased to accompany the children to the dressing rooms so they could get changed for the performance. The young woman looked at Alais and smiled at the little girl. She held out her hand. Alais thought that this was the most beautiful lady that she had ever seen and willingly took the proffered hand. As the entourage ascended the staircase, Alais whispered to the police officer that she needed the toilet. The young woman smiled and told Sally Roberts that she would accompany the little girl and they would only be a few minutes.

*

Still five minutes from the theatre, Jean-Luc grimaced as his mother's name flashed onto the screen of his phone. Expecting another telling off, he was alarmed at his mother's agonised voice telling him that Alais had been kidnapped. On the verge of tears, the young man told the rest of his small group what had happened. The four of them raced down the busy street. Opposite the theatre, Jean-Luc was horrified to see a policewoman carrying a struggling Alais to a limousine. The young man raced towards the car as it started to accelerate away; throwing himself into the path of the car, he reached up, his arms outstretched as if he could halt the car's progress. Miraculously, the driver of the vehicle swerved to avoid him and looked at a prostrate Jean-Luc. The young man's mind refused to accept the evidence before his eyes. The driver, his own eyes filled with misery, was Ted Green. Imanol Etcheverrie half dragged and half carried Jean-Luc into the theatre. Pushing their way through the crowd of happy theatre-goers blissfully unaware of the drama, they were met by Jean-Luc's parents who were still confused as to what had actually happened.

A senior police officer approached them and apologised that someone had dressed as a policewoman and kidnapped the little girl. Promising that at that very moment his men were combing the city, he turned to a distraught Gwenaelle and told her that her little girl would soon be back in her mother's arms. The significance of that remark was missed by everybody present.

Jean-Luc turned to Gwenaelle, he didn't know what to say. The young woman whose eyes were filled with tears held out her arms to him. The two of them clung together as Gwenaelle sobbed. Daniel Doissneau felt like crying himself as he thought how much his only grandchild had been through in such a short time. The practical side of him knew that they must not tell the other children and that for the sake of everybody there they must continue with the performance. He quickly conferred with Philip

Morrisson, who despite his own sadness, agreed that they must act as if nothing had happened.

A short distance away, in an area earmarked for demolition, an adolescent pushed a pram through the deserted streets. Eyes constantly on the interior of the small vehicle, the youngster obeyed instantly the orders that were given in an eerie silence. Suddenly the pram's progress was halted and quickly pulled into a dark alleyway. A limousine car glided to a halt outside one of the few complete buildings in the area. Watchful eyes saw a young policewoman drag a small girl from the back of the car and carry her into the building. The pram remained where it was for some minutes. The occupant half smiled as another car pulled up and the driver alighted the vehicle, the watcher shrank back into the interior of the pram and hissed at the driver as he went into the building.

Jean-Luc's mind replayed again and again what his eyes had seen just a few minutes before. He was sure that he had made a mistake thinking that Ted Green had been driving the vehicle that had carried Alais Dubois away. As he tried to make sense of it all, Daniel Doissneau appeared at his side.

'You are troubled my boy, is there something that you would like to share?'

Marie-Francoise took her son's arms from around Gwenaelle and quietly told him to go and talk with Daniel. As Jean-Luc started to tell the elderly doctor he had seen a dead man, the day of the bombing came back to him. With startling clarity, he remembered that Ted had told him over the phone that the last one of them into Dougeres had to buy the lunch. With Daniel prompting him, Jean-Luc realised that Ted Green couldn't have known of their change of plan as it had been a sudden decision made by Jean-Luc after he had spoken to Amandine Dubois. Daniel thought for a few minutes. Calling Imanol and the other Basques to him, he told them to be ready to act at his sign. Taking his mobile phone from his pocket he gave the same message in Basque to Xavier Aroztegi who was outside the theatre. He also told Xavier that he would need two cars. Turning back to Jean-Luc, he explained that he thought the kidnapping of Alais was part of a bigger plan which tied in with all the savage acts that had been carried out to destroy everybody connected with Dougeres.

'All the senseless murders of Sophie and Jerome, Susan Travers in London, and of course my daughter Amandine and the rest of the poor souls who perished in our village were all orchestrated by someone who is sure that there is something in Dougeres that will make all those barbaric acts worthwhile. Iker Aroztegi and Alan Munro had linked all those acts to the same person or group of people, but now I think we are close to finding out who is responsible and why. I am just waiting for the next step and we must all be ready. I believe that Alais is okay for the moment but I shudder to think what the madman who has her will do if he doesn't get what he wants.'

The children, like children do, quickly accepted the explanation that Alais was feeling sick and would not be able to join them on stage. There was so much to do and Philip Morrisson took charge of the children as he went over the show's itinerary with them. Only Molly Roberts was calm as she readied herself for her own performance. Adults marvelled at how the youngster had blossomed. Molly smiled as an agitated Sally Roberts fussed round her.

'Calm down Mum, everything will be fine. Amelie has promised to help me with my hair and make-up, and with Grandpa Philip guiding me, there is nothing to go wrong.'

In the foyer a police officer approached Gwenaelle and Jean-Luc. He waited as the couple, who were locked into their misery, looked up. Gwenaelle's eyes lit up as the officer told them that they had found the little girl safe and well. Before she could run to tell everybody, the policeman suggested that the couple join him and they could go and collect Alais who simply wanted her mother.

Listening intently a few feet away, Daniel Doissneau nodded his head slightly to the watching Imanol Etcheverrie. The young man spoke quickly to Amelie Morrisson who quickly kissed him and told him to be careful. Followed by his Basque friends, Imanol quickly exited the building and walked over to a waiting Xavier Aroztegi. All the men shook hands and quickly split into two groups. Xavier had chosen two old nondescript-looking cars in the car park. He took a piece of wire from his pocket, fashioned a loop in the end of the wire and to admiring glances from the group of Basques, quickly gained access to both of the cars. Soon the cars roared into life and full with the patient group of men, were held in wait.

Back in the theatre a young police officer approached Vincent Morrisson. The doctor had just told Molly and the rest of the children to 'break a leg'. The children giggled as it was explained to them that it was a theatrical term that meant good luck. They all thought these English sayings were really funny. Turning to the police officer, Vincent's face was ashen as he was told that Alais had been found, but a doctor was needed before she could be moved. His eyes full of tears, Vincent allowed the officer to lead him from the building.

Daniel had realised that the cunning plan to separate Gwenaelle, Jean-Luc and Vincent from the rest of the group had worked to perfection. One part of him admired the planning that had been executed perfectly, but at the same time he was horrified at the lengths that the madman behind all this mayhem would go to. Lifting his phone, he quickly told Xavier that Vincent was just leaving the theatre.

In the two cars the men watched as first Jean-Luc and Gwenaelle were escorted to a police car and driven away, closely followed by Vincent and his escort. Xavier signalled to Imanol that he would follow the car with Jean-Luc, while Imanol's group would keep close to the car containing Vincent.

An exultant Hugo de Beziers clapped his hands in satisfaction. His weeks of meticulous planning had almost come to fruition. His mood changed as he shouted at Ted Green.

'You almost ruined everything outside the theatre. You avoided Jean-Luc when it would have been easier to drive over him. By your act you let him see that you were still alive.'

De Beziers raised his pistol and pointed it at Ted's forehead. The Londoner stood there. He no longer feared what would happen to him as he knew that he was living on borrowed time.

'Go ahead, shoot. I will make it easier for you by turning my back. You are such an abject coward that shooting someone in the back should not be difficult for you.'

Ted stood and waited to die. De Beziers raged. His face first went red with the fury that threatened to consume him, then white as the realisation that he might still need Ted Green sank in. As quickly as the rage had descended, a sinister calm descended. De Beziers ordered Ted to face him. As the Londoner turned round, the monster's next words chilled him to the bone.

'Ted, your precious songbird is about to go on the stage. I have an explosives expert who at one word from me will blow the theatre with Molly, her mother, and all the people there into bits.'

Ted's shoulders slumped in despair, he knew that the man before him would carry out such a barbaric deed without another thought. A moment later, de Beziers ordered one of his men to lock Ted Green in the back room and to take his position while they waited for their guests.

Outside, the watcher waited patiently. Presently a police car pulled up. A stocky bald man who the watcher had never seen before exited the car and ran into the building. The police officer who had been driving pulled a pistol from its holster and followed him. Another car had followed the police vehicle and reversed into the shadows at the back of the street. The watcher tried to see who was in the car but it was in complete darkness. Within five minutes another police car arrived and in seconds a young couple that the watcher remembered from outside the newly built school in Dougeres rushed into the silent, dark building. Again, a plain-looking car rolled into the street and parked alongside the waiting car. Seven very capable-looking men slowly left their vehicles and looked all around the quiet area. They walked slowly towards the police cars and the building behind them. The youngster who had pushed the pram round Avignon for several days became very agitated. Stepping out from the darkened doorway, he stood before Imanol Etcheverrie.

The Basque stepped back in amazement. He couldn't believe his eyes. He embraced the youngster as if he was scared to let him go. All the men present, with the exception of Xavier Aroztegi, knew the boy and crowded round to tousle his hair and pat his back. Imanol turned to the huge Xavier.

'This is Yannick, in the mountains we call him the goat boy. Everybody thought that he had died in the Dougeres bombing. How on earth did he get here?'

The seven men jumped as a peculiar whispered voice told them that explanations would have to wait as events were sure to be moving very quickly inside. The young boy reacted to the outstretched arms and lifted his passenger from the pram. The watching men looked away, embarrassed as the watcher was set on the pavement. The sibilant voice told them that they would need to be careful as the man responsible for this evening's work was expecting one more guest.

'I think the safest place for the boy is with you. Give me a few minutes to get inside then follow me. Take great care as things are not as they seem.'

Painfully, the tiny figure walked slowly into the dark building. The watching group of men waited for around eight minutes, then followed slowly. Once inside they split up into two groups, three men with Imanol and two with the huge Xavier.

A dejected Jean-Luc stood alongside his equally dispirited brother as they realised that they had been very cleverly tricked. The two men stood protectively in front of Gwenaelle. The three police officers stood behind them with their hands on revolvers should the trio try to escape. Savouring this triumphant moment, Hugo de Beziers looked down from the pulpit of the derelict church. Hoardings had been erected down the passageways of the nave of the church. From within the hoardings came the cries of several people pleading to be set free. A tiny figure shuffled from behind a stone pillar. A cloak covered the twisted body and a large hood completely obscured the face. Even though he had set the trap that had ensnared the figure, Hugo de Beziers was shocked as he watched the painful progress of the one person who knew more about him than any living soul. The tortured voice came forth from the watcher.

'Noor, Noor Bishara, you might as well show yourself. I know that you are hiding in that pulpit.'

Almost shyly, the young woman stood up. At the same time the watcher pulled the hood from a shaved and horribly burnt head and face. All the features had melted into a lump. Two nostrils moved slightly above a thin, unrecognisable mouth. But the tiny eyes burned with an intensity that frightened the young woman in the pulpit.

'L-L-Lilian,' she stammered. 'I had no idea what

had happened to you.'

Hugo de Beziers, although horrified at the appearance of the horribly burnt woman, was curious as to how she had survived his savage attack. As if she had read his mind, Lilian Gregson, or L'Anglaise as she was known to the criminal element of the south of France, pulled the cloak from her shoulders. A horrible scar, intensely white against her charred skin, travelled the full width of her throat. Holding up a lump of skin and bone, she revealed that only the thumb remained on what had once been a working hand.

The three policemen and two other accomplices of Hugo de Beziers were engrossed in the drama that was being played out before them. Imperceptibly, Vincent and Jean-Luc were turning themselves around while all the time keeping in front of Gwenaelle. From each side of the church, two groups of men made their way slowly forward, moving between the stone pillars that afforded them some protection. Yannick, the young boy, caught sight of Hugo de Beziers. The youth became very agitated. He pointed at the man in the pulpit, his eyes bulging as his actions threatened to give them away. Xavier lifted a huge fist and silently begging the boy's forgiveness, knocked Yannick out with one blow. He caught the boy as he fell and laid him gently on the floor. As the group of men continued their silent progress, they realised that they were being aided by Lilian as her voice compelled both captors and captives to listen intently. Xavier's eyes carefully swept the nave of the church. He had a good view of all of the group who were listening intently to the painful whisper coming from the woman's throat.

'The scar is the legacy of when you tried to garrotte me, Hugo. If you had chosen to wait a few more minutes while the cocaine took hold of me, then I am sure that I would not be here now. I felt the wire come around my neck and managed to get my fingers in the way. The savagery of your attack took my fingers off. I can remember nothing after that. I don't know how long it took for me to recover, if you can call this a recovery, but I do know that I would certainly have died but for two things. One, the care and attention that was lavished on me by a silent boy, how he pulled me from the burning car and got me through the following weeks no-one will ever know. The desire for revenge has carried me through the sleepless, pain-filled nights and the battering my body has taken from first being carried round Avignon in a rackety old motorbike and then after we lost the bike, pushed round interminable cobbled streets in a pram.'

Xavier forced himself not to listen to the woman as he knew that there were armed men in the church. He looked upwards at the pulpit. The man called Hugo was staring down at the woman, his face a mixture of horror and contempt. The big man from the Pays Basque wondered why this Hugo chap seemed so familiar. Xavier looked curiously at the completely black eyes and wondered what strange quirk of nature had caused the phenomenon. His eyes darted all around the building as Hugo spoke.

'Your desire for revenge has got you nowhere. When I persuaded Noor to explain who the food parcels and the clothing were for, I realised that you had destroyed a large part of my property with the arson attacks. My family have waited centuries for the return of what is rightly ours. I have spent a considerable amount of money to ensure that everyone who tries to stop me achieving my objective will be crushed.'

The man's voice had risen during his speech. The finishing words were almost shouted making all those present realise that he was a maniac. De Beziers calmed himself with a great effort; turning back towards Lilian Gregson, he smiled.

'All your sabotage has been for nothing. I have manipulated you into revealing yourself. You have lost everything. If you were to walk through the streets people would look at you with fear and loathing. You have lost a comfortable standard of living with all the cocaine that you wanted. But most of all you have lost Noor Bishara, the only thing that your warped little mind has ever loved. Finally, you are about to lose your life.'

Hugo de Beziers raised his pistol and pointed it at Lilian Gregson. The woman stood there unflinching with a peculiar little smile on her face. Suddenly, Gwenaelle, who had stood there in silence since her entry into the church, begged de Beziers to let Alais go free.

'Ah yes, your little brat.' He shouted for Ted Green to bring the little girl out. A door in the newly built hoarding opened and a police officer holding a pistol ushered Ted forward. The beaten man held the hand of a little girl. Her tear-stained face was transformed into a beaming smile as she saw Gwenaelle Doissneau.

Ted Green's mind had gone into overdrive. During the short walk from the constructed lock-up he had seen a shadow behind a pillar. His own guard had obviously not seen it or all hell would have broken loose by now. Ted was desperate to somehow let Jean-Luc know that his mind had been turned by the amount of money that the man he now knew as Hugo de Beziers had offered him. He wasn't a greedy man but he had intended to give the money to Sally Roberts for all the kindnesses she had shown to him and his late wife. He knew that he must do everything in his power to aid the man, or men that remained in the shadows.

'Aunt Gwen, I was so scared and I waited and waited for you to take me home. Away from that naughty police lady.'

Faces turned towards Noor Bishara. She flushed at the looks of contempt aimed towards her. Jean-Luc and his brother could not understand how some people would use children to achieve their aims. Hugo de Beziers was uncharacteristically silent. In the midst of his triumph he had heard the little girl shout 'Aunt Gwen'. He knew in that moment that Amandine Dubois had indeed died in the bombing and he had spent an incredible amount of time and money trying to bring a ghost to Avignon. The scathing whisper of Lilian Gregson cut into his thoughts.

'Tell me Hugo de Beziers, how did you manage to corrupt so many people into working for you?'

De Beziers, anxious to regain his hold, smiled as he told an attentive audience that money is the answer to everything.

'Over many years from my days as a lowly policeman in Marseilles I discovered that powerful people will pay any amount of bribes to keep their private lives out of the public domain. At first I was happy with small sums of money to augment my salary, but thanks to my family I knew that knowledge is power and so I began to compile dossiers on every civil servant, public official, and police officer that I discovered had something to hide. Their secret desires were numerous, I found secret drinkers, gamblers, wife beaters, drug users, men who liked to visit houses of ill repute, men and women who indulged in every kind of vice that you can imagine. They all had one thing in common – they were susceptible to blackmail. The more powerful they were, the more they would pay. Soon my thoughts turned away from money, not for long I admit, as I realised that these senior officials were in a position to advance my career. And now here I am, Auguste Claudel, the commissioner of police of Avignon. Who knows how far I can go? Once I have removed you all from the face of the earth, I will continue adding to my considerable fortune that my many activities have brought me. Apart from my meteoric climb up the ladder, I will also have in my hands something that could destroy the Catholic Church.'

Xavier Aroztegi's brain was working furiously. He realised that the maniac in the pulpit was a master of disguise. Alesander Ibarague had told him that Claudel was a big man. The man before him only looked to be of an average height. He knew then that platform shoes would add height, padded jackets would bulk a figure out, and last but not least, the totally black eyes were obviously contact lenses designed to spread fear. Even the removal of all those elements left a very dangerous man along with an armed gang against unarmed men.

De Beziers again pointed his gun at Lilian Gregson. He reminded her that she was no shrinking violet and that she had killed many people in her time. Lilian tried desperately to straighten her burnt and twisted body. Finally, she pointed an accusing finger at de Beziers.

'It is true that I have killed lots of times, not least all those people in Dougeres. I offer no apologies and I neither want nor deserve forgiveness. I know that I am a psychopath, I have been told that often enough, but the one thing that I have never done is betray those closest to me. You and Noor Bishara are a perfect match. You have both stabbed me in the back. That is my raison d'être. The one thing that has helped me endure the miles of torture, the unrelenting pain and the knowledge that I am a dead woman walking, is to have my revenge on you both.'

De Beziers' voice was silky smooth as he told the woman before him that she had failed miserably. As his finger curled round the trigger, he looked into mocking eyes.

'Are you so sure, de Beziers? When you crowed earlier about manipulation are you convinced that you had manipulated me?'

For the first time the resolve of Hugo wavered. He looked at the woman, trying desperately to see what possible advantage she could gain from such a statement.

'All the random arson attacks were designed to

make you move your operations under one roof. After I started my campaign in the suburbs of this city, I knew that the only place that you could guard your illicit gains would have to be here in Avignon. The young boy who saved my life has pushed me round these streets countless times. I phoned Noor on several occasions, asking her to leave supplies in different parts of the city. Along with the food that she left for me I asked her to provide me with several objects that I have used many times before. I must say that Noor excelled herself, for along with all the provisions and the tools of my particular trade, she furnished me with the addresses of several empty buildings where the boy and I could shelter. We always moved after one night for fear of being discovered. But all of Noor's endeavours gave me a perfect chance to narrow down your options.

'I knew that you would choose an isolated place, but one that would be easily guarded by your tame police officers who could easily claim that they were guarding against vandalism. It was so kind of you to have a temporary prison built to hold the poor wretches that we can hear whimpering in the background. Your greed in wanting all your drugs, your contraband tobacco and alcohol, and lastly the people that you will sell to the highest bidder in one place has been your undoing. Before you pull that trigger, which I will be grateful for, remind yourself what my peculiar level of expertise is.' Lilian gloried in the indecision on the man's face. 'No? Well let me remind you. When I mentioned the newly built hoarding, I meant that it was kind of your workmen to leave their tools and a supply of timber here. The young boy who has ferried me about is very useful with carpenter's tools and he followed my mimed instructions to the letter. You and my dearest Noor are stood on a false floor. When I realised that Noor Bishara had betrayed me for the only thing that she loves, money, I had the boy construct a floor that would settle under your combined weights. Allied with the loop that I fixed to the underside of the false floor and to the top of an IED, well I think that you know what the outcome will be. As soon as either one of you steps from the pulpit, this church and all those in it will cease to exist. Before you ask how I knew where you would hide, that was easy. Your desire to always look down on people dictated the place where you would lie in wait for your victims.'

An improvised explosive device, or IED in short, was the weapon beloved by terrorists everywhere. They had been used for many years in every part of the world. Relatively easy to construct, they were just as easy to place and the subsequent explosions had the ability to kill and maim indiscriminately.

De Beziers' face wore the expression of a man that was beaten. He looked first at a weeping Noor Bishara, then at Lilian Gregson, and finally at his prisoners. Ted Green knew that now was the time to help the men in the shadows.

'I'm not staying here to be blown to pieces, I'll take my chances with the law.' Turning to Jean-Luc Morrisson, he winked and mouthed that he was so sorry. Whistling cheerfully, Ted started to walk towards the hoarding. He knew that all eyes would follow him. De Beziers screamed at him to stop. Hating the man for walking away, the maniac shot Ted Green three times in the back. A hysterical Noor

Bishara screamed at de Beziers to stand still; lashing out at him, she knocked the pistol from the startled man's hand.

Suddenly, men seemed to appear from every corner of the church. With the element of surprise they quickly overpowered some of the policemen controlled by de Beziers. Vincent Morrisson seized the opportunity to lash out with his foot at his guard. With all the force that Vincent could muster, the blow snapped the man's lower leg as if it was a twig. Screaming in agony, he collapsed to the floor. His colleague gazed stupidly at the scene, unable to comprehend what had happened. Jean-Luc, who had never raised a fist against anyone, pushed the man away and in the same moment pulled Gwenaelle and Alais to the floor, shielding them with his own body. The man that he had pushed fell over his fellow captor's legs and went down quickly. As he fell, his finger involuntarily squeezed the trigger of his gun. The bullet flew straight into Jean-Luc's chest.

As the last of de Beziers' force was overpowered, calm was quickly restored with Xavier Aroztegi taking charge. De Beziers, his head bowed, stood in silence. His mind was working furiously as he thought that his crooked lawyers would have to earn their retainer. He could not face the idea of spending the rest of his life locked up like a common criminal. With her curious twisted gait, Lilian Gregson stepped forward. As a concession to her struggle to raise her head, Xavier knelt. His eyes filled with compassion, he asked the woman if he could do anything for her.

'That is very kind of you, but no, there is nothing I need. You know that I can never allow de Beziers to walk from here. Clever lawyers, and he will have the best, believe me, will delay his trial for years and possibly get him a shorter sentence than he deserves. You need to get out of here immediately and take the people that Hugo de Beziers intended to be used as slaves and unwilling prostitutes with you. I know that these rogue policemen will go with you but be very careful who you contact in the police force here as nobody knows the depth of corruption.'

Xavier Aroztegi could say no more. Calling Imanol Etcheverrie to him, the two men walked towards the sounds of weeping from the makeshift prison. Lilian Gregson reminded the men that they didn't have much time. Xavier took the padlock in his massive hand. His face showed no strain at all as he simply twisted the lock until it shattered. Pulling open the door, the two men looked into the frightened faces of around thirty men, women, and children. Talking in Euskara, Xavier directed his friends to guide the refugees from the church. Two of the Basques guarded the corrupt police officers and the mass of people walked out into the dark night.

Chapter 9

Dougeres, Pays Basques, France.

Tears poured down Gwenaelle Doissneau's face. She clutched her father's arm as he too wiped tears from his eyes. Crying filled the packed church as people came to mourn one of their own. Marie-Francoise sobbed quietly as her husband Philip held her in his arms. Vincent Morrisson sat between a distraught Sally and Molly Roberts, his strong arms round their waists. People had come from miles around to pay tribute to a much-loved friend. The orphans filled an entire row as they huddled together, drawing comfort from their closeness. Amelie clutched the strong arm of Imanol. The Basque shepherds, uncomfortable in their dark suits, sat in silence as the priest, brought in for this solemn occasion, spoke of the short but glorious life of a soul who even now would be at God's side. The Aroztegis and the Ibaragues sat together. Unable to sit comfortably in a pew built for much smaller people, the huge Xavier stood respectfully at the back of the church. A small area at the back of the church had been left clear for a bed. Filled with antibiotics and other drugs to fight any infections that would attack a weakened body, the patient was unable to follow the proceedings. Jean-Luc had defied the very angry doctors in the Avignon hospital who had protested vehemently at his crazy insistence at leaving the hospital. Mercifully he had slept for the entire journey as his body struggled to recover. At the front of the church, holding the other arm of Gwenaelle, Damien Gaulthier fought to hold back the tears as he mourned his intended wife Elixabete Dicharry.

A sad group of people filed from the church to make their way to the small cemetery just two miles from Dougeres. Elderly people shook their heads at the tragic loss of such a young life. Following the interment they travelled back to the community centre. In truth, some of them had nowhere else to go. Alesander Ibarague had been the only witness to the sudden death of Elixabete. That fateful day, he had been walking happily towards the fish-filled rivers when he had heard a tremendous roaring noise. He had dropped all his fishing gear and hurried back towards Petit Dougeres. His horrified gaze had rested on Elixabete as she had stood transfixed with terror. A huge river of mud, soil, and water had come hurtling down the mountainside from where the overflowing mountain lake had burst its banks. The tiny hamlet had not stood a chance. The houses had collapsed under the enormous weight of the water until finally only Elixabete had stood in its way. Too late, the young woman tried to run to her car. She had been swallowed up by the sea of mud as it continued its relentless march down the slopes until its inevitable stop once it had reached the flat lands.

Now the residents of Petit Dougeres, along with

their guests, were homeless. Once again in the face of adversity, the indomitable spirit of the people of the communities came to the fore. Houses in the area were filled to overflowing as the refugees of the lost hamlet were welcomed into the homes of friends. The six completed houses in Dougeres took in as many of the homeless as they could, while the surplus, mostly younger people, took temporary shelter in the community centre. Daniel Doissneau and Philip Morrisson rose to the occasion magnificently. They begged and borrowed as many camping beds and sleeping bags as they could. Gifts of food and clothing arrived from Bayonne as Iker and Bihote Aroztegi galvanised the citizens of that city into once again digging deep into their pockets.

As they talked quietly in the community centre, people knew that despite their grief, they would have to put the tragic loss of Elixabete Dicharry into a corner of their minds and continue living. Madame Casillas insisted that for the moment Jean-Luc should stay in the cottage that she loved. However, Marie-Francoise had other ideas. She told the elderly lady that as Yannick had been restored to her family, she should devote her time to helping him settle into the community. Amelie responded to her mother's prompting by offering to move in with the old lady and help with the difficult task of housetraining the quite primitive Yannick. The silent boy had responded most to Amelie during the sad journey back from Avignon. To help her studies in child psychology, the young woman had learnt sign language and she sat with the frightened boy and prompted him with some simple exercises. Over the last few days Yannick had learnt to smile as people hugged him. Never allowed a childhood by his grandmother, the young boy was soon included in the children's games, mostly at the insistence of little Alais.

Among the adults there was a general air of despondency that the money falsely promised by Hugo de Beziers would never materialise. Nobody looked to apportion blame but now they were faced with the reality that the rebuilding of Dougeres would possibly take many years. Alesander Ibarague sat talking to Iker and Xavier Aroztegi. The young man blushed often as the two older men praised his cool head during the incident in Avignon. Of course Iker wondered why people were surprised at Xavier's conduct, because as everybody knew the boy was his son and he had inherited his father's logical mind.

Immediately after they had received the young man's report from that fateful night, the two older men had travelled to Avignon. As they drove to the city, Alesander was advising Xavier by phone which police officers he should contact to deal with the aftermath of the kidnapping and subsequent explosion at the church. Xavier Aroztegi had made out a very substantial report of the night's events. The young officer had impressed the older policeman who had taken charge. As prisoners were led to prison cells and rescuers and hostages were reunited with their overjoyed loved ones, Xavier had told that as he had left the church, Lilian Gregson had declared that she was lonely by herself and she would like to share the pulpit with Noor Bishara and Hugo de Beziers. A grim-faced Xavier had hurried from the area with the screams of the terrified couple begging L'Anglaise not to join them, as they knew that her tiny weight would push the false floor further down onto the rudimentary IED. The inevitable outcome was assured as soon as one of them moved.

The following morning Alesander Ibarague, joined by some of France's most senior policemen and indeed an advisor to the president, had made a preliminary report on the corruption that had permeated through the police force and the town hall. The resurrected Alesander Ibarague had been asked, in a way that he could not refuse, to take complete control of the investigation. He had insisted that a newly promoted Xavier Aroztegi should be seconded to his command and promised that no stone would be left unturned as he sought to cut the disease from the city that threatened to taint the whole of the force and the town hall. He knew that the majority of the civic officials and police officers were conscientious, hardworking people and he determined that before he was finished the spectre of corruption would be eradicated. Alesander had insisted to his superiors that he would return to Avignon only after he had paid his respects at the funeral of a much-loved young woman.

An exhausted Jean-Luc Morrisson weakly received the well-wishers at his bedside. He smiled gratefully as his friends filed past insisting that they needed him back at the building site as soon as possible. After the procession had moved away, the patient's smiling parents had moved to the bedside along with a blushing Gwenaelle Doissneau. Presently they were joined by the Ibaragues. Alesander asked the young man if he would consider a proposal for a moment without interrupting. Jean-Luc nodded.

'Firstly Jean-Luc, I have received a promise from none other than the president of France that any illicit monies we recover from the bank accounts of Hugo de Beziers will be given in full to the Dougeres rebuilding fund.'

Mouths dropped open at this incredibly generous offer. Moving on, Alesander told his audience that as he intended to retire as soon as his investigation into Hugo de Beziers was complete, he and his wife Ainhote would like to buy a house here in Dougeres. Everybody present looked at Jean-Luc in surprise as he shook his head negatively. Smiling weakly, he spoke.

'When the idea of rebuilding Dougeres was given to me, I knew that in a spirit of kindness the peoples of these small communities took my family and friends to their hearts. I knew that while I had a breath in my body, I would repay that kindness and offer homes to people who wanted to be part of this incredible movement that we have here. I never want the houses here to be owned, simply to be lived in and loved by the occupiers until such a time as they leave, when the dwellings will be occupied by other people who will cherish the houses and their community. So Alesander and Ainhote, on behalf of the citizens of Dougeres, welcome to your new home.'

Tears of gratitude were followed by laughter as Jean-Luc asked Alesander if he could use a cement mixer.

As people made the small talk that dominates large gatherings such as funerals, the orphans of Dougeres decided to give an impromptu concert. Philip

Morrisson smiled as the children asked if he would accompany them on the piano. The audience cheered as the children sang the songs so beloved of the Pays Basque. An understandably proud Sally Roberts told Gwenaelle that the concert in Avignon had been wonderful, with the orphans and Molly being called back again and again. Molly had become quite an accomplished performer, revelling in the hard work as she focussed on a future as a classical singer. Philip Morrisson had told her delighted mother many times that there would be no holding Molly once she started to receive formal training from a professional singing coach.

Asking Ainhote Ibarague to join her, Marie-Francoise took the hand of Gwenaelle and gently led her to the back of the room.

'My dear, you are physically and emotionally drained. It is no surprise as you never left my son's hospital bed for three days. The doctors told me that you talked to him constantly all the time that he was unconscious. Everybody can see the effect that the kidnapping of Alais had on you, thankfully like most children do she has bounced back, but you Gwenaelle, need to take care of yourself. So, and we will have no arguments, we have been talking about what we should do with you. Your father and Vincent as doctors have said that both you and Jean-Luc need peace and quiet to recover. Vincent and Sally have stocked the cabin in the mountains with supplies, we are a phone call away if you need anything, and Imanol Etcheverrie and his friends have promised to call in from time to time and check that you are coping. First thing tomorrow morning you will both be taken to the mountain retreat.'

Gwenaelle protested that the children needed her. Both Marie-Francoise and Ainhote smiled and told her that the children needed their much-loved teacher fit and well. Marie-Francoise added, 'If Ainhote is going to live among us, we need to put her to work. We don't want any idlers in Dougeres.'

The three women laughed and the matter was settled.

*

Jean-Luc slept for almost twenty-four hours. He woke in a strange bed but lay there listening to the sound of someone humming. Sunlight streamed through the windows and he listened appreciatively to the sounds of the birdsong coming through the open door. He couldn't work out where he was or how he had got here. He winced as the pain in his chest reminded him of his fragile state of health. Pushing the luxurious goose feather quilt from him, he slowly placed one foot on the floor. A voice, in a tone that would brook no argument, told him to stay exactly where he was. Gwenaelle's smiling face appeared above him.

'I was beginning to think that you would never wake up. Your mother told me that you always enjoyed a lie-in as a boy, but twenty-four hours is ridiculous.'

Jean-Luc stared in amazement at the young woman. As he looked carefully into her face, he could see the deep-rooted fatigue that had threatened her health. The horrors of the last few days revisited him. Although there were large chunks of the story missing for him, he knew that when he was ready he would ask Gwenaelle to tell him. He knew that he had come close to losing her, along with all of his family and friends. He remembered the brave sacrifice of Ted Green before his own particular world fell in on him. He told Gwenaelle that Sally and Molly must never know of Ted's involvement.

'It's okay Jean-Luc, before Alan Munro left for home he advised that for Sally's sake her last memories of Ted Green should be that he died in Dougeres all those months ago.'

The young woman marvelled at how this man she loved could think of the feelings of others despite his own pain. Turning away to hide the tears that threatened to flow, Gwenaelle told Jean-Luc that she had made some soup. The two of them laughed without embarrassment as she spoon fed him with the delicious soup. Enjoying each other's company in the peaceful surroundings, Gwenaelle and Jean-Luc spoke of their hopes for Dougeres now that the threat to their very existence had gone.

'Your mother had the presence of mind to pack your drawing pad and pencils among your things. She said that you could not go a day without drawing on something.' Gwenaelle didn't mention that she had looked through his sketchpad and had thrilled at the stunning images of herself on the first two pages. She reminded him that now the problem of finance for the rebirth of Dougeres had thankfully been settled, he needed to get his ideas down on paper. She reminded him that the work had never stopped and the whole community had thrown itself behind the project, knowing that they needed to finish some more houses before the onset of winter. Gwenaelle smiled as she saw that Jean-Luc had drifted off to sleep again. The woman knew that it was sleep that he needed more than anything and gently taking the sketchpad from his fingers, she stooped to kiss his forehead before pulling the quilt over him.

The next three days passed in a familiar routine. The two of them would discuss the project with Jean-Luc welcoming Gwenaelle's ideas for certain features to be added or taken away. Slowly she introduced some solid food into his diet as she saw that his strength was returning. They had both come to love the evenings. Gwenaelle would help the invalid out to the front porch where they would drink delicious hot chocolate and marvel at the magnificence of the night sky. She would point out particular stars and tell him of the myths and stories attributed to the particular heavenly objects. The wonders of the nature all around them began to work its magic as the young couple realised that their friendship was evolving. They would often just sit together in a comfortable silence. Their fingers would stray together and stay together as they enjoyed their solitude. Soon Jean-Luc was impatient to walk, he impressed on Gwenaelle that with her help, he could walk as far as the stream. She looked at him doubtfully.

'Cherie, your body has endured two massive shocks in less than six months, added to the stress that you have put yourself under planning the huge building project. You are exhausted. You have said many times that you want Dougeres to be here for many years to come, and so do I, but I also want you to be here for many years to come.'

Slowly, Jean-Luc walked, with Gwenaelle supporting him, the one hundred yards to the stream. The sweat poured from his face and body to remind him that he was as weak as a kitten. The young woman helped him to a large rock and knelt at his side as Jean-Luc sat gratefully. The early morning sun warmed their backs as they savoured the sounds of the bubbling stream. It almost seemed as if the water was giggling as it raced over the stones that sat on the stream's bed. Birds sang happily as they enjoyed a breakfast of the insects that lived by the water's edge. The couple both knew that each day spent together with family and friends would help them forget the horrors that had been visited on them so recently.

Gwenaelle ran back to the cabin for Jean-Luc's drawing pad and pencils and watched as he doodled for a few minutes until new ideas started to fill the paper. Watching the young woman as she knelt at the water's edge, Jean-Luc's pencil flew over the paper. Drawing from memory, he quickly put down on the paper a portrait that at first glance looked like a portrait of Gwenaelle gazing into a mirror. The young woman gasped as she knew that he had drawn herself and her late sister Amandine. She told him that even their closest friends had sometimes been unable to tell them apart. Jean-Luc declared emphatically that he would have known every time. At the woman's puzzled look, he cupped her chin in the palm of his hand.

'That day in the hospital in Bayonne, I thought at first that you were Amandine, but as I looked into your eyes I saw a competitive spirit that I don't think your sister had.'

Gwenaelle smiled as she remembered that her

beloved sister had been such a gentle soul, and indeed had always followed willingly as Gwenaelle got them into one scrape after another.

Before the couple knew it, a week had passed. A week filled with joy as Jean-Luc grew stronger. Like his brother Vincent before him. He explored the immediate surroundings. He admired the careful husbandry that had made the previous occupants of the cabin almost self-sufficient. As he looked at the vegetable garden enclosed by a fence, he filed a thought to the back of his mind. In the cabin itself he examined the simple but beautifully made furniture. Some carvings had been made on each piece of furniture. Jean-Luc admired the artistry of the works which depicted subjects such as birds, flowers, and animals. All the living things that the artist would have seen in the locale. Gwenaelle asked him if he was ready for his daily walk. She placed her arm around his waist as they opened the cabin door. She loved the feel of him and his smell as he held her. Jean-Luc felt that he could walk unaided as far as the stream but he wouldn't tell her that for fear she would let him.

Marie-Francoise had been up to the mountain retreat, as everybody in Dougeres had started calling it. Accompanied by her husband Philip and little Alais, Jean-Luc's mother was quietly satisfied as she saw the love that was growing between the younger couple. Philip joked that they mustn't hurry back as they finally had a teacher in Ainhote who was knocking the children into shape. Gwenaelle was alarmed until she saw the twinkle in Philip's eye. Alais told her aunt that Madame Ibarague was wonderful but all the children missed their own teacher.

Marie-Francoise looked at her son carefully, she saw that through the trauma of two life-threatening injuries he had lost so much weight. She was gratified to see that the fire in his eyes had never dimmed and when she gave him a progress report on the housebuilding backed up by lots of photographs that her husband had taken, Jean-Luc was delighted. His mother knew that he was torn between wanting to get back to his work in progress and staying here with this quite beautiful young woman. Philip remembered that his eldest son didn't know about Yannick or the goat boy as the Basque shepherds called him. With lots of interruptions from Alais who declared that she was doing sign language with Amelie and Madame Ibarague so that she could help her friend, the Morrissons explained the bizarre story of how Yannick had been found in Avignon. Jean-Luc was mystified as he heard that a fourteen-year-old boy who couldn't speak had been taken to the heart of a community who welcomed him back like the prodigal son.

As the evening drew in, the young couple were alone again. They had eaten a light but delicious supper and with their customary hot chocolate had snuggled up together on the porch. Jean-Luc showed Gwenaelle preliminary sketches of a house that he had designed that had several bedrooms. Pointing at one of the rooms, he explained what the sections through a drawing meant and how the plan displayed all the features, albeit scaled down. The young woman marvelled at how the simple explanation from Jean-Luc helped her to visualise what had been in the architect's mind. The two of them looked at each other for a long moment as Gwenaelle declared that they both needed some sleep. Reluctantly she turned towards her bed as Jean-Luc did the same.

Moments later she appeared at his bedside. Jean-Luc's mouth suddenly went dry as he saw that Gwenaelle had no clothes on.

'Is there room for another one in that bed?'

She giggled delightfully as he blushed, then laughed out loud as he placed a hand over his eyes but kept his fingers spread apart.

'Don't be shy, Cherie. You have seen me naked before.'

A stammering Jean-Luc asked her how she knew. Really enjoying his embarrassment, she told him that on one of her regular chats with Sally Roberts, the Englishwoman had brought the conversation round to the night of the storm. The night they had all discovered that Jean-Luc could walk.

'I told Sally that I had staggered into the church, freezing cold and soaked to the skin. With no heating in the church and stone floors, I would surely have died if you hadn't done something to help me.'

As the memory of that particular night came back to him he told how Sally had looked at him as if he had crawled from under a stone.

'How could either of you have known that it had been necessary for me to strip all your clothes off and dry you with the clerical vestments that my imaginary priest kept supplying me with?'

Gwenaelle laughed until her sides ached.

'Sally saw and I discovered when I undressed for

bed that you had put my shorts and underwear on back to front.' The two laughed together for a long time. As Jean-Luc moved over in the bed, Gwenaelle asked him to hold her like he had held her on the night of the storm that had almost killed her. As the sky pulled its veil of darkness down over the mountain, the couple, content in each other's arms, fell into a peaceful sleep.

Sunlight streamed through the window as Gwenaelle awoke. She looked at her companion who was lying on his side with a hand propped beneath his chin looking intently at the young woman.

'Are you thinking what a beautiful creature you have found, Jean-Luc?'

'Actually I was thinking that I have never heard a human being snore like you. It brought to mind a pig eating in a trough.' At the alarm in the woman's eyes, the young man burst out laughing and told her that he was joking. Gwenaelle asked Jean-Luc how long he had been learning the Basque language. With a puzzled expression on his face, the young man replied that he would like to learn Euskara but he had no knowledge of it at that particular time. He grew concerned as he saw the shock on the woman's face. In a quiet voice, she told him that as he had lain unconscious in his hospital bed, he had often uttered two expressions.

'You said repeatedly, but only when I was in the room, "Look ever homeward and where the water flows through the red stone." But you spoke in fluent Euskara.'

The couple looked at one another for several

minutes. It was another mystery to add to the strange happenings that seemed to follow Jean-Luc around. Gwenaelle rose from the bed and slipping his shirt onto her naked body, went to make some coffee. Jean-Luc's eyes followed her as she padded round the floor barefoot. She smiled as she remembered his mother telling her and Sally Roberts that both her sons needed showing what they wanted. By the side of the bed, Gwenaelle asked if Jean-Luc was hungry; she giggled as he growled that he was, but not for food. Reaching for her arm, he gently pulled the willing young woman towards him. Their desire for each other grew and their lips parted for their first kiss. Suddenly, a loud banging startled them. Both of them cursed as Vincent Morrisson opened the unlocked door. He blushed furiously as he realised that he had interrupted their lovemaking.

'You have to come down immediately. Alais heard the workmen discussing how they could clear the well of stones as there was nobody small enough to get down it. When their backs were turned the girl had climbed down the well and disappeared. Seconds later Yannick had climbed down after the child.'

Vincent went out to the jeep as the two dressed hurriedly. In a short time the vehicle was parked by the well as dozens of anxious faces peered down it, all shouting the names of the two youngsters. Suggestions came thick and fast as to the best way to clear the well. One by one they were discounted as people realised that if machinery was used, it could prove disastrous for Alais and Yannick. Jean-Luc stood in silence as he remembered listening on several occasions to the river that had been the source of water for both the church baptisms, and before that for the inhabitants of this commune over the centuries. As if in a trance, Jean-Luc walked slowly into the church and approached the font. He looked at the massive stone block that covered the top of the font. The builder of the church all those centuries before had understood the need for safety and had chiselled a hole through the huge block of stone that would allow a cup on a piece of rope to be lowered to the water below. Without a conscious thought Jean-Luc placed his hands on the sides of the stone block and simply slid it to one side. Quickly, he sat on the edge of the font and lowered himself down.

By this time Gwenaelle and her father Daniel had noticed the young man's absence and followed him into the church. The alarmed young woman turned to her father as they saw the white hair of Jean-Luc disappearing. Daniel put his finger to his lips as the two of them approached the font. After what seemed an eternity but was in fact just a few minutes, Jean-Luc hoisted Alais up towards her grandfather and aunt. The little girl beamed as she was safely lifted to the floor. A few seconds later, Yannick too was raised up into willing arms. The strain showing on his face, Jean-Luc struggled to climb out of the font. Gwenaelle shouted for Vincent. The doctor raced into the church and seeing his older brother's difficulty, swiftly pulled him from the font. Alais hugged her rescuer, an action that was imitated by Yannick. Her aunt asked the little girl if she had been scared.

'No Aunt Gwen, I wasn't the least bit scared because the nice man told me that Jean-Luc would come and help me and Yannick.'

'What nice man?'

'The man who looks like Jean-Luc, you know, the one with the scars on his arms.'

Father and daughter looked at one another. Daniel wondered why things that couldn't be explained rationally seemed to happen when Jean-Luc was near. A completely unperturbed Alais took Yannick's hand and allowed her aunt to lead them to the community centre and a change of clothes. People remarked at the incongruity of the sight of the boy who was on the cusp of manhood and the little girl who happily guided him. As she led her niece and Yannick away, Gwenaelle looked back at Jean-Luc and shrugged her shoulders at the missed opportunity for them to go wherever their emotions would take them. She giggled as Jean-Luc mouthed the word 'later' to her. Daniel Doissneau insisted that Jean-Luc allow him to drive them back to the mountain retreat as the younger man needed rest. With a twinkle in his eye, Daniel remarked that he wouldn't exactly be the company that the young man wanted, but at least Jean-Luc would be able to sleep.

The following morning Daniel Doissneau woke to an empty cabin. Dressing quickly, he opened the door and was pleasantly surprised to find Jean-Luc sat by the stream with his drawing pad in his lap and a thoughtful expression on his face. As he looked at Jean-Luc's latest sketch, a question came quickly to Daniel's lips.

'So my boy, tell me about your little adventure when you disappeared into the church font.'

Jean-Luc deliberated for a few moments as if to

get his thoughts in order.

'When I lowered myself through the font, I reasoned that I should have waited for professionals with safety harnesses and floodlights, but it was almost as if I had no control over my actions. As my feet touched the ground, I was immediately bathed in light. Where the light came from, I don't know. I saw that I was stood in a small underground cave. I stood there while my breath came back and I saw...'

Daniel held his hand up, immediately silencing the younger man. The elderly doctor simply pointed at Jean-Luc's sketchpad. Daniel asked the younger man if the sketch on the pad was what he had seen. Jean-Luc nodded. Daniel gazed at a flowing stream that ran through the middle of a natural stone archway.

'What colour is the stone Jean-Luc?'

Daniel smiled as the young man replied that it was red.

'Professional men and doubters would say that you had drawn a scene that you had spoken of in your sleep. They would also dismiss your supposed lack of knowledge of the Basque language, insisting that you must have learnt a few words while you have been here. Gwenaelle has told me of the gift that was given to you for her in Avignon. Sadly Alais, my granddaughter, is as curious as a kitten and she opened the parcel. Much to her disappointment, it wasn't a silk blouse or some sparkling jewellery which girls, no matter their age, set such store by. It was simply this.'

As Daniel finished speaking he delved into the carrier bag and withdrew a wooden object about twelve inches square. Jean-Luc realised it was a picture frame. As the doctor turned it round the younger man saw that it was a painting. Jean-Luc gasped as he saw that the painting was identical to his sketch of the stream flowing through a red stone archway. Putting the painting and the sketch pad into his carrier bag, Daniel Doissneau told the stunned man that the story wasn't quite over as he would like Jean-Luc to read the newspaper that the framed painting had been wrapped in in Avignon.

For several minutes, a mystified Jean-Luc read and re-read the newspaper's front cover. The leading article told of a stunning discovery by an archaeological team that had been delving into the chequered past of the Palais des Papes. Some grains had been found in the garden started by Pope Benedict VII that had given the teams of researchers more clues as to how life had been lived in the papal palace almost seven hundred years earlier. Almost as an addition to the main article, the report told of how a small area of stonework unconnected to the building had been opened up to reveal a wooden box encased in pitch. The pitch had obviously been intended to preserve the box in much the same way as ancient sailors had used pitch to waterproof their boats. The archaeologists had carefully melted the pitch to open the box which had revealed a quite beautiful carving of a river flowing beneath a stone archway. A tiny carved inscription in the Basque language read, 'Where the river flows through the red stone.' Learned historians had surmised that the artist had simply left an example of his talent in much the same way as men have done since time immemorial.

The elderly doctor asked Jean-Luc if he would

draw a sketch of his mother. The puzzled young man looked at his friend.

'Humour an old man please my boy, and do you think you could age the drawing by adding a few lines that your beautiful mother will undoubtedly acquire as the years go by?'

As the architect followed the doctor's request, Daniel Doissneau smiled with satisfaction. Taking his phone from his pocket, he made two brief calls. Jean-Luc was full of questions but his friend simply smiled and told him that patience was a virtue. As they drove back towards the village, Daniel asked Jean-Luc to tell him some more of his ideas for the Dougeres project. Twenty minutes later Alesander Ibarague met them at the church. The three men shook hands and sat as Daniel began to speak.

'Before the advent of television and newspapers and now the internet, families' only way of preserving the past was by handing down their stories through the generations. My own family was no different. My origins, as far as I know, started in Wales. However, the first of my ancestors in France arrived here in Dougeres around seven hundred years ago. He built this church for the community as a token of his gratitude at the warm welcome that he and his family were given. Simon the mason lived out the rest of his long life here amidst the rivers and mountains that he loved. Along with his own children, he and his wife Gwyneth raised the baby son of Simon's greatest friend. The boy grew and followed his adopted father and brothers into the building profession. A devout man, Simon had built the font of the church over an underground river, realising that the equally religious families in this area would need a source of water for christenings. Simon and Gwyneth told the boy about the presumed death from the plague of his natural father in Avignon and of his mother's death in childbirth. The boy, Mathieu, grew up never knowing his birth parents but received the unconditional love that Simon and Gwyneth gave to their own children. In time Mathieu married and raised his own family, blissfully unaware of his family history. The only knowledge he had was that his mother Eleanor had wanted him to be raised in the birthplace of his ancestors. The centuries passed and successive generations departed this earth, hopefully leaving a better world for their children. The one constant that every generation of the families of Mathieu and Eleanor and Simon and Gwyneth had, were the two phrases that all of the children learned by heart.'

A voice rang out from the doorway, 'Look ever homeward and where the water flows through the red stone.'

A smiling Marie-Francoise Morrisson entered the church. She kissed her two friends and embraced her son. After sitting down, she wondered aloud why Daniel had taken her away from the children. The old doctor smiled and asked Jean-Luc to reveal his earlier sketch.

The small group of people stared at the sketch that Jean-Luc had drawn earlier. He had portrayed his mother as an elderly lady. Everybody present saw the striking resemblance that Marie-Francoise and Madame Casillas shared.

Daniel Doissneau told his stunned audience of the night that Marie-Francoise had come to Petit

Dougeres. One of his Basque friends had told him that she had stared at the landscape as they drove through the Pays Basque and muttered several times, 'Look ever homewards,' in the native tongue. As her grief over the death of her daughter Sophie had eased, she had quickly remembered the traditions, sayings, and folk songs of the Basque people.

Marie-Francoise was more composed now and started to tell the attentive audience her story.

'My grandmother had a huge impact on me when I was small. Because my own parents had to work, she taught me all the skills that I would need in my adult life. She also taught me the Basque language, which I admit is a little rusty, and the beautiful songs and traditions of this proud race of people. When I heard of the bomb, I thought that nobody could have survived so I kept quiet. My grandmother had left this area pregnant and unmarried. There was a lot of stigma attached to such a situation in those days. When I learned of the survival of Madame Casillas, I didn't know what kind of reception I would get from her.'

Aware that something eventful was taking place inside the church, the Morrisson family had started to filter into the building. The elderly lady under discussion had arrived in time to hear this last statement. Madame Casillas kissed Marie-Francoise and told her that her grandmother had simply fallen in love.

'Eleanor, your grandmother was my mother's sister, in fact I was named after her. My mother would often say that one must always listen to their heart. Besides, my dear, there have always been illegitimate babies even in the best families.'

All those present smiled then grew serious as the old lady, her voice trembling, said that she had to tell them of the skeletons in her own family cupboard.

'I have told you that my sister Agathe lived in your mountain retreat. She really was a bad apple. She seemed to derive satisfaction from hurting people and it was a great relief when she moved to the mountain. We came to see her less and less, which I am ashamed to say suited our family perfectly. It was a great shock when she moved back to the village to have her baby. Her daughter Helene was a beautiful child. When Agathe announced that she was going back to her mountain we begged her to leave the child with us. Our pleas fell on deaf ears. As the girl grew she was treated simply as a drudge. The rare occasions that we did see her, the child, starved of affection, simply followed her mother around. She was not allowed to mix with other children and we worried for her safety. As she approached her thirties, cowed into submission by an uncaring mother, Helene ran off with one of the local shepherds. Oh how we cheered at the news.

'Sadly, a few months later, the girl returned alone, a baby boy in her arms and with no knowledge of how to care for the child, she turned to the only person she could think of who would give her a bed. Agathe crowed and immediately banned us all from seeing Helene or the boy. We knew that a familiar pattern would dictate the child's life but we were powerless to do anything as we feared for Yannick's very existence. Soon after, Helene disappeared again. We were pleased but at the same time alarmed for the toddler. When I learned of the graves that had been found near the cabin, I suspected that foul play had taken place. The relief that the only bodies found were those of some goats was only temporary as one of the local shepherds told me that human bones were recovered from a ravine. I know in my heart what fate had befallen my poor niece Helene. The next few years passed with Agathe only coming down to the village on market days to barter her goat's cheese and vegetables for necessary supplies and fuel for her damned motorbike and sidecar. Yannick would sit in the sidecar, a feeble-minded boy unable to communicate with anyone. Agathe once said, in what for her must have been a moment of weakness, that taking care of her simpleton grandson was her punishment from God.'

The usually quiet Vincent Morrisson spoke up.

'Any boy that can get a motorbike and sidecar from here and negotiate the traffic in a large city such as Avignon is not in my opinion simple-minded.' Taking the hands of Madame Casillas in his own, Vincent asked to be allowed to take the boy to a hospital in Bayonne. He added that although he had an opinion as to Yannick's silence, he would like the boy to undergo extensive tests. When asked what his thoughts were on the boy's condition, Vincent told the group that both he and Daniel had noticed a change in Yannick's demeanour over the last few days.

'We have both seen that he is not so quick to smile. I believe that in his mind, Yannick is experiencing a sense of isolation. He has been taken from his mountain home and seen sights in just a few weeks that must have bewildered him. He has gone from a daily routine looking after his goats and growing vegetables to first riding, then walking round a big city with sights that were obviously beyond his understanding. Now he just follows Alais around without knowing what any of us are doing in his life.'

Madame Casillas cried quietly as she thought of the miserable existence that the youngster had endured. She begged Vincent to help Yannick. The young doctor promised that he would take the boy to Bayonne the following day.

Marie-Francoise would have hated to be called a schemer but as she heard Vincent's plans her mind went into overdrive. Telling those present that she needed to make an important telephone call, she walked outside and quickly selected a contact on her phone. In just a few seconds she had sent the same text to three recipients. As she walked back into the church, she heard Daniel invite Alesander Ibarague to tell them of his own particular discovery.

'Because of your unwitting involvement in the crimes of the maniac who tried to destroy this community, I have been given permission to inform you of an investigation that will never be released into the public domain. I can tell you that due to his obsessive need to document every part of his life, our task has been made so much easier. His web of corruption had spread through both the police force and the town hall in Avignon. Again because of his skill at documenting every fact about his accomplices, we were able to remove them from their posts. The worst among them, and by that I mean the police officers who carried out his every wish, including murder, were themselves killed on the orders of that madman. In this way he kept those loyal to him terrified that they would be next and he also removed those who knew about his criminal activities. We were able to persuade his minions to admit the parts they played for the chance of reduced prison sentences. Some of them will never see the outside world again whilst others will retire from public life. They have become pariahs to the many decent police officers and public officials who strive to do their best for the citizens of Avignon. Our continuing investigation has given us the chance to remove some of the worst drug dealers and people traffickers that have blighted the south of France and beyond for many years.

'We may never know who the man who called himself Auguste Claudel really was as he had very skilfully hidden his true identity. The real Auguste died in a childhood accident. Psychologists have ventured that this unknown man had submerged himself into the personas of Hugo de Beziers and Auguste Claudel so much that eventually he came to believe that he really was the last surviving member of that medieval family. Our research showed that every one of the de Beziers perished during the plague. We believe that, in the absence of his real name, we will refer to him as de Beziers. Hugo read of the amazing discovery at the palace of the Popes and put a very clever scheme into place.

'I was intrigued to find that part of the newspaper article mentioned a rather good carving on an old wooden box, but as I read more about the de Beziers family I was horrified to discover the lengths that they had gone to over the centuries to achieve their aims. When I read that de Beziers had secured the services of Amandine Dubois to provide a Basque translation I knew that all of the horrific events of the past few months had been engineered by him to clear every soul from this village, and allow him unfettered access to end a centuries-old search. I am still in the dark as to what this much searched-for object actually is, but I hope that as soon as my work in Avignon is done then perhaps together we can try to solve the puzzle.'

As no objections were raised, Alesander told them all that he needed to get back to Avignon as soon as possible. Daniel asked him if he knew how long the investigation was likely to take. Alesander laughed and told them that was the least of his worries.

'My daughter Katallin has been keeping house for Xavier and I while her mother does nothing but sit in the sunshine here. Katallin and Xavier took an instant dislike to one another and I am sure that by now blood will be flowing. Poor Xavier doesn't stand a chance. My dear wife hoped that Xavier and our daughter would get together, but quite frankly I think that there is more chance of the Pope getting married.'

Everybody laughed at the tongue in cheek remarks from the senior policeman.

At Jean-Luc's request, Daniel Doissneau was telling him the story behind his family crest that had been carved on the end of each of the pews down one side of the nave of the church. Daniel explained that out of deference to his family's history, they had kept the crest of Simon the mason over the centuries. Taking Jean-Luc's hand, the elderly man asked for a pledge.

'Promise me, my boy, that when I depart this earth, you will find someone to carve a copy of the crest and include my name. As the last male member of my family, I want all the different surnames to be remembered as belonging to that one family. Jean-Luc, there are two family crests in this church. The families whose lives have been entwined for around seven hundred years. You know by now that Eleanor Casillas is your relative. Her ancestor was the boy Mathieu, who was raised by Simon and Gwyneth, his family name was Charpentier. You are also a Charpentier.'

The younger man was awestruck as he tried to digest this piece of information. He wondered if some long forgotten memory or instinct had led his feet here. At Daniel's request Jean-Luc studied the pews on the opposite side of the aisle and saw that like Daniel's family, the surnames had changed many times over the centuries, but had always kept the same carving of a hand holding a wood chisel.

Jean-Luc promised the older man that his name would never be forgotten while he, Jean-Luc Morrisson, lived. Gently guiding the doctor away from the rest of the group, he whispered that he needed to make a request. Neither of the men noticed that the eyes of Marie-Francoise followed them. She seemed to have a sixth sense when something important was about to happen to her family members and she smiled with satisfaction as the elderly doctor embraced her son.

Several hours later and back in the church, Jean-Luc was thinking back to the conversation that he had had with Daniel Doissneau. His fingers ran over the woodcarvings that adorned each of the pews. He also remembered the words of the horribly burnt woman they had called L'Anglaise when she spoke of Yannick. Jean-Luc jumped as Gwenaelle sat beside him. He had been so wrapped up in his thoughts that he hadn't heard the young woman's footsteps.

'You are deep in thought, Cherie?'

'Gwenaelle, I was just running recent events through in my mind and thinking how lucky we have been to survive the actions of that madman. I know that we have all suffered great personal losses. You more than most I think.'

The young woman's eyes filled with tears at the words of the gentle man that she loved so much. She rose and walked aimlessly along the front of the pews. Stopping suddenly, she stared at the pew below her. An alarmed Jean-Luc joined her. The two of them gazed at the dust-covered seat and the names Gwenaelle and Jean-Luc surrounded by a heart. The young woman looked in wonder at the man beside her.

'I did that on the night of the storm before you staggered in here. I was sure that I had wiped that pew clean. I knew I loved you that night, but I thought that you hated me. I don't have a ring at the moment, and I can't quite get down on one knee yet, but will you do me the honour of becoming my wife?'

The old fashioned proposal endeared Jean-Luc to the young woman by his side. Her eyes glistened with tears of happiness as she silently mouthed the word yes. Finally, the couple kissed. A shiver ran through both their bodies as they embraced.

A stifled giggle caused the couple to turn towards

the door. Alais stood with one hand over her mouth. Slowly the little girl walked towards her aunt and Jean-Luc. Throwing herself into their joint embrace, she asked point blank if she could be a bridesmaid. The adults laughed as they saw the excitement that filled the eyes of Alais. Squirming from their grasp, she ran to the door, declaring that she needed to tell her grandfather. With a look of resignation, Jean-Luc told the young woman in his arms that the news would be all over the Pays Basque by the morning. Knowing the reception that they would face, the couple walked slowly into the community centre. The excited crowd raced towards them with Marie-Francoise leading by a long way. Tears of joy streamed down her face as she hugged the couple, then admonished Jean-Luc for taking so long. Family and friends kissed and hugged the overwhelmed couple as plans were made for the biggest wedding party that the Pays Basque had ever seen.

Sally Roberts and her daughter Molly embraced their friends. As Sally turned around, Marie-Francoise whispered to the young woman that she would never have a better moment than this. Almost as if she was talking to herself the Englishwoman declared that as soon as the wedding was over, she and Molly would return home. Vincent Morrisson, his face as white as a sheet, looked at Sally.

'H-H-Home? But I thought that this was your home now Sally. I have told Daniel that I intend to stay here and take over the practice when he retires. I assumed that you would stay as my nurse.'

'Do you only want me for your nurse, Vincent?'

The young doctor, his face red with embarrassment,

looked round at the silent group of people as they all waited for him to speak. He gasped for air as he tried desperately to frame his words.

'I think I fell in love with you the moment I met you at the airport, but I thought that you and Jean-Luc were together. As we worked together I knew that I wanted to spend the rest of my life with you but you never spoke of the future. I know that the people of this community want you to stay and I want you to be my wife. Sally, I love you, will you marry me?'

Her face radiant, Sally Roberts stated that she had fallen in love with a man not much given to words, but a man who by his actions alone brought out the very best in those people lucky enough to know him.

'Yes Vincent, I will be your wife but I don't think that I can carry on as your nurse. At least not for a while. I am going to be very busy looking after our baby.'

'Baby? How has that happened?'

Daniel Doissneau brought laughter to the room as he wondered aloud what kind of a doctor didn't know how babies were made.

The impromptu party lasted long into the night. Bottles of locally produced cider were opened with great ceremony to toast the two happy couples. A bewildered Yannick sat at the side of Alais Dubois. The little girl kept hold of his hand as the boy watched the happy group of people dancing together. He had never known that people reacted to one another in this way.

Finally the party came to an end as Jean-Luc reminded the villagers that they still had some houses to build. Groans of disappointment swept the room as Gwenaelle, in her best schoolteacher's voice, told the children that there would still be lessons in the morning. Madame Eleanor Casillas smiled as Ainhote and Jean-Luc linked her arms to escort her home to her cottage. Yannick dutifully followed the trio as they slowly walked the few hundred yards. The elderly lady had spent a long part of the evening with Ainhote Ibarague who had given Eleanor hope that Yannick would one day be an active member of this community. She thrilled as the younger woman repeated part of what she had spoken of earlier.

'Thankfully, education chiefs are much more enlightened when it comes to dealing with children with special needs. They have realised that in order for people with a handicap to live as normal a life as possible, it is necessary to integrate them into mainstream education as soon as they can. In schools across France, and indeed most countries of the world, children with disabilities work and play alongside pupils more fortunate than themselves. This has two advantages, it helps the children with special needs and it also lets the able-bodied children see that the old fashioned idea of keeping disadvantaged children in seclusion is extremely cruel.'

After an exhausting two weeks Jean-Luc had gratefully taken his mother's orders to heart when she had told him to make himself scarce while the women planned the final details of the church service that was set for the following morning. Craving solitude, the young man walked into the silent church. His eyes looked round the building that had come to mean so much to him, although his mind was trying to make sense of the recent events. As soon as marriage proposals had been accepted, Marie-Francoise Morrisson had started to organise the two weddings with a precision that left all those around her breathless. The bans had been published in Bayonne where Jean-Luc and Gwenaelle and Vincent and Sally had taken part in the civil arrangement that was necessary in France. Both the couples had laughed as Amelie Morrisson had turned up to meet them in Bayonne. Accompanied as usual by Imanol Etcheverrie, the young woman laughed as she told her brothers and their brides that her mother had a degree in scheming. The other two members of the group were Ainhote Ibarague and the silent Yannick. Vincent had made an appointment for the boy to see a specialist at the local hospital, and Ainhote, who had quickly built a rapport with the youngster, had volunteered to look after the boy. Iker and Bihote Aroztegi had insisted that the entire group should stay with them.

Feeling a kindly presence behind him, Jean-Luc turned to see the man he now knew had rescued him from an early death all those months ago in the village. The man before him smiled kindly as the younger man stood.

'You have achieved so much my son, in just a short time. Once again this village has children running through it. The excitement at the forthcoming weddings is heavy in the air. The houses are well on their way to completion and many more babies will be born here to keep ancient lineages going. The village will welcome a new priest soon. Originally, the church had intended that he would simply give you and Vincent and your brides a proper church blessing. I know that the church will ensure that Father Thierry will stay here.'

A puzzled Jean-Luc wondered who this man was and how he could know what was going to happen. The young man was oblivious to the fact that two men dressed in clerical garb had just entered the church and were stood in silence in the doorway.

'How can you know what will happen?'

The man with the heavily scarred forearms reached behind Jean-Luc and lifted the sketch pad from the pew. He selected a page and turned it towards the bewildered younger man. Jean-Luc stared at the drawing he had done of the river flowing through the red stone archway. The keystone at the top of the arch had disappeared. As if he was in a trance, Jean-Luc walked over to the font and effortlessly moved the huge stone cover to one side. Slowly, he lowered himself into the font. He reappeared a few minutes later holding a jute sack in one hand. Climbing from the font, he approached the stranger.

'Open the sack, my son. It contains a gift that was given to me by my friend and teacher a long time ago. Many murders have been committed by maniacs desperate to claim this object for their own twisted purposes.'

As he pulled the long-sought treasure from the sack, Jean-Luc stared in astonishment at the small earthenware dish in his hands. His face mirrored his disappointment as he looked up at his companion.

'Did you expect gold and silver Jean-Luc, or perhaps diamonds and rubies?'

'I am not sure what I expected, but are you telling me that Sophie and Jerome and their unborn child, Amandine, Susan, and countless other innocent people were murdered for an earthenware dish?'

'Tell me Jean-Luc, why the pilgrims you were accompanying to Santiago de Compostela were so intent on making that journey. Why the terminally ill people on the coach wanted desperately to go to Lourdes. Why do Muslims make their own pilgrimage to Mecca, Jews to the wailing wall in Jerusalem or Sikhs to Amritsar and countless millions of people of every religious persuasion endure ridicule, hatred, and physical violence in order to do as their holy books decree? It is quite simple my son, it is faith. A branch of your own family pursued this dish, killing those who stood in their way, in order to use this relic as a blackmail tool against the Catholic Church. Imagine how the faith of the countless millions of pilgrims who have walked the Via Compostela would have been shaken if the legend of Saint James had been shown as just a story invented by some imaginative people. For centuries men have decried the holy books of every religion on Earth, seeking to convince believers that those books are just works of fiction. They have all missed the point. It is a belief in something far greater than man's understanding that leads the masses to the synagogues, mosques and churches and all the other houses of worship. A black-hearted family of mass murderers tried to destroy that faith in the fourteenth century, and over the last few months a man just as evil sought to continue that quest.'

One of the two men in the doorway looked at

Jean-Luc with a compassionate gaze. He thought that the young man was obviously mentally ill. Why would he walk round in an agitated state, talking to himself? His companion, an elderly man, saw exactly the same scene but thought that there was more to this tableau than met the eye. He noticed that the man stood in the nave of the church would first speak and then stand as if he was receiving a reply. Unlike his young companion, the elderly man had seen and heard things that couldn't be explained rationally and his strong beliefs helped him to accept the mysteries of life. The two men listened carefully as Jean-Luc rather stupidly repeated that the object in his hands was simply a dish.

'You are correct Jean-Luc, it is just a dish. A dish that was given to me as an act of kindness after I had broken my own.'

Suddenly a bright light enveloped the dish. A frightened Jean-Luc carefully put the earthenware plate down. Three mystified men looked at the dish as the light played all around it. An image appeared on the dish, a face with eyes that had seen much sadness. The light increased in strength and settled on the wall behind the font. None of the men present would ever understand the events of the next few minutes. In the midst of the illuminated wall, scenes appeared. Starting with a double beheading, the images told a silent story as they changed to show how a wooden board carrying a headless corpse had washed up on a beach. The tableau changed, the wall was filled with images of scallops, the universal symbol of the pilgrimage to Santiago de Compostela. The images, in just a few minutes had told the story of the origins of the earthenware dish and one of the imaginative legends that had grown up around that area of northern Spain. As quick as they had appeared, the images were gone and the bright light with them. Aware of another presence, Jean-Luc turned to the doorway. The two men had fallen to their knees and were praying. As the younger priest helped his companion to his feet, the older man took hold of Jean-Luc's face in his two hands and looked into his eyes.

'I am Cardinal Claudio Mazzola. A friend of yours, Alesander Ibarague, contacted me through the church and told me a rather sad yet uplifting story of how a small community had triumphed over great adversity. I needed to see this place for myself. I defy anyone to explain rationally what we have just witnessed. Alesander tried to tell me what kind of man you are, Jean-Luc, a man whose love for others continues to inspire people to achieve so much. His words did not do you justice.'

The cardinal signalled for his companion to join them. As the two young men shook hands, Jean-Luc shocked the two priests as he said, 'I am pleased to meet you Father Thierry, this is a wonderful community and I am sure that you will be with us for a long time.'

Cardinal Mazzola, his hands shaking, accepted the earthenware plate that Jean-Luc held out to him.

Chapter 10

The morning of the double wedding shone with the promise of a beautiful day. Jean-Luc had received a phone call and after dressing hurriedly raced down to the outskirts of the village where he met an elderly Basque couple. The three of them walked to the back of the truck where a smiling Jean-Luc nodded his head in satisfaction. As he took his wallet from his pocket, the older man placed his hand on his forearm and shook his head. The elderly lady nodded her head in agreement as her husband insisted that it was a gift. The couple were pleased to accept an invitation from Jean-Luc to attend the wedding ceremony. One hour later a convoy of cars drove slowly into the village as all the residents rushed to greet the passengers. Amelie Morrisson, her face radiant, helped Yannick from the lead vehicle. The youngster smiled happily as Alais rushed towards him closely followed by Madame Casillas. Tears flowed as the boy made the sign for hello. His great-aunt cried with happiness as he placed his hand on his heart and pointed towards her. Daniel Doissneau promised that there would be a lot to speak of after the wedding ceremony.

In a prearranged movement the whole community

followed Jean-Luc as he walked towards the perimeter of the village. A mystified Yannick could only follow in their wake as Amelie and Ainhote, his two patient teachers, held his hands firmly. The entourage stopped outside a newly constructed building. Jean-Luc opened his drawing pad and showed his latest sketch to Yannick. A smile appeared on his face as he looked at a drawing of a goat. Suddenly his nose started to twitch as a familiar smell entered his nostrils. Alais had opened the door of the barn and in the doorway stood a young goat. Nervously it walked forward as Yannick, his face wreathed in smiles, sank to his knees to embrace the creature. Nobody minded that the boy had got his new clothes dirty.

At Jean-Luc's beckoning, Yannick followed him into the barn. Down one wall was a pen, where the goats could be kept at night, which housed another six of the creatures. The other wall had an area for making the goats cheese that Eleanor Casillas insisted was the best in the Pays Basque. The boy stared at the last thing in the barn. Away from all things pertaining to the goats was a sturdy bench with a vice at each end and a beautifully made box that contained all the tools associated with woodcarving. Jean-Luc explained to the villagers that both he and Vincent had realised that the boy had made the furniture in the mountain cabin and decorated it with carvings of animals and birds. Yannick stared at the box of tools, wanting to hold them in his hands but uncertain who they were for. Jean-Luc quickly drew an owl on his sketchpad and offered it to the boy. Yannick walked slowly to the bench and with a chisel and mallet in his hands and a piece of soft timber, set to work. Many voices commented that the tools that Yannick were holding seemed to be an extension of his hands. He quickly duplicated the owl on the wood. The villagers crowded round, all anxious to see the work that the boy had produced. More than one tear was shed as Yannick took up the carving and gave it to his great-aunt Eleanor.

Marie-Francoise Morrisson told all those present that there was a double wedding to attend and the happy group of people filed from the barn. Understandably, Yannick was reluctant to leave until Jean-Luc gave him the lock and key to the barn's door. The boy, hand in hand with Alais, walked happily towards the community centre. Gwenaelle kissed her husband passionately as they lingered at the back of the group.

'Cherie, should we just slip away to our mountain retreat?'

Jean-Luc was just about to agree when his mother, with a twinkle in her eye, declared that they were required to attend their own wedding ceremony.

The tiny church of Dougeres shook to deafening applause as the two happy couples ran from the building. It had been standing room only in the church with scores more people filling the doorway and the close proximity. A very nervous priest had conducted his first blessing in his new parish. People surged forward to shake his hand and welcome him to their community. Many photographs were taken of the priest with the two radiant couples.

The wedding feast went on long into the night as speeches were made and numerous toasts offered to the two ecstatic couples. The orphans performed the songs of the Pays Basque, followed by Molly Roberts who, accompanied by her, as she loved to call him, Grandfather Philip, thrilled the audience with her beautiful songs. Everybody laughed as a slightly drunk Father Thierry slurred that Molly had the voice of an angel. A rather fearful elderly lady wondered aloud if Jean-Luc, as a much in-demand architect, would take Gwenaelle from her home. The young man rose and faced the audience.

'From the moment I walked down from the hills into Dougeres just before the bomb, I felt that I had come home. The kindness and friendship and dare I say the love that has been bestowed onto me and my family and friends, all of us total strangers, by the people of this wonderful community, has left me with a sense of fulfilment. I have worked all over the world, in major cities and on huge projects. At times I have lived with a packed suitcase by my bed waiting for a phone call and some plane tickets to go who knows where. Always, despite the satisfaction of my work, there has been an emptiness inside of me. I don't know what the future holds for me, thankfully none of us do, but I hope that it will be a future spent in a tiny Basque village where everyone knows and looks out for their neighbours. I want to watch, God willing, my children playing happily in the streets, exploring the mountains and growing up with lots of aunts and uncles, by proxy, watching out for them.'

Vincent Morrisson had a captive audience as he explained the outcome of the tests that Yannick had undergone in Bayonne.

'It seems probable that the boy had mumps as a toddler. With a simple vaccination, he would have been fine. I am sure that his grandmother would have insisted on treating him herself using remedies that people have used for centuries. Unfortunately mumps can be very serious indeed for a child, and although the boy pulled through, he has been left totally deaf. If this deafness had been noticed earlier, much could have been done to ensure that the boy would have had a normal childhood. His life was far from normal, and as a result of his seclusion, he has only ever known a world of silence. Happily, the specialists at the hospital discovered that Yannick has a very high level of intelligence, which I think many of us had already realised, and they think that there is nothing to stop him taking his rightful place in society. Ainhote has agreed to continue working with the boy and I am sure that there will be another teacher with the required skills who will agree to help the boy.'

As Vincent spoke this last sentence, all eyes turned to a blushing Amelie Morrisson. The young woman laughed as she held her hands up.

'As soon as I have got my degree I will be delighted to work with Ainhote and Yannick.'

Rather coyly, Amelie wondered if there would be anyone to protect her as the Pays Basque could be quite a dangerous place. Again eyes turned to rest on Imanol Etcheverrie. The Basque shepherd had fallen in love with Amelie soon after going to Paris to keep watch over her. A proud man, he was determined that he would wear the trousers in his family. Silently he looked back at the young woman. Amelie knew that she had met her match.

'Imanol, in those early days I resented my mother's insistence that I should have a bodyguard. All my classmates laughed at you for following me round like a faithful dog. As the days and weeks passed I saw a man determined to ensure that his promise to my family would be kept. I am ashamed to say that I too laughed at you. I soon began to see your strength and the quietly dignified way that you conduct yourself. I see now what my mother saw in those terrible days following the loss of my dear sister Sophie. I hope, Imanol, that you will always be in my life, as I couldn't bear the thought of losing you.'

The shepherd gathered her in his strong arms and told her that he would be at her side for as long as she needed him. The orphans asked Gwenaelle if they could learn sign language to help Yannick. Smiling at her charges, the school principal told them that she thought the whole community would want to learn how to sign.

Friends insisted that more photographs should be taken. The Morrissons gathered for group shots and individual pictures. As Vincent and Jean-Luc stood together, a third person came between them. As he felt one of the heavily scarred forearms go round his shoulders, Jean-Luc knew that their companion would not appear on the photograph of himself and Vincent. He also knew that nobody else heard the words spoken by his ancestor.

'Jean-Luc, I am pleased to tell you that you will soon be a father. The first of many children that you and Gwenaelle will bring to this tiny community. Thank you for making Dougeres a haven of safety for the descendants of my descendants.'

*

Excitement filled her face as Madame Morrisson opened her front door. Dressed casually in jeans and a blouse, Molly Giardelli, accompanied by her three teenage children, hugged her grandmother to her. Hugs and kisses were exchanged as the elderly lady greeted Molly's three daughters. Marie-Francoise had never made any distinction between her natural grandchildren and Molly. The three girls busily arranged the masses of flowers they had brought with them as Molly caught up on all the local news. She smiled as she told her grandmother that they would soon have visitors as the curtains in the two adjoining cottages had twitched as she had parked her car outside. Within minutes knocks sounded at the door and in walked Ainhote Ibarague and Bihote Aroztegi. The dearest friends of Marie-Francoise hugged Molly and her children delightedly. Everybody talked at once until Madame Morrisson declared that they must be going. Molly promised Bihote and Ainhote that she was staying for a week and there would be lots of time to chat, but for now she needed to meet up with the rest of the family.

A short car ride took them to the cemetery on the outskirts of the village. Molly's eyes mirrored her concern as she helped her grandmother from the car. She worried at the old lady's increasing frailty. Molly's three daughters respectfully stayed a few yards behind their mother and great-grandmother. Marie-Francoise smiled as Molly knelt at Philip Morrisson's graveside. She had loved the special bond that had existed between her husband and Molly right until his death. On hearing of her beloved grandfather's serious illness, the world-renowned opera singer had immediately cancelled all her appointments, declaring that the furious organisers could sue her, to be with Philip. She had stated categorically that she would nurse him for however long it took. As his final minutes on Earth had approached, Molly had taken his hand in hers and sung to him. Philip listened as his granddaughter sang one of his favourite songs from the musical 'Carousel'. As the final notes of 'If I Loved You' finished, Philip died with a smile on his face.

Molly had delivered a moving eulogy at the funeral, telling the silent audience of how Philip had moved with her to Italy for three months to help her cope with life in another country and another language. His love of music had broken down many barriers for her and after receiving an invitation to study with one of the world's foremost singing coaches, the scared young girl had gradually adapted to her new life. Although Molly had travelled all over the world, she had made her home in Italy after falling in love with her pianist and musical arranger. As often as she could Molly returned to the place and the people that would always have a piece of her heart. Every year a generous donation was paid into the bank account that was used solely for the upkeep of Dougeres and for any future building work that would be undertaken. At Molly's insistence, these donations were never publicised, although they were always gratefully received.

While Molly tended her grandfather's grave, Marie-Francoise looked round the graveyard that would soon need to be extended. A solitary tear rolled down her cheek as she gently touched the headstone that bore the names of Sophie and Jerome and their unborn child. At Gwenaelle Morrisson's request,

Yannick Casillas had carved the inscription that had delighted Marie-Francoise. Although only symbolic, as there had been no bodies interred there, it gave comfort to the Morrisson family that they could see a physical resting place for a much-loved daughter. On hearing her daughter's voices, Molly rose and turned to embrace her parents. Sally cried joyfully as she hugged her daughter to her.

'Hi Mum, hi Dad. Sorry that we didn't come over right away, but I needed to say hello to Grandad.'

Vincent and Sally brushed the apology aside as they hugged their eldest daughter. Both women made an appraisal of the other. Molly thought that her mother looked so content, but then she had done since she had married Vincent. The village doctor, although still a stocky man, had kept himself in good shape. He laughingly grumbled that Sally only fed him enough to keep a sparrow alive. Despite his complaints, his daughter thought that he looked the picture of health. The mother of four girls besides Molly, Sally had embraced the simple lifestyle of the Pays Basque. Far beyond the confines of the village, she had made enduring friendships. A fluent French and Basque speaker, she fought passionately to keep the ancient language alive. She attended women's groups and spoke to children in the classroom, explaining that their culture and language was the beating heart of the Pays Basque. She warned them that if their language was lost, then they would very easily lose their identity.

The small procession made their way from the cemetery. As they arrived back in the village, friends rushed to greet them. Questions were fired thick and fast as to the length of their stay. Would Molly sing for them, and importantly for them all, could they have a party in the community centre? Molly and her daughters laughed as Marie-Francoise insisted that her granddaughter was on holiday and needed to rest. The crowd smiled as they went about their daily routines, they knew that Molly would want to sing for them soon.

Blissfully unaware of the commotion, Yannick Charpentier worked happily in his barn. He had tended to his goats and now his fingers caressed the piece of timber he was about to work on. There was much demand for Yannick's woodcarvings and he sold his products worldwide. He looked briefly at the photograph of a much-loved family pet. As the picture was quickly memorised, Yannick sighed with contentment as his chisel bit into the wood. Gone was the nervous young boy who inhabited a silent world. With the help of all the villagers and particularly Ainhote Ibarague and Amelie Etcheverrie, he had become a confident man, able to communicate and to travel to various parts of the Pays Basque as he sold his works at markets in the cities, towns, and villages of the department.

Yannick still loved to embrace all those he met, it had become the best way for him to show his friendship. A shadow filled the doorway and the woodcarver smiled as he looked up. The two small boys raced into his arms. Expertly, they signed to him and told him that they loved him. Bending to kiss each of his sons, Yannick watched as they ran to meet friends on their way to school. Their mother embraced her husband as she mouthed some words to him.

Reading her lips, his face lit up as she told him that Molly had arrived. Quickly, he wiped his hands on his apron and Yannick and Alais Charpentier walked hand in hand into the village. As the pair followed their sons towards the village centre, Yannick looked with pride at the communal vegetable garden. During the building of the first new houses all those years ago, Jean-Luc had remembered the small vegetable patch outside the mountain cabin and had known that the villagers would need to be as self-sufficient as possible. He had realised that Yannick had grown the vegetables for himself and his grandmother, so it had seemed a natural progression for the mute boy to show the orphans of Dougeres the much needed skills that their own parents would have taught them at the required time. There had been lots of laughter over the years as the villagers tried to find ways to keep the goats out of the continually extending garden.

Word of Molly's arrival had spread and the school and community centre quickly emptied as the principal gave her permission for the teaching staff to greet their friend. The doors were flung open as Amelie Etcheverrie led the way. Alone in the school, the principal quickly turned to her computer. Selecting one of the numerous social messaging sites, she sent a short message to several contacts. Finally, she joined her friends and family in the village square as it quickly filled with people when a laughing Molly Giardelli and her three daughters left the tiny cottage of Marie-Francoise Morrisson.

Molly's three daughters looked in amazement as a car disgorged its occupants. Xavier Aroztegi and his wife kissed the three elderly ladies enjoying the sunshine that bathed the three cottages. The Giardelli sisters looked appreciatively at the huge teenage boy who was being teased by his grandmothers that three of Italy's most beautiful young women had heard about him and had come to see for themselves. Xavier swept Molly into his arms as if she was a baby. The huge man had had a long and distinguished career as a policeman back in his hometown of Bayonne. A frequent visitor for many years, he had often joined his late father Iker and his best friend Alesander Ibarague fishing the rivers that surrounded the area.

Iker and Bihote had lost their bar to a fire, and not having the heart to start another bar, had gratefully accepted Jean-Luc's offer to move into the village of Dougeres. Iker had laughed when Jean-Luc told him that they needed more pensioners for the children to harass.

Alan Munro had often been a welcome guest until the travelling had become too much for him. Out walking one day in his beloved Scottish highlands with his dogs for company, Alan had suffered a massive heart attack and died instantly. Within two years Iker and Alesander had followed him.

Molly's daughters listened wide-eyed as Bihote and Ainhote told them how Xavier had met his match. The two elderly ladies laughed as they regaled the girls with the often told story. Back when Xavier was staying at the apartment of Katallin Ibarague, the two had been having a furious row, well in actual fact the young woman was furious and Xavier was laughing at her. This had enraged her even more. She had retorted that if she could reach him she would slap his stupid face. Ever the gentleman, Xavier had knelt before her. True to her word, Katallin slapped him and he had kissed her in return. This had been repeated three times until the by now much calmer young woman had looked into his eyes and then started to laugh. Ainhote and Bihote chuckled as they remembered Alesander's words that the young couple detested one another. They had just celebrated twenty-six years of marriage and had a fine son in nineteen-year-old Iker to prove their lasting love.

As the late afternoon sun started to bid farewell to the day, delicious smells filled the air and men rushed from their homes to the community centre and back to do their wives' bidding. Molly laughed as she thought that these wonderful people didn't need much of a reason to throw a party. Cars began to park outside the community centre and excited families joined their friends and relatives.

Everyone who had received the message from Sophie Morrisson had responded. Vincent's first born daughter had been named for her deceased aunt at Sally's insistence. Sophie was now the school principal, and was as well-loved as her Aunt Gwenaelle. Great excitement filled the faces of a certain bunch of adults, pleased that their good friend Molly was home and as the orphans of Dougeres walked past the lovingly rebuilt well, they remarked how successive generations had maintained the garden of remembrance that they, the orphans, had asked to build. It had been a labour of love as each one of the children had planted a tree in memory of their parents. Yannick Charpentier and Jean-Luc had made some beautiful benches that were placed around the perimeter of the remembrance garden. Despite these comfortable seats the elderly ladies of the village, by some unspoken agreement with tradition, would insist on sitting on the walls of the well to do their knitting and watch over the children as they played.

Seats were quickly filled and small children raced round excitedly. A rather stout Father Thierry accepted with thanks a glass of locally brewed cider. The older residents laughed as they remarked that two glasses of the potent brew would see the priest under the table. Vincent made a quick call, demanding that the recipient join the party.

Jean-Luc was talking to the son of the building contractor who had built the first houses in Dougeres. The young man was busy overseeing the arrival of some more building material as the village grew outwards. Numbering around forty houses, much deliberation had been needed before the village committee had agreed to the latest proposal. The objections had been raised solely because people did not want to lessen the majesty of the mountains as houses were built upon the slopes. The bombing of Dougeres had largely been forgotten by the outside world, but it remained in the memories of those it had affected the most. Many of the villagers had opened their houses as bed and breakfast accommodations for tourists. This helped the village retain their desired self-sufficiency by swelling the collective bank account. The builder gratefully accepted Gwenaelle's invitation to raise a glass with them in the community centre and with his workers, preceded the couple into the building.

In their early sixties, Gwenaelle and Jean-Luc, dressed simply in shorts and tee-shirts, walked hand in hand into the recently extended school. Thirty years ago Jean-Luc had decided that the school could be extended upwards should the need arise. Now the valley rang with the sounds of children who came from all over the community. Gwenaelle had retired but insisted on helping out when she was needed. The parents of six children, both Gwenaelle and Jean-Luc were slim and tanned as they spent quite a lot of time in the village's mountain retreat. Four of their children had chosen to find their way in the bigger world. The eldest offspring, Mathieu and Eleanor, lived in the village with their respective spouses. Eleanor worked alongside her uncle Vincent as a village doctor, while Mathieu had joined his father in a busy architect's practice. Gwenaelle laughed as a small boy raced to his grandmother. Two and a half years old, Samuel Morrisson was a bundle of mischief. Shortly before his death his great-grandfather, the much-loved Daniel Doissneau had laughed and declared that the child had the face of an angel and the mind of a devil. In his short life, Sam had done his best to live up to Daniel's prophecy. Now his bottom lip trembled and his eyes filled with tears as his nana asked him if he was ready to start school the next day.

Before entering the party, Gwenaelle and Jean-Luc looked at one another. The colour of her hair matched that of her husband's, although he still wore his hair long. The last thirty years had passed so quickly, but their love for one another had never dimmed. They knew that their four absent children were busy with their own lives, but each of their offspring had quickly learned that wherever their feet took them, they should always look ever homewards.

Dougeres, Pays Basque, France, 2044.

As if by magic, the front doors to the three adjoining cottages opened at exactly the same time. The three elderly ladies smiled and kissed each other as they slowly made their way towards the well opposite their dwellings. They each took out needles and wool from their bags and settled down to continue knitting the garments for the baby that was expected soon to the granddaughter of one of the trio.

They smiled as they grumbled about the arthritis that afflicted them. The three ladies had been great friends for many years. Not one of them minded that they had heard each other's stories many times. They had never moved from the village for many years, nor had they wanted to. They made disparaging comments about the weekly market that would arrive the following day, and yearned for the days when the produce sold was so much better than now. They had raised their families together, helping each other out in times of hardship, and cried for one another through the inevitable widowhood as it touched each one of them. They tended the graves of the men who had shared so much with them and spoke fondly of their children and grandchildren. And now another generation was about to be born bringing joy to the tiny hamlets that surrounded Dougeres. The trio looked back into their memories; each of them knew that they had many years behind them and that in their long journey, time was slowly but inexorably catching them up.

14768159R00162

Printed in Great Britain
by Amazon.co.uk, Ltd.,
Marston Gate.